MW00564150

MORE THAN DARE YOU

A MORE THAN WORDS NOVEL

SHAYLA BLACK

more than

DARE YOU

A MORE THAN WORDS NOVEL

SHAYLA BLACK

Steamy. Emotional. Forever.

MORE THAN DARE YOU
More Than Words, Book 6
Written by Shayla Black

This book is an original publication by Shayla Black.

Copyright 2020 Shelley Bradley LLC

Cover Design by: Rachel Connolly
Photographer: Sara Eirew Photographer
Edited by: Amy Knupp of Blue Otter
Proofread by: Fedora Chen

ISBN: 978-1-936596-61-4

The characters and events portrayed in this book are fictional. Any similarity to real persons, living or dead, is purely coincidental and not intended by the author. All rights reserved. No part of this book may be reproduced in any form by an electronic or mechanical means—except for brief quotations embedded in critical articles or reviews—without express written permission.

eBooks are not transferable. They cannot be sold, shared, or given away, as it is illegal and an infringement on the copyright of this work.

All rights reserved.

PRAISE FOR *MORE THAN WANT YOU*

"Amazing! Everything I didn't even know I needed or wanted in a romance novel. Hot. Spicy. Addicting." - Rachel Van Dyken, #1 New York Times Bestselling Author

"Sexy, passionate and oh-so-clever! An intriguing love story!" - Lauren Blakely, #1 New York Times Bestselling Author

"You'll hate him and then you'll love him! A sexy read with a surprising twist." - Carly Phillips, New York Times Bestselling Author

PRAISE FOR *MORE THAN NEED YOU*

5 Stars! "I adore Shayla Black! She masterfully delivers story after story full of passion, love, heartbreak, and redemption." - Chasing Away Reality

5 Stars! "I love this book!!! It has all the elements that takes you on an emotional rollercoaster." -Romance Between The Sheets

PRAISE FOR *MORE THAN LOVE YOU*

5 Stars! "The perfect blend of romance, lust, love and standing in your own way. I love the story." – Alpha Book Club

5 Stars! "One of the best books I've read in months! I love this book!" – Magic Beyond The Covers Book Blog

PRAISE FOR *MORE THAN CRAVE YOU*

5 Stars! "With beautifully written characters and a storyline that I could not put down this was a fabulous read. It needs more than 5 stars!!" –The Overflowing Bookcase

5 Stars! "...fun, hot and really hard to put down...loved it!"– Sissy's Romance Book Review

PRAISE FOR *MORE THAN TEMPT YOU*

5 Stars! "The More Than Words series is Shayla Black at her best —and this book is absolutely my favorite of the series so far." – USA Today bestselling author Angel Payne

5 Stars! "I nibbled my nails to nubs one minute and had to turn up the A/C the next. I enjoyed the hell out of every step of their journey and was sad to turn the final page. I wasn't ready for the goodness to end...sigh."– iScream Books Blog

ABOUT *MORE THAN DARE YOU*

I dared her to spend a hot, no-strings night with me. Now I'm determined to keep her forever.

I'm Trace Weston, recently reformed womanizer. In the blink of an eye, I went from busy bachelor to full-time single dad. My life was already complicated before my sister-in-law asked me to show off my bedroom skills to her bestie, who's wanting to experience real pleasure now that her one-and-only long-term relationship is over. Gorgeous Masey Garrett isn't my "usual." She's shy, sassy, driven, and incredibly kind. Suddenly I'm falling fast...but she's only mine for a night.

What's a former player to do? Change the rules.

Now she's under my roof night after night, letting me into her body and her life. Her heart? Not so much. She loves my newborn son. Me? I can't tell. I'm pulling out all the stops to win her over, but she's not taking me seriously. Other than passion, how can I reach her? Every attempt only pulls me deeper under her spell. Sure, I could drop an L bomb...except that once imploded my heart. But when her past collides with my desired future, can I risk everything and dare Masey to stay with me forever?

FOREWORD

There are infinite ways to tell someone you love them. Some of the most powerful don't require words at all. This was the truth rolling through my head when I first conceived of this series, writing about a love so complete that mere letters strung together to make sentences weren't an adequate communicator of those feelings. Instead, for this series, music was my go-to choice.

I *love* music. I'm always immersed in it and spend hours a day with my ear buds plugged in. I write to music. I think to music. I even sleep to music. I was thrilled to incorporate songs into the story I felt were meaningful to the journey. I think of it this way: a movie has a soundtrack. Why shouldn't a book?

So I created one.

Some of the songs I've selected will be familiar. Some are old. Some are newer. Some popular. Some obscure. They all just fit (in my opinion) and came straight from the heart. I listened to many of these songs as I wrote the book.

For maximum understanding (and feels), I seriously recommend becoming familiar with these songs and either playing them or rolling them around in your head as you read. Due to copyright laws, I can't use exact lyrics, but I tried to give you the gist of those most meaningful to Clint and Bethany's story. I've also made it simple for you to give these songs a listen by creating a Spotify playlist.

Hugs and happy reading!

SCREAM - Usher
WAITING FOR A GIRL LIKE YOU - Foreigner
CAN'T STOP THIS FEELING - Justin Timberlake
YOU ARE THE WOMAN - Firefall
AFTERNOON DELIGHT - Starland Vocal Band
SHAPE OF YOU - Ed Sheeran
MEANT TO BE - Florida Georgia Line
COME AWAY WITH ME - Norah Jones
A THOUSAND YEARS - Christina Perri
BEST DAY OF MY LIFE - American Authors

BEST PART - Daniel Caeser feat. H.E.R.

LOVE SHACK - B-52s

LET ME LOVE YOU - DJ Snake feat. Justin Bieber

CHAPTER ONE

Trace

Friday, April 6
Maui, Hawaii

"You ready for a night of meaningless sex?" My brother, Noah, swallows back his whiskey neat, then turns to me at the swanky hotel's bar with a sly smile.

Normally, I would be all in. Well, let's be honest; I still am… but with less hedonistic abandon. "Why not? Mom is watching Ranger this weekend, so this is the first time in five months I won't be a slave to a tiny human's whims or erratic sleep schedule."

"I get you, man. Being a new dad has been hell on my sex life, too. I literally counted the minutes until Harlow's doctor said we could 'resume normal activity,' but it took a few days before my wife and I got enough sleep to feel like it." Noah snorts. "I can't even imagine how rough it's been on you to suddenly become a single dad."

He's not kidding. One minute, I was a single, footloose bachelor, playing the field and having fun. Getting lucky was never a matter of actual luck, just showing up with decent conversation and a smile. Yeah, I'm advantaged. I've got good genes. My job as a charter boat owner-operator helps me keep fit. I grew up the less sports-inclined younger brother to a local football god who eventually turned pro and made a shit ton of money. So if I wanted to score off the field, I had to be creative. I learned charm. Flirting is like breathing. And I usually do all right. Or I did.

But ever since learning that I fathered a son during a drunken one-night stand and Ranger's mother giving me permanent full-time custody, my life has been upside down. I've been living like a monk.

"I'm so out of practice, man. I'm worried my parts are rusty."

My older brother laughs. "I'm sure your hand has ensured your parts work just fine. Besides, it's like riding a bike."

"Well, since I left all the athletic shit to you, that doesn't make me feel better. So what's the deal with this girl?"

"Masey Garrett—that's her name—just arrived here from Cali. Like my wife said when she called to ask if you'd, um… show her a good time, she and Harlow were sorority sisters. And they're besties. Masey is a beauty influencer, whatever that is."

"Her name is helpful. The rest…" I shrug. "Not really important. I just want to know why she's looking for a one-night stand." And exactly what I'm getting myself into.

Noah leans in. "I'm not totally sure. I haven't met Masey. She didn't attend our wedding last June because her dad had just died, and this douche broke up with her a few days later. Nice guy, huh?"

"Sounds like a real prince."

"But I know she's had the same boyfriend since she was fifteen, so Harlow's take is that Masey is finally ready to get back up and ride a bike or two of her own."

Neglected and lonely. I've done girls like her. I'm doing Masey as a weird favor to my sister-in-law, but helping out shouldn't be a hardship. "Do you know what she looks like?"

"I've only seen pictures." But he's smiling. With Noah, that's either a really good thing…or really bad.

"Out with it. Is she a troll?"

"No. She's not your usual, bro, but I think you'll like her. Little thing. Pale. Huge blue eyes. Sassy. She's got good girl written all over her."

Interesting. She sounds fun to corrupt. I shift in my seat to hide my suddenly hard dick, and my brother laughs. Clearly, I'm not fooling him.

"Anything else?"

On the bar in front of Noah, his phone dings. He glances at it. "You can ask Harlow. She's on her way in."

"With Masey?"

"No. She was running a few errands, so she's coming in her own rental car. You'll get a chance to grill my wife first."

One thing I appreciate about Harlow? She's a straight-to-the-point girl. I never have to guess where I stand with her. If she's mad, she'll tell me to my face. And if she has information, she'll give me the unvarnished truth. "Perfect."

"Then I'm taking Harlow home. Since Maxon and Keeley offered to watch our little rug rat tonight, I'm totally going to take advantage of my wife…who looks gorgeous." Noah stares past me with a leer. "Hi, baby. Wanna fuck?"

"Hell yeah. I hope you took your vitamins this morning, mister. You're going to need them." She winks.

My sister-in-law is fantastic. Gorgeous, smart, funny—the all-around package. My brother is lucky, and I'm thrilled for them. They're deliriously happy, and they deserve it. I won't bullshit myself; I'd like what they have. Someday. I'm not desperate. Ranger and I have been baching it for months, and we're okay. But seeing my brother's bliss has made me aware that…yeah, I'd love something similar eventually.

Never thought I'd say that, but things change. Time heals all wounds and—

Nope. Not thinking about *her*.

"Hey." I kiss Harlow's cheek. "Look at you. A dress *and* makeup?"

"Right? I finally don't look like a sleep-deprived new mom, thanks to Masey. She's a magician with makeup. But that *is* her business."

"Anything I should know about her?"

Harlow doesn't mind that we get right to it. "I'm sure my husband gave you the basics, but the important part is, she's really nervous."

"Why?" I'm not scary or anything. "She's just wanting a one-night thing, right?"

"Yeah. She's looking to pop her post-Thom cherry with a man whore who can show her everything she's been missing. I told her you'd be perfect."

I try not to let Harlow's words sting. Normally, I'd grin at that description and own it. I can't deny that's who I am. Well, who I was. But being a dad has made me look at life more seriously. I have my eye on the future now. Not the endless pussy I can chase but the actual months and years in front of me…and what I should fill them with. For Harlow, though, I'll do this favor and help her friend feel good.

"Sure."

She winces. "Sorry if I offended you. I didn't mean to."

"It's fine. So she wants to know what it's like to have someone other than Thom fuck her?"

"Yes and no. Yes, she wants to know what it's like for someone other than the selfish douche she dated for ten years to fuck her." Harlow leans in and drops her voice. "But when Thom dumped her for a chick who masturbates online for a living, he told Masey she sucked in bed. It's not good for a girl's confidence."

I don't know Masey and I don't know Thom, but I'm pretty sure I know who the asshole is in this scenario. "I'm sure it's not."

Ninety-nine times out of a hundred when some guy tells a girl that she sucks in the sack, it's not her issue. But Thom is probably one of those without a self-reflective bone in his body and he can't see how he contributed to their lackluster sex life. I'm not expecting Masey to be the best lay ever. But I doubt she actually needs more than a few orgasms and a confidence boost.

"Even so, she wants to know what she could be doing better."

If Masey is looking for pointers, that's easy enough. "No problem. Anything else?"

"There's a guy back home, apparently. Her hot neighbor. He asked her out right before she left home, and they plan to get together when she returns. Not that she thinks they'll hop into the sack right away, but…better to be prepared, you know. Other than that?" Harlow shakes her head. "She's not looking for more than a good time tonight, so don't worry she'll turn into a clinging vine."

Somehow, Harlow's assurance makes me even more uncomfortable. But she's merely asking me to help a friend in need, so I let it go. "Got it."

"Great. Just...be nice. I know you will. But she's been through a lot with Thom. Even though she's glued herself back together, she's more fragile than she lets on."

It's not a problem since I'm not usually an asshole. "Absolutely."

"I appreciate you doing this. If you'll send her off in the morning with a loopy grin, I'll be eternally grateful."

"One loopy grin, coming right up," I reassure her. "If you'd like, I'll make sure she's bow-legged, too."

Harlow flashes me a megawatt smile. "That would be great! I knew there was a reason you're my favorite brother-in-law."

"I'm your only brother-in-law."

"Details." She gives me a playful wave of her hand. "Anyway, she wanted me to assure you that if you don't find her attractive, there won't be any hard feelings. Buy her a drink and tell her you're busy tonight after all. Just do it gently."

At this point, I can't picture that. Masey sounds like she needs TLC, and my sudden misgivings aside, I need to get laid after a five-month dry spell. It's not a match made in heaven, but we can make it work for a night. "I'm sure it won't be a problem. I'm assuming that if she doesn't find me attractive, she'll let me down easy, too?"

"Sure." Harlow shakes her head. "But that won't be an issue."

"Why do you say that?"

She leans in with a conspiratorial whisper. "I showed her your picture. I think I had to wipe the drool off her chin."

"Well, at least she has good taste," I quip. "Got one of her? I haven't seen—"

A woman walks into my line of vision, a mere dozen feet away. Instantly, she ends my speech, stops my heart, and makes my dick jerk like a divining rod in her direction. She's got reddish-brown curls that sway around her shoulders, a delicate profile, lush lashes that fan the palest porcelain cheeks, a red bow of a mouth that nearly has me crying for relief, and curves for days under her clinging, va-voom red dress.

"Holy shit," I mutter.

Harlow turns and follows my line of vision. When her gaze lands on the brunette, she flashes a smile. "Masey!"

The bombshell turns, recognition lighting her face. Then her stare lands on me. Her breath catches. A tremor wracks her. She bites her lip, then sends me a searching smile.

I get to fuck *her?* All night? Standing without any conscious thought, I grin back as my feet automatically take me to her until I'm staring straight down into her eyes, my heart pounding like a drum.

In retrospect, I should have known in that moment how hard I was going to fall.

"Hi." Fuck, it's suddenly hard to breathe.

"Hi," she returns softly. "Trace?"

I nod and finally remember to stick out my hand. "Nice to meet you, Masey."

She tucks her palm against mine, and lightning zips up my arm to shock my heart. "Same."

Damn, she's even more striking up close. Her big eyes are a deep ocean blue. They seem huge in her soft oval face. They convey innocence, just like the dusting of freckles on her nose. Then there's her lush mouth that says *fuck me hard, fuck me now.* I'm totally happy to comply.

Tonight is going to be beyond; I already know.

"Hello?" Harlow snaps, then extends her hand between our faces to break our stare. "Can you two hear me?"

I release Masey's hand and flash my sister-in-law a self-deprecating grin. "Loud and clear. You and Noah heading out?"

"Yep." She nods. "He's going to take me to dinner, where we'll pretend to eat while he mercilessly eye-fucks me to insanity. Then we'll go home and do the real thing."

I grimace. "I didn't need to know that."

Harlow laughs. "Your brother's a stud."

"I didn't need to know that, either."

"I only told you because you look so adorably uncomfortable every time I bring it up. You two good here?"

As I glance in Masey's direction, our eyes meet again. She gives me a little nod. I try to ignore the subtle signs of her attraction and focus on the conversation. The sooner I do, the sooner my brother and sister-in-law will leave us.

"We're good. Enjoy your night." I clap my brother on the back. "I don't want details."

"Nope. Not sharing those," Noah assures as he wraps his hand around his wife's elbow and drags her away. "She's said enough, and I'll be sure to put that sassy mouth to better use tonight."

Ugh. I could have done without knowing that, too. "Shut up. You're not helping."

Masey grimaces. "At all. Just...bye. I'll call you."

Harlow blows her a kiss and gives me a wave. "I'd tell you not to do anything I wouldn't do, but..."

"We know," Masey says. "Please leave now. K? Thanks. Bye."

Then Noah smiles as he wraps his arm around Harlow's waist and mercifully leads her outside the open-air bar, toward the parking lot. Now it's just this gorgeous stranger, the glass-and-chrome hot spot, and a whole lot of unspoken expectations between us.

"You want to go and…"

Her blush tells me she's reluctant to finish that sentence by suggesting the obvious. Her uncertainty is cute on the one hand but troubling on the other. I like the idea that she's off-balance, but if it's because she's lacking confidence, I want to fix it.

Of course, I could just take her from here, find the nearest bed, and fuck her brains out. But this will go a whole lot better if she gets comfortable on a verbally intimate level with me. Besides, we've got all night, and I want to savor her.

"Let's sit and have a drink first." I gesture her toward the stools Noah and I just vacated. "I was having a beer. You want something?"

Masey looks a little crestfallen, but tries not to. "Merlot."

I call the bartender over and order, then turn to Masey when he leaves to uncork a bottle. "Tell me about you."

She bites that pouty red lip again. Far away, the gesture caught my eye. Up close, it fucking hypnotizes me. "There's not much to say, and I hate to bore you. Look, if you're not interested—"

"Honey, I'm so interested that, if we were alone, I'd lick you from the tips of your pretty toes all the way to that lip you keep sinking your teeth into. I promise I'd focus on all the best parts in between until you screamed for me."

"Oh." She blinks, looking stunned. "Okay, then."

"So don't think I'm not interested."

She smiles up at me from under her lashes. There's a lot of sweet angel in her stare…but I see the devil lurking, too. "I'm definitely interested myself."

Since I've read her body, I didn't need the verbal affirmation, but it's nice. "We're on the same page. So let's just take a few minutes to sit down and get to know each other before we have a hell of a night, huh?"

"All right." She slips onto the barstool Noah vacated, then turns to me with a shrug. "Not much to say. I went to college with Harlow. Communications major. While she stayed in and got her master's, I couldn't find a job I liked. Well, that's not true. I couldn't find one that paid enough to cover my rent and didn't have me working for a complete douche. I've always loved makeup. Not sure why, except there's something artistic and transformative about it. It helps you to feel like whoever you want to be. Right after high school, I started a YouTube channel, mostly for fun, but I put out videos pretty regularly. By the time I was out of college, I had over one hundred thousand followers. It was both growing and making me a decent income stream, so I took a part-time job and devoted the rest of my energy into doing what I love. Over the next two years, I grew my channel by leaps and bounds. Now I have over one point five million followers, and the rest of my social media reach has multiplied."

I only understand about half of what she said. I'm the weird guy who prefers human interaction over staring at the screen of my phone. But even so, I realize what she's accomplished in the past handful of years is pretty amazing. "You must have busted your ass."

She nods. "It's often a seven-day-a-week job to keep the videos flowing. Not everyone understands."

Translation: the ex wasn't supportive and trying to work around him was a fight. Why? I don't get the reason some men are threatened by a woman's sense of purpose or success. Is their own confidence so lacking that they can't deal?

"I get it. I'm self-employed and I keep weird hours, too."

That perks her up as the bartender sets her wine in front of her and I gesture to him to add that to my tab. "Really? What do you do?"

"I run a charter boat service. I take vacationers and corporate types out deep-sea fishing, scuba diving, or on a houseboat for anywhere between a few hours and a few weeks." I shrug. "Just depends. I love the water and I like facilitating a good time, so this works for me. Between us, there's nothing funnier than a bunch of uptight suits getting on board day one, talking shop, then seeing them two days later all drunk and telling fart jokes."

Masey laughs. It's light and feminine and real. The sound does something to me. And if she didn't both need and deserve a guy to seduce the hell out of her, I would be ready to skip the conversation and get busy now.

"They really do that?"

"Every. Single. Time. Put a beer in one hand and a fishing pole in the other for a few hours, and it's predictable. Families are interesting, too. You can see the ones who are genuinely close and appreciate the time together. But you can also tell the ones where someone, usually Mom, insists they're going to have some togetherness, damn it. By the end of a week, I'm often texting my brother with my bet about who will turn ax murderer first."

She winces. "That sounds uncomfortable."

"You have no idea. I had to learn real quick how to dodge becoming the referee."

"I'm sure." Masey cocks her head and slants me a stare. "So no wild spring break crews, bachelorette parties, or single girls?"

"No." Never fucking again. "I'm in a position to take jobs when I want from the people I want, so I avoid girl-drama like the plague. No offense, but pair a bunch of young females with a few gallons of booze…and nothing good happens."

"I can't argue with that." She laughs. "It's one reason my salt circle has gotten so small over the last few years. In college, I had to deal with all my sorority sisters. And most were great. But now that I live alone and I'm independently employed, I can pick and choose who I talk to every day. Being in the beauty community is no cakewalk. There's a lot of pressure to be perfect, which isn't realistic. And you're dealing with the public, who feels it's their right—their responsibility, even—to comment on every single thing you say and do behind their anonymous online accounts. If a rival influencer doesn't like you for some reason, their fans may come after you. And they can be vicious. That part sucks. And don't start me on drama channels… I try to ignore all their tea spilling as much as I can, be an adult, and do my job."

"And what is that exactly?"

"I review makeup, do tutorials, test a variety of products, talk about skin care… It's a little bit of everything beauty related."

"You might as well have been speaking Greek." I laugh, then take a swig of beer. "So you want to talk about your sex life with Thom?"

She nearly chokes on her merlot. "Not really."

She doesn't elaborate, and her face, for once, is almost impossible to read. What is she not saying?

"You sure? No judgment here."

"I'd rather not revisit the past, cloud your opinion, or dwell on something hurtful."

"I get it." I really do…but I need information, so I try another tactic. "Maybe you should tell me what you want, then. It's most important for me to know that anyway."

"Sex. Isn't that the point of us meeting?"

"Yeah, but that's a broad topic. What are your turnoffs?"

"Thom."

Masey shares Harlow's bluntness, and I like that. She's a bit more tactful...but not much.

I laugh. "Since I've never met the guy, I don't know what that means. What did he do that turned you off so much?"

She sighs. "I always felt rushed. And if I ever tried to tell him I didn't like something, he got defensive and told me the problem was mine."

"So he had a small ego?" And I'm guessing he had a small dick to match.

"Yes. He had this...germ thing. He didn't like kissing much. He always came to bed smelling like hand sanitizer. And he always showered immediately afterward. It was kind of insulting."

What a dipshit. "So I'm guessing he wasn't spontaneous?"

Masey shakes her head emphatically. "Not at all. I'm not terribly spur-of-the-moment myself, so it didn't bother me much. But his schedule was very precise, so if I was even ten minutes late, then he—"

"Wait," I insist. She couldn't have meant that the way it sounded. "You had an appointment to have sex with your own boyfriend?"

She grimaces. "That sounds horrible, but yeah. We just kept really different schedules, so it became a necessity. Otherwise, he'd have meetings all day, but I often filmed and edited videos at night or sometimes I had parties and launch events to attend. He also traveled. Sadly, we'd look up, and a month had gone by. So unless we both committed to a time in advance, the sex just wasn't happening."

I don't know this guy since we've never met, but odds are

Thom wasn't going without...just going without Masey. But I keep that thought to myself. "No early-morning quickies?"

Masey shakes her head. "He likes to be at the gym by five thirty a.m. No one who values their life should talk to me that early."

"Same." I laugh. "And no late-night nookie?"

"I sometimes worked until midnight or beyond, but he was usually in bed by ten."

I don't get this guy. If someone said I could have an extra couple of hours of sleep or a couple of hot hours with Masey, I would pass on sleep every time. "Okay, so you made appointments and if you were late he...what? Bailed?"

She nods. "He doesn't like to be kept waiting. He's always said sex shouldn't take more than twenty minutes or so anyway, but—"

I choke on my beer. "Excuse me?"

"Thom looks at sex from a financial perspective since he's an entertainment and intellectual property attorney. He's very in demand and bills out at four fifty an hour. By his calculations, even that twenty minutes of being with me cost him a hundred and fifty dollars." She wrinkles her nose. "He said at that rate it was like paying for sex."

I'm speechless. Seriously. The basic math involved is easy to understand, but the sentiment is fucking ridiculous. "That might be the most unromantic thing I've ever heard. And you put up with this?"

She sighs. "He wasn't always like that. When I was in high school and he was just starting college, everything was different. We both had demanding academic tracks, plus I had activities, parents, friends... He had his frat stuff. We made it work, even though we couldn't see each other all that often. But once I finished college and he started practicing law, we moved in together. Our relationship got more complicated. I think I expected everything between us would be 'normal,' that we'd finally have time together. Instead, it seemed like we both got busy and sex became less of a priority."

"Wow." *He sounds like an asshole, and I'm guessing your relationship sucked.* "Tell me what a typical 'appointment' was like."

"I'd rather not." She grimaces. "It's really personal."

"I totally get that. But I don't know how else to make sure I give you what you want." *And probably need.*

Has this girl ever had a decent orgasm in her life?

She rolls her eyes, reluctantly and silently admitting that I have a point. "He insisted I brush my teeth and take a shower after dinner. Then about nine, we'd meet in the bedroom."

"Always the bedroom?"

"Yes. He couldn't handle the thought of germs or bodily fluids anywhere else in the apartment."

So he'd treated her like she had cooties? "What then?"

"We'd kiss a little, and sometimes he'd touch me. Then he'd put on a condom, and…you know."

"I do." And that must have been dull as fuck. "I take it he wasn't much for oral sex?"

"Receiving it, sure."

So Thom was uptight and selfish? "Not a lot of foreplay, huh?"

"Not as much as I would have liked."

"Did you tell him that?"

She nodded. "He told me I shouldn't be self-absorbed and that what he did had worked for his former girlfriends."

He doesn't just sound like an asshole; he clearly is one.

Based on everything Masey said, anal was obviously out of the equation. Hell, she'd never even enjoyed a raunchy fuck at midnight, much less rung in a blissfully sated dawn.

As gorgeous as she is, that's a total waste.

"Damn it, the more I talk about this, the more pathetic I sound," she grumbles.

"No. If he's the only sexual partner you've ever had…"

"He is."

"And he's had others…"

"A few."

My guess is more than a few, but no sense in making her feel any more self-defeated than she does. "Then in my mind, it was his responsibility to help you have the best experience you could."

"I think he tried."

No, he hadn't. "So what happened if you said you wanted to explore a different position?"

"He preferred to be on top."

Mr. Missionary, huh? "Or you wore something slinky to bed?"

"He thought lacy lingerie was low-class and didn't suit me. He preferred me to be reserved. Ladylike."

Since he dumped Masey for a girl who masturbates on the internet, I'm calling bullshit. "So you wore what before an appointment for sex?"

"A bathrobe."

That makes no sense to me, and I can't avoid shaking my head. The notion of Masey in something plunging, lacy, and see-through in the same shade of red as her dress has me sweating.

"What's the thing he did in bed you liked most?"

She doesn't even hesitate. "Sometimes he would cuddle me afterward."

The cuddling was better than the sex? Given what she'd described, I shouldn't be shocked, but holy shit… "Thing you liked the least?"

"He wasn't really into kissing. Not like deep, passionate kisses. He'd press his lips to mine, brush them over mine, and even nip at my bottom lip every so often. But he never…" She winces like what she's about to admit is really difficult and embarrassing.

"Never what?"

"French kissed me."

There's no stopping the shock. "Never?"

"No."

"Not even once?"

"No."

Fuck me. This girl might not be a virgin in the strictest sense of the word, but she's distinctly inexperienced. If she's still game, it's my job—my duty, even—to show her exactly what she's been missing. And I'll be damned if I don't do it so fucking right she can't see straight. In fact, I'm looking forward to it.

"You think that's crazy." She looks embarrassed as she stares down into her nearly empty glass of wine.

"Crazy isn't the right word. I think your ex is a self-centered jack-off, and it will be my distinct pleasure to show you everything you've been missing."

"So…" She fingers the rim of her glass and cocks her head at me. "What qualifies you? Harlow said you were a man whore, but that doesn't make you actually good in bed."

It's hard not to cringe, but I somehow manage a smile because Masey's question proves she's thinking. Experience doesn't automatically make a person good. "Man whore is probably a strong word. I won't say I haven't had a lot of sex. I have. But that's not what qualifies me. It's my focus."

"What does that mean?"

"My brother concentrated on football—peewee, high school, college, pro—for nearly three decades. I knew from the time I was little that I didn't have Noah's ability with a pigskin. I played a little, but it wasn't where I directed my attention."

"But girls were?" She arches a brow at me.

"Oh, yeah. Well, that and boats. I love anything to do with the water."

She wrinkles her nose. "Not me. I can barely swim."

Seriously? "You didn't take lessons as a kid?"

I picture her growing up in some upscale suburban community with a mom who carted her to all kinds of lessons, including instructive dips in the pool.

"Water has always intimidated me, so I never really wanted to try. Anyway, you were saying…"

Too bad I won't be with her longer; I could show her the joys of more than sex. She seems like she'd be fun to hang out with. But I brush the thought aside. She isn't looking for anything except a good time. Neither am I.

"Early on, one thing became clear to me: my brother was built for sports. I was built for sex." It probably sounds cocky, but that's the best way I know how to put it.

"So you're God's gift?"

I laugh. "No. It's that focus thing. He put all his attention and energy into throwing a ball. And I put mine into—"

"Getting laid."

"Not exactly. I mean, I definitely put energy into getting girls into bed," I admit. "But to me, sex isn't about the conquest or even getting off. It's about figuring out my partner's body, learning what she responds to, then making her come apart for me." I definitely get off on it.

Masey's cheeks turn pink. "And what do you do with a woman who doesn't come apart at all?"

"You don't orgasm during sex?"

"Not really. I'm just…in my head too much."

Because her ex didn't give her enough time or stimulation to get out of it. That's not her fault. But at some point, it doesn't make sense to keep talking about sex. It only makes sense to show her. "Let's see about fixing that. If you're still interested?"

There she goes, biting that pouty lip again. I shift in my chair thinking about all the ways I can make love to that virgin tongue.

She downs the last of her wine and nods. "It's probably crazy, but I am."

I push her wineglass toward the bartender. "I'd offer to get you another one, but I want you to have a clear head tonight."

"I'd like that, too. But…"

"But?"

She sighs. "I've never even kissed a man I don't know well, much less…"

Had sex with one. I get it. "You need to know me to feel comfortable?"

Masey grimaces. "If I don't, I worry it could be a real problem. I'll just be uptight that I'm screwing a stranger and—"

"It's fine," I assure her and launch in with the basics. "I grew up on Oahu with Noah and my sister, Samaria. My parents were great. My dad passed away a few years ago, so my mom moved here to Maui to be closer to me. And you know my brother joined us here after he retired from pro football and left Texas. So we're all pretty close. I went into business for myself about ten years ago. I do all right. I'm generally happy."

"No girlfriend?"

"No."

"No long-term relationship or fiancées along the way?"

I came close once but… "No."

Masey doesn't need to know about that disaster to have a good time with me in bed. She also doesn't need to know about my son. I like this girl—really, I do—and some part of me is already wishing we had more than a night, because I think our chemistry has serious potential to be a major win in bed. But if this is purely a one-time hookup, then telling her about Ranger now is a potential overshare.

She nods consideringly. "How old were you the first time…"

"I had sex? Fourteen."

Her big blue eyes go wide. "Seriously?"

"Yeah. When I was a freshman, I had a buddy, Mike, who had an older sister. Sometimes, I'd spend the weekend with him playing video games and stuff. But this one night, he fell asleep, his parents had gone to bed hours ago, and Megan and I…"

"Were bored and had sex?"

"Something like that."

I leave out the part where she'd just broken up with her boyfriend and used me to get back at him. At first, it was awesome that she told everyone at school I'd done her good—a total lie since I was a typical disastrous first-timer—so it would get back to her ex-boyfriend. All my friends thought I was the man—except her brother. Mike stopped talking to me, which sucked because, up until then, he was my best friend. And then Megan's ex decided he needed to beat the shit out of me. Thankfully, Noah stepped in and saved me, but it was close. And it wasn't pleasant.

After that, anytime a girl wanted to make her boyfriend jealous, was curious about sex with someone new, or wanted to drop her V-card with a guy who "knew what he was doing," they came to me. The good news was, I had sex with a lot of different girls in high school. The bad news, I never had an actual girlfriend. No female took me seriously. They all saw me purely as a fuck boy.

"Wow, I was eighteen my first time. Thom was older than me, so he insisted we wait until I was 'legal.'"

Probably wise, but the way Masey puts it makes it sound like Thom was more concerned about being arrested than making sure his girlfriend was actually ready for the adult ramifications of sex.

"How was it?"

She shrugs. "Doesn't it always hurt the first time?"

That's hardly a glowing review, and I could tell her that it definitely didn't have to, but it's irrelevant now. We're going to spend a night together, and this conversation is probably more personal than it needs to be.

I shrug. "Masey, listen… If you're not ready for this, just say so. I'll get you another glass of wine, we'll laugh a little, then I'll make sure you get home alone and in one piece. But if you want to spend the night with me and experience some of the possibilities of sex for yourself, then I think you should let me close out this tab, put your hand in mine, and tell me where I can undress you and make you feel good all night."

CHAPTER TWO

Following Masey's sensible white rented sedan, I cruise south down the Piilani Highway, deeper into the heart of Wailea, tapping my thumb against the steering wheel. My playlist flips from Imagine Dragons to Usher, who straight-up croons to the woman he's eyeing that if she wants to scream, to let him know and he'll take her there. A smile tugs at my lips as I take a right and follow her into a gated community.

Harlow told me that Masey rented a place for her Maui stay since she tends to work and film at night and didn't want to risk keeping her and Noah or their newborn awake. I expected a cute little condo with an iffy view of the water. After all, even that costs a fortune here in paradise, and most people who come to the island for a vacation spend their time on the beach anyway.

But when I pull up in front of a plush white villa that looks like an upscale haven in the moonlight, it's obvious Masey thought bigger and better.

In front of me, she stops the car and slides out, locking it with a press of her fob and a beep. I follow suit and sidle up behind her. When she glances over her shoulder at me, I see she's not just nervous but visibly tense. Her eyes look huge in her delicate face.

Reluctantly, I refrain from touching her. "Second thoughts?"

She unlocks the door and slowly opens it before turning to me and pulling it wide. Since a full ten seconds go by before she responds, it definitely qualifies as a hesitation. "No."

Bullshit. She had time to think during her drive. I get it. I'm a stranger and I make her nervous. "It's okay if you are."

"It's not. I'm not a coward."

"No one said you were." I step in and close the door as she flips on a light. I'm not at all surprised when she steps back, putting distance between us. "There's a difference between being afraid and not being ready. But either is okay. Honestly, we can spend the night talking. Just talking. I'm happy to tell you what you should look for and expect in a future partner. Harlow tells me you're interested in one of your neighbors back home?"

"Yes."

I nod. "I can help you be ready for whatever happens with him without ever laying a finger on you if that makes you more comfortable."

My assurance seems to set her at ease. "I appreciate that, but I wanted this for a reason. I have to stop freaking out that I'm 'cheating' or doing something wrong. I'm a single woman, and it's perfectly normal to want to know what real pleasure feels like."

I nod. "If that's what you want, that's what I'll give you. But there's no reason to rush. We'll do this at your pace."

Suddenly, she laughs at herself. "All my hang-ups must be a real turn-on for you."

"I already said that desiring you isn't a problem."

She gives me an artificially bright smile. "So you did. Can I get you something to drink?"

I don't need her to play hostess, but I sense she isn't comfortable enough yet for me to start the seduction. "No, thanks. Tell me what relaxes you."

"Honestly? Nothing." She shrugs. "I'm a little driven and high-strung even on a good day."

And this isn't a good day, at least in her head. I can tell.

I meander to the French doors at the back of the magazine-worthy neutral living room and stare out at the dark ocean rolling beyond her lanai. "Let's walk."

"What?"

I open the doors and motion to her. "Come on. Come with me."

She frowns, then locks the front door, pockets her keys, and follows me. "What are you doing?"

"Ditch the shoes." I toe mine off, leaving them just outside the back door.

Masey follows suit, and when I hold out my hand, I'm gratified she takes it. That's a start. I hang on to that as we trek past the lanai and hit the sand.

The beach is deserted and mysterious, illuminated only by the moon. We walk in silence for a bit, the sand filtering between my toes, and I wait. When it's clear I'm not going to immediately maul her, the tension begins to leave her.

"What do you think of Maui so far?"

"I love it. It's so much quieter here. It's one of the first things I noticed when I arrived. I'm so used to LA, you know? The people and the smog, the traffic—ugh, the traffic—the cars, the noise, and the airplanes since I live pretty close to the airport. But when I got here, I walked the beach that first night. I felt like the only person in this corner of the world."

"It helps that you have your own beach."

She concedes the point with a self-deprecating nod. "There is that. So...how come a seemingly nice, sexually gifted guy like you isn't taken?"

It's a fair question, but not an easy one. "I don't meet a lot of women taking corporate stiffs out for team-building excursions, and the few I do are usually tourists. Here today, back to the mainland tomorrow. My brother and Harlow are damn lucky to have each other. It's great—for them. But I'm not in a hurry for marital bliss, so I'm okay with being alone."

Well, I used to be. Now...I'm rethinking. My reasons for not getting serious about women are definitely more complicated than I've let on, but nothing I've said is untrue.

She nods. "I don't meet many men in my line of work, either. Some, but no one I've been attracted to. And since my job so often consumes me, I'll sometimes look up and realize I haven't left my house for days. Grocery and food delivery services are the best things ever. My cute neighbor moving in two doors down was a nice surprise, too."

"Why do you think you put up with so much of your ex's bullshit?"

"Honestly? I convinced myself as a starry-eyed teenager that we were 'meant to be.' So when he did something that upset or annoyed me, I made excuses or wrote it off. Law school was stressful, and his job even more so. No one is perfect, and to spend your life with another person, you have to compromise. I had lots of excuses like that. But I thought we were on the same page about sharing our future."

"Were you happy?"

She's quiet, staring out at the moonlight falling onto the ocean waves as they roll in gently. Then she sighs. "I thought I was. In retrospect, I was in the whirlwind of growing my business and trying to keep our relationship together. I didn't really take time to think. Every once in a while, when I couldn't sleep at night, I'd ask myself if I was where I should be in life. But I couldn't picture where else—or with who else—I should be. So I'd silence any questions that arose."

"He ended it, right?"

"Yes."

When she tenses, I squeeze her hand. "Tell me how you felt about that. Not the day it happened, because I'm sure that was a shock. But after you managed to process it all."

"Actually, I was relieved." She slants a glance up at me and holds my stare. "Did you guess that?"

"More or less. Since Harlow set us up for the night, I figured you wanted this for one of two reasons. Either you wanted to make him jealous with some revenge sex or—"

"No." She blanches. "I guess people do that, but it's horrible. I'm a very loyal person, and I cared about Thom once. No matter what he did or how it ended, I would never intentionally cause him pain."

Wow, that puts her ahead of ninety-eight percent of the women I've slept with.

"Or I figured you were genuinely over him and ready to move on. And the most likely reason for you to be over him now was if you weren't completely invested in the first place."

She looks stunned. "That's incredibly astute."

To lighten the mood, I flash her a grin. "Did you think my only good quality would be my cock?"

She bites her lip and blushes enough for me to see her cheeks turn rosy in the moonlight. "This will sound horrible, but I didn't think of you beyond the sex at all. I didn't expect you would think of me beyond what we did in the bedroom, either."

"We can approach tonight that way. I just don't think you'll like it."

"Because you're convinced I'm the kind of girl who wants to know her partner before we hop into bed?"

It's more than that. "Because you're the kind of girl who needs to be emotionally connected to your partner before you let him into your body. You want safety and trust and some level of assurance that he's not a douchebag."

She blinks at me. "How did you know?"

I stop walking and face her. The wind lilts, and I can't resist brushing away a reddish-brown strand of hair from her cheek. God, she really has the most hypnotic eyes—big and blue and fathomless as the ocean behind her. I could stare into them for hours. Of course, I'd like to do that while I'm buried deep inside her, but I don't know if we'll get there tonight. Or even if we should.

"Being good in bed isn't about having the best equipment around or learning the most practiced technique. Not that it hurts." I wink, gratified when I get a smile out of her. "It's about being patient, honest, and intuitive. I'd be every kind of asshole if I took you to bed, no questions asked."

"I didn't think it would matter to you. That *I* would matter."

Wow, her ex must have been a complete asshole if that's her expectation. "I don't want you to ever regret me."

Her smile softens before turning wry. "I was prepared to, you know? I'd already scheduled my post-fling guilt breakdown about noon tomorrow."

Masey is gorgeous, but she's especially cute when she pokes fun at herself. "If I could free up that slot in your schedule for something more…worthwhile, I'd call that a win."

"Do you mean doing something like you?" She winces. "Sorry. Sometimes, I tell corny jokes when I'm nervous."

I smile. "It's fine. You can throw me out whenever you want, but if I'm still around at noon, I hope you're still letting me make you sigh and smile…"

"That might be nice."

Doubt and uncertainty linger on her face. She thinks she's hiding it, I'm sure. But I can read her. Somewhere, deep down, she believed her ex's BS about her prowess and she's taken it to heart.

Would I like to spend a night in bed with Masey? Um…is oxygen necessary for breathing? Of course I want her. But I also really hope she lets me show her she's neither unsexy nor broken or whatever she thinks.

We meander down the beach a bit more, her hand still in mine. There's silence, but it's not awkward. She's feeling out what it's like to be next to me. And she's beginning to relax. I see it in the set of her shoulders and the subtle sway of her hips.

"Noah has been good for Harlow," she says.

"She's been really good for him, too."

"When Harlow was engaged to Simon, I knew he wasn't right for her and that she wasn't happy. Thom and I double-dated with them once." She rolls her eyes.

"Disaster?"

"Simon thought Thom was uptight."

"Isn't that true?"

Masey bobs her head like I've got a point. "I suppose so. And Thom thought Simon was, in his words, a prick."

"I saw the video Harlow played before she ran out on their wedding, so I *know* that's true."

"Oh, it is."

I'm guessing neither liked their respective boyfriends because they both saw too much of themselves in the other. I'm glad they're both free of their exes.

"But it's funny," she continues. "In college, Harlow and I thought I would be the first one married and pregnant. Now, I don't know if that will ever happen for me."

"Is that something you want?"

"Yeah. It probably sounds old-fashioned. And after everything that's happened, I should probably rethink my long-term plans, but family has always been important to me. I've always wanted one of my own, but..." She sounds somewhere between wistful and resigned.

I feel for her. But she's wrong. "It will happen, just not with Thom."

"That alone is a blessing. My mom has been telling me for years that Thom wasn't the man for me. I didn't want to hear it. She also told me that everything happens for a reason. When he broke up with me, I didn't see what purpose there could possibly be for me to lose the future I'd envisioned for myself. Now, I'm grateful. Ever marrying him would have been a big mistake. Having kids with him, even worse. I just don't know where that leaves me. My brother, Chase, is way less poetic. He just threatened to kill Thom. And since he's some badass special ops guy, I'm sure he could." Then she seems to realize where she is, and that I'm a relative stranger. She flashes me an awkward smile. "Sorry. *Way* more than you wanted to hear."

"You're fine. I'm happy to listen." After making a mental note to avoid her brother, I lean in and whisper, "Like I said, more than my penis functions."

She laughs. "It would seem. You're easy to talk to."

"You're interesting to be with."

Masey scoffs. "Woe-is-me crap is never interesting."

"You're not woe-is-me. I don't hear you crying and blaming Thom for everything. You were with him for ten years. It's normal to wonder where you're going next in life."

"Thanks for understanding. At least I still have work. That's been my constant."

"Harlow told me you're filming while you're here. You brought all the equipment with you? That's dedication."

"Testing product and filming helps me keep my mind off things. And it's not that much stuff to ship over. Well, the product is. I've got *so* much of that. Spring launches are here, and I'm super behind."

I don't understand makeup, so I don't grasp what she's saying. "Spring launches? How many tubes of mascara does one person need?"

"You'd be surprised. But it's way more than that. I have so many palettes, foundations, and lip stains, not to mention self-tanners, sunscreens, and masques. Body creams, nail polishes… I could go on."

What the… "You buy all this stuff?"

"I buy some, but most brands send me free product to test and review. Despite that, I give my honest opinion—always. Some influencers are too beholden to various brands to be unvarnished. They want the cash, trips, and other perks that come with kissing ass. But I've always prided myself on giving praise or criticism to products whenever it's warranted. That means I've been blacklisted by certain brands for being too honest. That's fine. My sole responsibility is to my followers. I only want them to spend their hard-earned money on the good stuff. I wouldn't have a channel without them, after all. They seem to appreciate how seriously I take my role."

"That makes sense…but how does that equate to money?"

"Mostly YouTube ad revenue. I also speak to various entrepreneurial and women's groups. I do some online personal beauty consulting. Next month, I'll be starting negotiation on a collaboration that I'm not allowed to talk about yet but it's beyond exciting. I have a few sponsored videos about products, but only those I stand behind one hundred percent."

And that's enough to afford swanky digs like her vacation rental? "Before you explained it, I would have thought it was just slapping on some makeup and talking to the camera but—"

Her laugh interrupts me. "It used to be. Now I have an upload schedule people count on. So I sometimes film multiple videos a day, which means changing outfits, washing off the makeup I just put on, and starting over again. Then add on hours of editing video, responding to comments on existing uploads, not to mention growing Instagram, Pinterest, Twitch…"

"Could you speak English, please?"

She shakes her head with a self-conscious laugh. "I'll stop boring you."

"You're not. Seriously, it's fascinating, even if I don't totally understand."

"Now I know you're BSing me." She rolls her eyes. "Guys like you don't find makeup interesting."

"Not the makeup itself. You're right. I'm lost about all that. But the way you juggle product, filming, social media, and outside ventures to grow your passion into a self-supporting business. That's amazing."

"Didn't you do the same with boats?"

"Kind of. But I don't have to…apply any craftsmanship to make the boat different. I just sail her as is."

"Maybe you don't need to apply craftsmanship because your boat is naturally prettier than mine," she teases.

"Ha! Floating heaps of fiberglass are downright ugly compared to you. Trust me on that."

"But you love your boats, don't you?"

"Yep." I stop and turn to her again, this time cupping her

cheek. "That should tell you something about how gorgeous I think you are."

She frowns. "You don't have to ply me with compliments or try to seduce me. I already said yes."

"So…what? You don't need me to be nice to you?" I'm trying to follow her logic, but it doesn't make any sense. "Seems like you've had enough of someone who didn't properly appreciate you. Even if we only have tonight, I want you to feel better about yourself when I leave here."

She wraps her fingers around my wrist. They're small and gentle. And chilled. "I only need your honesty."

"Honey, I don't know how to be any more honest than that. When I first saw you, I was talking to Harlow and literally lost my train of thought. I couldn't speak. I couldn't breathe. I could only think about how beautiful you were." And still are.

For a moment, her eyes soften. Then abruptly she rolls them and starts walking again. "Okay, Casanova."

I grab her arm and urge her back. "I'm serious. Thom may have made you feel less than desirable for some fucked-up reason that served his interests. I have no reason to lie. Like you pointed out, you already said yes. But if you want me to teach you how to be better in bed, the first step is to be confident. That means you need to know your worth. You're a diamond, honey. Don't ever let a man tell you any different."

She blinks up at me with big, questioning eyes. Maybe I shouldn't cup her cheek again, but I can't keep my hands off her. Hell, it takes all my self-control not to kiss her senseless and prove just how interested I am. But she's not ready for that. Not yet.

At least she's listening. It's a start.

"I thought you'd tell me everything I'm doing wrong—not to

be a dead fish while we're having sex or that my blow job technique is terrible. I never imagined you'd be…nice. Why?"

I'm not even sure how to answer her question. I could say that Thom already put her through enough, but I've said it. Reminding her would only give her the impression I'm with her out of pity. What I'm feeling has nothing to do with that. Would I like the chance to have a man-to-man with Thom? Yes. Self-centered pieces of shit like him don't really grasp anyone's needs but their own. I know that firsthand.

I could also tell Masey that I'm typically a nice person. I prefer to get along with others. I don't have much of a temper. Throwing down isn't a sport for me. In fact, it often seems really fucking juvenile. I have other ways to make my point than with a fist. But that's not really what she's asking.

"What you want is beyond sex. You want intimacy."

Before I've even finished speaking, she's shaking her head. "No, I—"

"Yes. You've had detached, one-sided sex. I don't need to show you anything about that; you could probably write a book. What you want—and need—to know is what it's like when two people in bed together are fully engaged and fully committed to pleasing each other."

Masey suddenly closes her mouth. "You're right."

"I can see from your expression that you're realizing, from where we stand right now, it won't be easy."

She looks somewhere between frustrated and defeated. "Yes."

"And we don't have time to build the kind of intimacy that comes from getting to know each other and slowly dating, dipping our toe in the water, or going through personal crises to see if the other person will be there for us. That takes somewhere between weeks and years, depending. We have tonight."

"So what do we do? Now that you've pointed all this out, it seems so obvious. I think I've known it in the back of my head and simply didn't want to admit it. But I haven't trusted Thom with my emotions in a long time." She frowns. "Maybe I never really did."

"It's probably one reason you are where you find yourself now."

"You really are insightful. Thom had the emotional range of a nailhead. Where did you—"

"My mother. When my dad was alive, he sometimes took jobs away from home for weeks, even months. My mom raised us kids with a lot of love and understanding. My brother and I would sometimes exclude our little sister. Not on purpose, but Noah and I wanted to play with balls and trucks and bugs. Samaria wanted to play with dresses, dolls, and finger paints. Whenever we had disagreements, Mom would always make us explain ourselves to whomever we squabbled with. They would be expected to do the same. It made me think about *why* I felt the way I felt."

"You knew you would be asked."

"Yep. And I also had to listen to someone else's perspective, try to understand it, and compromise. That's the way everything worked in my house. I think being the middle kid, the brunt of that fell on me. At the time, I hated it, but it's served me well over the years. Since you and I have been talking, I've listened and tried to hear your side of the breakup, understand what wasn't working for you, and come up with solutions."

"What did you decide?"

I shake my head. "It's not for me to decide. I have suggestions. But we both have to agree."

"Or they're pointless." Masey nods, the motion sending

moonlight gleaming off her dark hair. "That makes sense. When one person tries to run the show…"

"That's the only person who ends up happy. So you and I both have to promise that we'll go into our night together with open minds, in good faith. No holding back. No playing games. No agendas other than mutual pleasure."

"I can't argue with that."

"Good. This is where you need to be honest—with me and yourself. Are you ready to do that?"

She takes a deep breath. I sense her soul searching. She's taking this seriously, and I commend that…until she nibbles on that lip again. It makes me hard and drives me to distraction.

I've done my best to be as academic about tonight as I can be, but she's so fucking gorgeous. I'm already imagining what's under her clothes and how much access she'll grant me once they're gone. Will she blush pink when I stare at her? Turn rosy as she nears climax? Is she a moaner? A screamer? A discreet glance tells me she has pretty painted fingernails I'm hoping she'll dig into my back as she gets close…

"I have to try. Really try. Otherwise, I'm wasting your time and doing us both a disservice."

"Yeah."

"And who knows when this kind of opportunity will come around again?"

When someone else will be the lucky guy in her bed?

It's a knee-jerk reaction, but the whole question pisses me off. We haven't even kissed yet, and I'm already feeling as if I'll fuck up the first asshole who dares to put his hands on her, much less play games that mess with her head.

Chill, buddy. She's not yours.

"Maybe tomorrow." I force myself to shrug.

She sends me a reproving stare. "Probably never. I mean,

you're available. You seem honest and understanding. You're my best friend's brother-in-law, and she says you're a great guy. That goes a long way with me…"

That's the kind of language someone uses to describe a dependable used car, not someone you want to get hot, sweaty, and deep into pleasure with.

"If you're not attracted to me, this won't work." It kills me to even suggest that maybe I'm not the guy she needs tonight. All signs have pointed to yes, and I don't want to give her any reason to walk away from me before I've even touched her. But I have to let her choose. I have to give her the chance to be brutally honest.

Tonight's all about that.

Even in the moonlight, I see a little smile flirt with her bow of a mouth before she looks down as if she can't quite meet my stare. "I am. When I first saw you in the bar, I couldn't breathe or speak, either."

Thank fuck.

I let out a sigh of relief I don't realize I've been holding and plant a finger under her chin to lift it. "Good. Are we in agreement, then? Do you still want to try this?"

"I think I need to."

She's right, and on the one hand, now that I've seen her and now that we've talked, I am more than happy to bestow all the pleasure on her I can until tomorrow. On the other hand, I'm already dreading that I may be paving the way for her to enjoy the hell out of sex with someone else.

What are you saying, you want a girlfriend now? When you and Ranger are still figuring life out? Where in your schedule would you fit her?

I stifle the voice of reason and curl my finger in, bringing her closer. "So that's a yes?"

"Yes."

The breathy way she replies doesn't just make my cock harder, it seems to squeeze something inside my chest.

I'm going to get my hands on her. She'll be mine—at least for tonight. I'll worry about tomorrow then. Hell, maybe by the time the sun comes up, this crazy draw I feel to her will be broken.

"Then let's go." I hold out my hand.

She looks at it with a frown. The wind blows, the surf crashes, the leaves rustle. I know exactly what she's thinking.

"But I thought—"

"No, I'm not going to kiss you here, Masey. I don't know how this is going to go. I want you someplace where you'll be comfortable, where we can do whatever feels good when it feels right."

"In public isn't it. Good point," she agrees as she puts her hand in mine and leads me back to her villa with a teasing smile. "Just say it. You're worried if things get carried away, we'll end up having sex on the beach."

The way I'm feeling now? "It's a distinct possibility."

She laughs me off. "I was kidding."

"I'm not."

"Oh, please. I'm nowhere near the sexiest woman you've ever met. And since I doubt very much you're worried about controlling yourself around me—"

"I wouldn't take that bet if I were you."

My words register. The smile slides off her face. She blinks. "You're serious?"

"Absolutely."

"You're not worried about me behaving like some dog in heat and climbing all over you?"

"Worried isn't the word I'd use." Leaving our shoes on the

lanai, I hold the back door open, watching as Masey slides inside the vacation rental. "Hopeful. Excited." I shut the door between us and the outside world, directing all my focus on her. "Turned on…"

"Pfft. I'm the girl desperate enough to ask her best friend if she knew a guy willing to spend tonight with me so I could experience sex without my ex. You can't actually be interested in me beyond the fact I'm an easy lay."

I don't know whether I should wring Thom's neck or hers. "You're going to learn to stop selling yourself short, even if I have to spend all night kissing the bad habit out of you…"

She swallows. "Why?"

Because we have chemistry for days, honey. But I'm not going to waste the breath looking for the right words to convince her I think she's sexy as fuck when I've got a better way. I crook my finger at her. "Come closer and let me demonstrate." When she hesitates, I grin her way. "I dare you."

CHAPTER THREE

*M*asey draws in a sharp, shallow breath and holds it as she searches my face. Her pulse pounds. A tremor shudders through her. She licks her lips.

I have the distinct impression she's nervous…but tempted. The attraction is getting to her, wearing down her hesitation. Or maybe she's considering giving in because the alternative is merely the status quo. Whatever. Knowing she's nearly in the palm of my hand is a fucking turn-on.

My stare drops to her mouth. It was made for kissing. For sex. Everything about it tempts me. She's still wearing the remnants of a rosy gloss that accentuates the pout of her full lips. I want to kiss them, feel them glide across my skin, see them wrap around my cock.

"You dare me?" She raises an arched brow.

I drag in a breath to cool the lust burning my veins. "Yeah."

Slowly, she sinks her teeth into that bottom lip again. The gesture brings a rush of red to her pouty mouth. Is her unconscious habit the reason it always looks swollen? Or is that simply the normal plumpness of her lips?

For some reason I can't fathom, I need the answer to that question—and a ton of others about her. What does she look like when she's completely bare-faced and relaxed? When she first wakes and stretches? When she comes? I'm dying to understand what makes her tick and what it is about her that gets to me.

Masey is nothing like my "usual." She's not a blonde. She's not flirty. She's not loud or laughing or trying to be the center of everyone's attention. She doesn't have a wild streak. She doesn't have the kind of sexuality that makes me think that, once I get my hands on her, she'll be a bucking bronco I'll need to hold tight to handle her fierce, unbridled ride.

Instead, she has an appeal I've never encountered. She's not an explosion of sex on my senses but a slow, constant burn. Without even taking Masey to bed, I'm pretty sure that once with her won't dim this flame. What draws me isn't purely her killer cleavage, though it's damn tempting, or the gorgeous legs her short skirt reveals. She hasn't laughed loudly, downed shots, then cast me a flirty glance and suggested we fuck. No, Masey is measured, deliberate, and driven. Our candid conversation gave me a glimpse of the real her, and I'm sure she didn't ask Harlow to help her find the perfect one-night stand without a lot of consideration. My guess is she thought about this for weeks, maybe months. And despite Masey not being the kind of woman I'd normally pursue, I'm drawn to her. Her innate caution and her hint of something almost pure is a fascinating part of her allure.

And no one has touched it.

I want to be the first. I want to hoard it. Keep it. I want to study the origami of her personality and figure out everything about her that attracts me.

It makes no sense, but I'm aching for her in a way that doesn't feel strictly like sex.

Finally, she raises her chin as if she's reached a decision. Then she steps into my personal space. "You dared me. I can't say no to that. So, are you going to kiss me already?"

"Hell yeah. Oh, honey, if you knew everything racing through my head, you'd probably run."

A little furrow of worry appears between her brows. "Why? You're not going to hurt me, right?"

"Never."

"Then—"

"Let's not dissect whatever this is. Let's just let it happen."

"I've never been good at that."

Because she's never had the chance; Thom didn't make it possible. I have a feeling that she's tried to fantasize her way into the experience she wanted with her ex—and failed. Her anxiety is an unspoken ache bleeding between us. I feel her wondering... What will she do if I can't give her what she craves? If she's not capable of feeling real pleasure and she has to face the fact she's been blaming her ex all this time?

And underneath her worries lies a yearning I can't resist. Not for me specifically...but if I do everything right, is there any chance it could be? Is it at all possible she wakes up tomorrow and wants me to stay longer?

What the... Why am I thinking this shit? She's only here for a couple of weeks while she puts her ex behind her enough to date her new neighbor. Masey and I have nothing beyond tonight. I need to remember that.

But she's in my head and under my skin. Sure, I'm attracted. But this is...different.

It feels like more.

"I have no doubt you're better than you think," I finally say as I cradle her cheek and slowly slide my fingers around her nape, curling the tips along the soft column. "But let me help you. Tonight, tell me everything you think. If something I do feels good, say so. If it doesn't, I want to hear that, too."

She licks her lips again, and at the thought of her tongue on my skin, I feel my knees start to buckle. "You do?"

Masey breathes the question like she's not sure whether to believe me. I do my best to give her a reassuring smile when what I really want is to strip her bare, kiss her breathless, then rake my lips all over her body and focus on the parts that will make her sigh and moan and ultimately scream.

"Yeah."

"You won't feel criticized?"

"Positive."

"All right. I will."

"Good. Last chance."

"To back out?" She shakes her head. "No. I-I want this."

"This?" I know what she's getting at. I have every intention of being the most accommodating lover she's ever imagined. But I'm going to be an absolute bastard about one thing: she can't just want sex. I've hardly touched her and I already know that's not enough for me anymore.

"I want you," she admits softly, sending my triumph spiking. "It feels incredibly intimate to admit that. I barely know you and I already want you so much I don't understand…"

My fingers tighten on her nape as I start to lean in. "Same, honey. I want you, too. Now stop talking so I can kiss you."

She braces herself by clutching my shoulders. Her palms are like ghosts, barely whispering over my shirt. But her fingers dig into me, as if she can't quite keep her anxiety and her need to herself. "Oh, god."

"It's going to be good, Masey. I promise."

I have no doubt about that.

She stops breathing again. Her eyes slide shut. She tilts her face up to me. Without her heels, she's a tiny thing. I bend closer, closer, watching her lips softly purse.

My heart chugs. My blood races through my veins, searing muscle and skin. My cock, which has been hard since we met, turns unbearably stony as I inhale her scent. The beach clings to her—salt and wind and something sweet that's purely her.

What if I've been looking at the wrong kind of woman my whole life? What if everything I've been seeking is now right in front of me?

It's a ridiculous, out-of-nowhere thought—my last before I cover her rosy mouth with my own.

She conforms to me in an instant, like warm butter. Where I jut, she softens. Where I press, she yields. She leans into me and rises on her tiptoes. Her palms still float over me, but her fingers squeeze tighter as if she needs to be closer, as if she's testing whether I'll really be solid enough to give her what she's aching for. And she's so subtly sweet she's addictive.

With a groan, I urge her back to the nearest wall, pinning her against it, inhaling more of her as I cover her body with mine. I'm not at all shocked that she fits against me, that the swells of her breasts press perfectly against my chest and my hips settle against her exactly where they should. She gasps at the contact, breath shuddering through our kiss as she momentarily stiffens.

Fuck, is she having second thoughts? Is she going to pull away?

Then suddenly, she exhales and melts into me. Her lips soften even more as they part gently in the shiest welcome.

Oh, honey. That's all I need to barge right in.

I work my lips between hers and urge them apart. She's

there—she and her virgin tongue—now pressing against me, fingers creeping up to my neck, into my hair.

Her next exhalation is a shaky little moan. She grips me tighter. Yeah, she knows what's next, and I can't believe I'm going to be the first man to truly kiss her.

With the heady thought rolling through my brain, I work my way into her mouth, seeking, exploring, aching for her to meet me. And yes, there she is with a bashful glide of her tongue, another unsteady inhalation, and a grip around me that's beginning to feel desperate.

I tilt my head, go deeper. Again, she conforms, the answering slant of her lips the perfect counterbalance to give me unfettered access to all her flavors and secrets.

As I delve deeper still, we breathe together. She's sweet in my nose, honey against my tongue, a drug in my veins.

My hands glide down her curves before settling at her hips. Tonight isn't about me, and I want to make her feel so fucking good she never stops craving me, but I yank her against my aching cock and grind into her.

Her shaking sighs become an unsteady moan as she parts her legs to accommodate me, rocking up to meet me as I press right where she needs it, too.

Oh, fuck.

I dig my fingers into her, working them back until I'm gripping her ass and lifting her against me, surging, squeezing, thrusting.

Heat spikes. Lust jolts. Jesus, I'm so fucking dizzy I tear my lips from hers, but only long enough to suck in a giant draft of air. It doesn't clear my head. I doubt anything will. And I don't even care right now if I fall the fuck onto the floor. I'll take Masey with me, sink as deep into her mouth as I can, crawl on top of her, bury myself inside her…

"Trace," she pants, clinging tighter as she tosses her head back.

It's an offering. She's inviting me to put my lips on her skin and taste her. She's being vulnerable to me, giving herself to me.

No way I'm refusing that.

I wrap one hand around her nape again and squeeze, compelling her to tilt her head back. *Yes…* Now, she's utterly mine, and I drag my lips up her soft, so-pale throat, skating my way across her jaw as I work my fingers into her long tresses and slowly close my fist, then tug her in exactly where I want her. As she gasps and her eyes flare wide with surprise, I swallow the sound with a growl and my kiss.

Then I consume her.

I work her lips open until she can't possibly part wider, then I barge in, leaving her no defense against my onslaught.

Yes, I'm being ruthless. I can't seem to stop myself. Whatever hesitations she has, I want them gone. Whatever barriers or protections she might have erected against men in general or me specifically, those need to go, too. I want to leave no part of her untouched by my hands, my mouth, my passion. I want to delve into her, drown inside her.

I've lost my fucking mind. But it feels too good to care, much less stop.

Masey arches, crushing her breasts against me as she whimpers into my kiss. She clings, her fingers latching on to my shoulders like a growing vine spreading across a fence and claiming its territory. I'm all too happy to be hers.

She's too tempting not to tease, so with a last brush of my lips over hers, I pull back. She moans and lunges for me like I'm her air and she won't be able to breathe without me. Her lips part, seeking mine in an insistent rush. I catch her chin in my grip, denying her another kiss while I study her dilated eyes and flushed cheeks. So female. So sensual.

I swipe my thumb across her bottom lip and draw it down, then begin dipping my head to her slowly. Her audible breaths fill the air between us as I cover her mouth and dive deep. When I drag my tongue against hers, the kiss turns wilder, more fiery than the last. So fucking hot I think I'm going to melt.

Jesus, this is insane.

With a shudder, she grips at my short hair and rubs her breasts against me like she needs relief only I can give her and rocks against my desperate cock, silently pleading.

I eat at her until I can't think straight. Until I can barely breathe. It's all I can do not to lower her to the floor, shove our clothes aside, forget the fact there's a bed somewhere in this villa, and fuck her blind. But I promised her way more than a hot quickie. I promised her everything.

Time to get my head on straight and deliver.

Reluctantly, I pull my mouth free, tightening my fist in her hair to prevent her from suckering me in with another one of her kisses I find so damn hard to resist. "Bedroom?"

"Down the hall. On the right."

I nod. "Wrap your legs around me."

She seems confused until I haul her against my body and straighten upright. Then she curls herself around me, arms and legs clinging. Before I even take a step, she starts nuzzling my neck. I shudder and hold in a groan. Her lips burn a path until she reaches the seam of my shoulder. She kisses me there, sweeping my shirt aside so she has more skin to worship. Another shiver wracks me when she surprises me with a drag of her tongue.

Shit. I'm barely halfway down the hall. How am I going to make it the rest of the way without losing my sanity?

And this woman has been unsure about her appeal? About her sexuality? Does she have any idea I'm burning alive?

I try to get a grip on my self-control. Mostly, I end up clutching her ass tighter and dragging my demanding lips along her jaw as I take ground-eating strides into the bedroom.

When I force myself to set Masey down in front of the bed, she's panting and staring at me as if she's convinced everything about tonight will be different than anything she's ever felt. It both terrifies her and turns her on. Suddenly, I'm feeling the same as I lose myself in her eyes.

I've never seen a more expressive woman. Or maybe I'm just reading her better because I'm so in tune with her. I can't say, and I can't spare the energy to figure it out now. Whatever it is about her, about us together, it makes me ache and sweat.

With our gazes fused, I reach for the buttons of my shirt. As they start to slip free, her stare follows, sliding lower and lower, until I'm pulling my shirttails free from my jeans and shrugging out of the starched cotton. As I drape it on a nearby chair, her eyes flare wide. She skates her fingertips down the bulge of my shoulder, over the ridge of my biceps, sending tremors through me again. I tingle everywhere she's touched. Every cell of my body is on fire.

"More?" My voice comes out rough, just shy of a growl.

She licks her top lip, bites the lower one. That habit of hers is going to undo me. "Yes."

I nod as I step into her space, then crouch in front of her, wrapping my hands around her sleek thighs. Her body tightens as I glide my palms up her legs. She sways closer, her eyes fluttering shut as I inch my fingers under her hem…up, up. Her silken red skirt drapes over my forearms as I curl my fingers around the waistband of her panties. I watch her, gratified to see her heart beat every bit as hard as mine and hear her labored breaths fill the still between us.

She blinks at me as if she's in danger of falling and only I can save her.

"You want me to take these off? Here? Now?" Once I do, there's no going back. I'll explore her pussy in every way until I've redefined pleasure for her and she's so addicted she doesn't remember Thom ever touching her.

"Do it." Her voice shakes.

I can't help the devilish smile spreading across my face as I tug the garment down her thighs and direct her to step out of it. I toss aside the tiny hot-pink thong trimmed with lace and bows. I have no doubt she looks incredible in it, and I'll get an eyeful— later. Now…I step back and sweep my gaze up her body. She doesn't look any different than she did the moment I first saw her in the bar, but I know that under her softly sexy, almost ladylike dress, her pussy is bare. And probably wet and pouty, too.

I step closer, drop a hand to the small of her back, and work down her smooth, round ass, laving my way across her collar-bones until I'm filling my palm with her surprisingly lush cheek.

She melts against me. "Trace…"

"You're hot as fuck without panties. If I didn't want you so damn much right now, I'd love going back to that bar and seducing you, all the while being the only man in the place to know that all I'd have to do to touch you is drop my hand onto your thigh and slide my way under your skirt. What if I made you come at the bar? What if I kissed you to swallow your screams so that only you and I knew you'd had an orgasm for me in public?"

Masey swallows hard. "You wouldn't."

"Oh, I would. And you'd let me."

She shakes her head. "What if someone saw?"

"Not happening. Even though we'd be in public, that orgasm would be mine—and mine alone."

"What if I couldn't climax? Some days I just can't…" She looks away.

I cup her cheek and bring her back to face me. "Maybe some days in the past. Forget about then. Focus on now." I settle a lingering, featherlight kiss over her lips. "Think about us."

As much as I enjoy verbally seducing Masey, I love touching her even more. I definitely can't resist kissing her again.

I settle my mouth over hers and sink deep. She opens hungrily and welcomes me by pressing her body into mine, meeting the lash of my tongue with a little whimper. She fits herself into my palm as I press my hand up her curves. Suddenly, I'm so close to her breast I'm nearly cradling it. I fucking want to touch her. As if she can read my mind, she wriggles and arches, silently begging me to take her in hand.

I have to know just how aroused she is.

My thumb wanders and…yes. Her nipple is hard. When I strum it, her breath catches. She digs her nails into my shoulders. She rubs against me again like she needs me to cure her ache.

I can't suppress my ruthless smile as I step away to sit on the edge of her bed. I have a vague impression of white linens and bright moonlight streaming in through a wall of windows around us before I pull her down to my lap. She falls back against my chest with a little squeak. Before she can recover or adjust, I've positioned her legs on either side of mine. I flare my knees out—and part her thighs wide. The only thing between my touch and her pussy is one little bitty skirt.

It's toast.

I drop one hand to her knee…and start skimming my fingertips up the inside of her thigh so, so slowly.

She gasps and clutches my hand. "Trace."

"Close your eyes. We're back at the bar." I shake her fingers off and gather her skirt in my hand as I creep up her leg. "The bartender wants to know if you want another merlot."

"Um…"

"I'll take another beer," I say as I flatten my free hand against her chest, just above her breasts, plastering her back to me. Under my palm, her heart beats ferociously. My fingertips dip over her nipple again.

She's even harder.

"Last call, honey," I whisper in her ear. "Wine…or something harder?"

"Harder," she breathes out.

"You got it. I'll come up"—I press my aching cock into her wriggling ass—"with something you'll like. Okay?"

She gives me a shaky nod. "Yes."

"The crowd is thinning out, and the bartender isn't looking at us now. I want something sweet."

"What—"

I grip her head and turn her chin to me, sinking my lips onto hers at the same moment my fingers get impatient and zip up her inner thigh to settle on her pussy. Slick, swollen, open. Perfect.

I've died and gone to heaven.

"Like that, honey?" I ask as I circle the hard bud of her clit.

"Yes. Oh…" She writhes on my lap. "Yes."

I clamp a hand on her thigh to still her. "Glad to hear it. You can't move too much. You can't be too loud. Or people will guess I have my hand on your pussy and that I'm making you feel good."

"We shouldn't." She whines the words.

"But it feels too good to stop," I argue.

She hesitates, and I see her mercilessly biting that swollen lower lip before she lifts her hips with a wheedling cry. "Way too good."

Fuck, this game, meant to get her out of her head, is going straight to mine.

"That's right," I pant in her ear. "You're so juicy against my fingers. Still worried I can't make you come?"

When I circle her sensitive nubbin again, she only answers with a gasp. Her head falls back to my shoulder. Rhythmically, she rocks her hips back onto my cock, then up against my fingers, back and forth, driving us both within an inch of sanity.

I wish like fuck I could see her. I imagine her cheeks are flushed and her eyes heavy-lidded. I'll bet her pussy is glossy and pink, lushly female as she parts her legs wider for me and invites me even deeper.

I slip a finger past her engorged folds and into her tight, sweltering heat. She closes around my digit with a cry and clamps down. Fuck, when I work my cock inside her, she's going to be like a fist. And as much as that idea turns me on, the way she's riding my fingers and calling my name fucking unhinges me.

"Think you'll come for me now?"

"Maybe." Her voice shakes. "Probably. Trace…"

"What do you want?"

"So much. Your clothes off. Your lips on mine. Your body against me."

"Me inside you?" I scissor and swirl my fingers inside her to press my point. "Fucking you until you scream?"

She nods earnestly. "Please. Yes."

"So polite… But I know there's a dirty girl in there."

She shakes her head. "No. I'm not—"

"You're letting me finger you at the bar," I point out, working my digits deeper inside her and teasing her clit with my thumb until her wail fills my ears. "If you don't want it, tell me." Other than her harsh breathing, total silence. "Masey?"

Her chest rises and falls with every breath. She gushes into my palm.

Yeah, she's close.

"You'll come for me right here, won't you?"

"If you keep touching me, I-I don't know how I'll stop it."

"You can't." I could get her off in seconds. The signs are all there. She's primed. She's ready. But I have another plan. "And god, you're so fucking sexy."

Head tossed back, she lifts to my hand. "You make me feel that way."

Though she's panting, I hear wonder in her tone. She's never felt particularly sexual or desirable—something else I'd like to punch Thom for.

I kiss my way up her neck and murmur in her ear. "You going to let me touch more of you?"

"Yes."

With a moan and another brush of her clit, I glide my palm down her thighs, toward her knees, then completely withdraw my hands from under her skirt.

"W-what are you doing?"

She's too polite to ask why I'm not making her come now. "There's so much of you I haven't explored yet, honey. And I think the guy in the corner was watching me touch your pussy. I don't want him seeing your pleasure or anything under your skirt. Tonight, that's mine."

"But—"

"I'll continue once it's safe," I murmur, gripping her hips. "If we don't give that perv a reason to look at us, something else will distract him. Just give it a few minutes…" Which will give her time to cool down.

Before I start ramping her up again.

"Okay."

Her voice tells me she's wondering where I'm going with this scenario, but she's playing along. I'll take it. She might have denied being a dirty girl, and she might lack the experience. But the instincts are there.

"Don't worry, honey. Nothing I want more than to watch you come. But I think, until then, I can touch you in other ways without anyone seeing…" I murmur as I lift my hands to the button at her nape. The moment I inhale, I smell her tang on my fingers. My mouth waters. My desire revs. I want her on my tongue.

Patience. Stick to the plan.

My fingers shake as I work the pearl button free from its mooring. Then I slide the fabric apart, spreading both ends toward her shoulders. The keyhole back expands to reveal exactly what I was looking for—the clasps of her matching pink bra.

With one hand, I unhook the three metal catches. With the other, I wrap my fingers around her throat and lean her head back until I'm whispering in her ear. "Take your bra off under your dress. Can you do that? Slide one strap down your arm at a time and slip it free. Don't let anyone see."

"Trace…"

When she cocks her head in my direction, I tighten my fingers around her jaw. "What? I'll block you with my body, but do it quick, while the guy in the corner is busy and the bartender has his back turned."

Masey hesitates. "Okay."

But she does exactly what I ask, sliding the delicate pink strap free from one arm before shrugging the dress back onto her shoulder. She repeats the process on the other side, then slips the wiry pink contraption through the other armhole and quickly adjusts the dress back into place. I pluck the bra from her grasp. It's still warm from her body. It even smells like her, somehow beachy and coconutty and fresh. The cups hint at breasts that will definitely fill my hands.

I can't wait.

After dropping the garment to the floor, I gather the closure of her dress around her neck again, bringing the ends together.

She gasps as the silk brushes her sensitive nipples. Then she melts back into me.

I smile. Masey's response is exactly what I anticipated.

"Feel good?" I ask, though I know it does.

"Yes. And unexpected."

"You're sitting at a bar with a man you just met, wearing a pretty, perfectly respectable dress—and absolutely nothing on underneath. Want to tell me again you're not a dirty girl? We both know I can touch any part of you now. And something else I know? You won't stop me."

"It feels so wrong." Her voice trembles. "But so good."

"Mmm, honey. I think the guy in the corner is busy hitting on the cocktail waitress. I want to see how else I can touch you without anyone noticing." I slip my hand into the keyhole back, smooth my palm over her shoulder, down her ribs, then slide around her body until I'm skimming my way up her abdomen and cradling her breast in my hand.

"Trace…"

"Feel good?" I stroke my thumb across the so-hard tip.

"Yes," she answers with a catch of her breath.

"Your nipples sensitive?"

"Not usually."

Because Thom, the dipshit, didn't take the time to arouse all her erogenous zones.

"Hmm. They must be pretty," I croon. "They're so firm and taut."

I demonstrate by pinching one. Masey wriggles in my lap. She's killing me with her breathy little moans and that pretty ass. I don't know how much more I can take...but it's too delicious to give up. And most important, she's not thinking about the fact that we're here in her rented bedroom to have pre-scheduled sex. In her mind, we're together in a bar, and I'm with her because I care only about her pleasure.

Given her lousy experiences, this is a good place for her mind to be.

"I-I never thought about my nipples."

And I'm hardly thinking about anything else right now. I'll see them—and study them, touch them, taste them—in good time.

"I'm sure they're luscious. Are they symmetrical?" I slide one hand out from the back of her dress, then insert the other, easing around to the front and cupping her other breast.

"I d-don't know. I think so."

With a slow drag, I thumb her other nipple. "If I can get both hands on them at once, I'll find out. I'll do my best to make sure no one sees."

Thank fuck the fabric of her dress is stretchy and easily accommodates the first hand joining the second around her ribs and kneading her breasts. No question, they're definitely symmetrical and capped with stiff tips that I'll bet are so engorged they're red. And I'm equally sure they'll be sweet as fuck in my mouth.

I pluck them between my thumbs and fingers, elongating

and tugging gently. Her wriggling on my lap starts in earnest again.

"More." Her voice breaks.

"Are you sure they're not sensitive? They feel that way to me. Every time I touch you"—I glide my fingertips over the hard crests again, earning another gasp—"I swear they get harder. You feel that, right?"

"Yes." She digs her nails into my thigh. "I do."

"You're definitely sensitive, honey. Very." I slide my lips against her ear. "I'm betting that a lot of what you thought about your body and the way it works isn't true."

She squirms again. "I'm wondering if you're right."

I absolutely am. But if she needs more convincing, I have all night to prove my point.

Rubbing and tweaking her nipples between my fingers, I ply my lips at her neck, nip at her lobe, breathe across her skin. Like before, her breaths turn audible. She writhes and tries to press her thighs together for relief, but with her legs still tangled with mine, I don't let her.

"Trace," she pants.

The sound of her arousal is so heady.

"Honey?"

"I don't think I can take much more of this. I ache. I need—"

"Shh. We're doing all we dare here at the bar now. Besides, I don't think you've ever been truly aroused in your life. I'm going to change that."

"I'm aroused now. Really."

More than usual, sure. But… "I'm not convinced you're aroused enough."

"It's more than I need. I swear. Can't we leave here, go somewhere alone, and take our clothes off?"

Masey is more assertive than I thought she'd be. I give her

points for going out on a limb. But I also think her courage is a measure of her growing trust in me. She wouldn't risk telling me how she feels if she believed I'd only shoot her down, like Thom.

"If that's what you want…"

She nods emphatically. "Please."

Once we drop the pretense of being in public, I suspect things between us will heat up—fast. "I need a few minutes to finish this beer and close out the tab."

"Trace…" She sighs in frustration.

"I'll make it worth the wait. I promise," I whisper in her ear. "Hey, the guy in the corner is gone. You still wet for me?"

"Yes." Then she turns to look at me over her shoulder. Even in the shadows, I can tell her lips are swollen and her cheeks a scorching pink. But it's her dilated eyes that grab me by the cock and squeeze. "Want to check?"

I can't resist smiling at her. "Oh, I plan to."

With one last tug of her nipple, I snake one hand from inside her dress and feel my way down her body, up under her skirt again. I skim an unerring path to her sex. If I thought she was wet before, she's drenched now. And so swollen she's downright puffy with need.

One touch of her clit earns me a wrenching moan and tells me she's dangerously close to orgasm.

My grin becomes a smile. "That is one juicy pussy. You ready to get out of here and let me make you feel so good?"

"Yes. Hurry."

All her earlier hesitation is gone. She was willing at the onset, but I wasn't convinced she actually wanted sex beyond a curiosity to see how it felt with someone else. And I hated the idea of her flaying herself with guilt afterward. When I leave her, I want her to focus on the pleasure and not linger over remorse. Sex shouldn't be bound by hang-ups and barricaded by inhibitions. She put up with Thom's germaphobe thing and his busy career, not to mention his moronic outlook on how much time sex should take from his "busy" schedule. I want to blow past all those stupid obstacles and show her ecstasy.

She deserves it.

"Let's go." I urge her to her feet and stand behind her.

Masey turns to face me. "Where?"

"Where do you want to be? We can imagine ourselves anywhere…"

"In my bedroom. With you. I don't know how you knew I needed to be someplace else for a bit—"

"It was obvious you were struggling to face it head on." I shrug. "I just tried to help."

"Thanks," she murmurs before sinking her teeth into that bottom lip again.

"You know that drives me insane, right?"

Her frown looks genuinely perplexed. "What?"

"The way you bite your lip."

She stops. "Sorry. I didn't realize."

"I didn't say I wanted you to stop. I said it drives me utterly batshit. And after the way I've riled and aroused you tonight, do you really feel bad about paying me back?"

A little smile creeps across her face. "Not a lot."

"Good. Don't change for me—or anyone. You're great the way you are." I cup her cheek. "And now I get to prove you're orgasmic, too."

"What do I get to do to you in return?"

"Keep being you. You'll drive me even wilder."

She tsks. "No, I won't."

"Wanna bet? I'm staring at you in this red dress. It's perfectly modest…except that it's clinging to your hard nipples and I know you're fucking bare underneath it. It drives my desire, which motivates me to provoke yours, even higher. And once I do, you'll undoubtedly make some move that torques me up even more. Get it?"

Masey cocks her head. "Does that work in reverse?"

What is she asking? If I turn her loose on my body, let her do whatever she wants, will she arouse the ever-loving fuck out of me? "Yeah."

Her smile gives me more than a little pause. "Good to know. So you coming home with me?"

"I'm already here. You going to let me take that dress off?"

She blinks. "I'll be totally naked."

"Yes, you will." I bring her body against me and cover her lips with mine, forging my way inside and remembering just how sweet she tastes.

"But what about you?" She glances down. "Those jeans can't be comfortable."

Then she surprises the hell out of me when she cups my cock through the denim.

I suck in a sharp breath and try to maintain my cool. If I don't, I'll be ripping through my button-fly, shucking these pants, throwing her down on the bed, tossing up her skirt…and remembering too late that this isn't just about easing the need broiling in my balls. Harlow asked me to do Masey right. She needs it. My impatience doesn't get to override that…but she's making it hard to resist.

I'll stop her—in a minute.

Through the thick fabric, I feel her curious fingers slide and squeeze up, caressing when she reaches the sensitive head, then gripping her way back down. I groan and toss my head back, digging my desperate fingers into her shoulders and trying so hard not to tear off everything we're wearing and find relief now.

I'm usually cool and patient. The five-month abstinence isn't helping, but I know this is mostly about Masey. She's making me crave more.

"It's nice to know I can get to you, too," she murmurs as she kisses her way across my shoulder, down to one pec, then sucks my nipple in her mouth.

I rise to my toes, my body stiffening. Desire detonates like a bomb in my gut.

Too damn fast. "Jesus, Masey…"

I can't stop myself, I thumb her breast through her dress, twisting and tugging on her nipple.

She freezes. Her breaths seesaws from her chest. "How quickly can you get these jeans off? I can be naked in ten seconds."

My whole plan tonight was to take my time, inundate her with pleasure, and saturate her with sheer sensation. Now, a quickie sounds perfect. I can still give her all that other stuff in round two, right?

There's no way this is over after one quick tumble. Hell, the way I'm feeling now, I don't see how this ever ends.

Shit, that's a complicated thought in and of itself.

We'll cross that bridge later.

"I can be in the bed, condom on, and ready by then."

"Thank god." She reaches for the hem of her dress and starts to pull it up.

I'm determined to watch her every move as I attack my button fly.

But my phone rings. I'd ignore it except it's the chime I assigned my mother, and she never calls unless it's important, especially this time of night.

"Fuck," I hiss as I reach for the device.

"Do you need to get that now?" I hear the whine in Masey's voice. She's not happy.

That makes two of us.

"Unfortunately, yeah. Hopefully, this will just take a minute." Maybe Ranger is just being fussy or she has a question about where I packed the extra diapers.

Please be simple, I silently pray as I press the button to answer.

CHAPTER FOUR

"*Makuahine?*" I mutter as I grip the phone, then hold up a finger to Masey and mouth, *Give me a minute.*

As I walk into the hall for privacy—where I won't be tempted by the sight of Masey getting naked—my mother says, "I'm sorry to call. I know you're…busy."

Of course she knows. I didn't tell her I planned to spend the night in bed with Harlow's best friend, but my mother raised two boys with active sex drives. I haven't been out in months. She doesn't have to try too hard to guess what I'm up to.

"What's wrong?" I ask.

"I put Ranger in his playpen in the living room with his toys while I finished my dinner dishes. Somehow, I splashed water on the floor, and when I turned to put away the clean pots, I slipped in it and fell. I think I broke my ankle. I can't get myself up."

Oh, shit. I can't leave my mom hurting and stranded on the cold tile, and my son shouldn't be unsupervised. What if he puts something in his mouth and chokes?

I tamp down worry. "Did you call an ambulance?"

"Not for a broken ankle. I'm not dying, *keikikāne*."

I sigh. She's right.

"Any blood?" Please, god, don't let the fractured bone have punctured her skin.

"No. But it has swelled. And it's painful."

While I'm relieved it's not a compound break, the fact she's hurting isn't good news.

"Okay, don't move. I'm on my way. Can you call one of your neighbors until I can get there? What about Mrs. Palakiko?"

"She left for the mainland yesterday to visit her son."

Damn it. "I'm on my way, but I'm at least fifteen minutes out." I march back into the bedroom, where Masey has already flipped on a bedside lamp. I try to ignore the fact she looks deliciously disheveled as I reach for my shirt on the floor and send her a deeply apologetic glance.

"I can wait," my mother says in my ear. "It took me that long just to crawl for my phone so I could call you."

Fuck. That's bad. This evening has gone from spectacular to shit show in two minutes.

"I'll hurry. Just...don't move. Call me back immediately if anything else happens. And call 911 if you need to."

She agrees, and I hang up, already doing a one-handed shrug into my shirt and gazing at Masey with regret. "I'm so sorry. I have to go. My mom fell and hurt herself. She lives alone and..."

Harlow's bestie doesn't hesitate, just grabs her bra and panties off the floor. "Then you need to go. I totally understand."

"Rain check tomorrow?" I don't know how I'm going to

make that work if my mom can't watch Ranger. Maybe Noah and Harlow will volunteer?

"Sure. I'm here until the eighteenth, so whenever. I'll just be doing some product testing and filming."

"Thanks for understanding. I'm going to make this up to you, honey. I promised you pleasure, and I intend to come through."

She waves that concern away. "It's fine. Do you want me to come with you? Do you need help?

It's tempting, but probably not a good idea. If I introduce Masey to Makuahine, she'll start hearing wedding bells. I love Ranger more than anything, but he's turned my life upside down. I still don't know what day it is half the time. The situation is improving, but the struggle of going from bachelor to single dad has been real. I can't take on more now.

"I appreciate that, but I should be okay. She thinks she broke her ankle, so I just need to get her to the ER for an X-ray."

"Okay…well, if you can make it back here some other time, let me know. Harlow has my number."

"Thanks. I'll call you tomorrow." Then I dash out of the bedroom, holding my shirt together with one hand and grabbing my discarded shoes off the lanai with the other. Back in the living room, I hop into them and turn to find Masey nearby, clearly wearing her bra again and holding the front door open for me.

"I hope your mom is all right."

It's two seconds I probably shouldn't spend, but I can't resist leaning in for a quick kiss. I want to say something beyond *thank you* or *I'll call you.* I've said that, and there's something more bubbling inside me. Something deeper. Now isn't the time, so I simply nod and head out, jogging toward my car.

Pressing the fob to unlock my door, I race around to the driver's side—only to be stopped short. My front left tire is completely flat. Apparently, that *was* glass I ran over on my way to the bar.

"Fuck!" With a frustrated huff, I shove my keys in my pocket. What the hell do I do now? I don't have time to change a damn tire.

"What's wrong?" Masey asks softly, stepping out onto the covered, stone-paved porch.

I sift through all my possible options. Calling Noah and Harlow, even if I managed to interrupt their alone time, would take too long. My sister, Samaria, lives on Oahu. I hate to bother my sister-in-law's extended family. Her brothers, Maxon, Griff, and Evan, are all great, but they each have newborns with their wives. Bethany, her sister, is with her fiancé, Clint, in LA. They'll return to Maui midweek before their wedding next Saturday. There's no one else I trust on the island. And Ranger is *my* son. *My* responsibility.

One I haven't told Masey about.

But at this point, I don't think I have a choice.

"My tire is flat."

"If you need to borrow my car…"

It will be stranded at my mom's house if I do, since Masey doesn't have a car seat for my son. "That won't work. I know I'm asking a lot—"

"You're not. Do you want me to take you? I'm happy to help."

As I suspected, despite her hidden bad-girl streak, she's actually very sweet. That's something I've never found particularly appealing…but I'm rethinking it now. And I'm definitely grateful that she's kind enough to lend me a hand. Most of the women I've spent my time with in the past probably wouldn't have cared enough to spit on me if I was on fire.

"I appreciate that."

"Let me grab my purse and keys. I'll be right back."

Masey disappears inside the house again, then emerges moments later, shoes on, purse slung over her shoulder. As I hover near the passenger door of her white rental, she tosses me the keys. "Do you mind driving? I still have no idea where I'm going since I've only been on the island a couple of days."

I didn't even think about that. "Sure."

After opening the passenger door for her, I dash around the back of the sedan and slide into the driver's seat. I have to adjust everything before I can even sit down. Normally, I'd tease her about being short. Not to make fun of her but because I think she's really cute. And sexy, too. Right now, I'm too focused on reaching my mother and son.

And deciding how I tell her about Ranger.

I back out of her driveway and screech out of her secluded neighborhood. Am I overthinking this? As much as I've been into this woman this evening, that doesn't mean I'll feel the same after we've "done the deed." Or that Masey will *ever* feel that way. Best to simply be factual.

"I need to tell you something." When I look over, she's flipped the visor down and turned on the accompanying light so she can freshen her face. Her cheeks are still rosy. Her lips are even more swollen than the last time I looked. Her dark hair is a wild, curled mass.

There's no way my mother won't take one look at her and know exactly what we've been doing, then ask me a million probing questions about my feelings.

Shit.

Masey looks my way. "What?"

I swallow. Telling her about Ranger means explaining something that happened over a year ago. It's one of the nights I'm least proud of. On the other hand, my fuckup brought me one of my greatest blessings. Yes, that little boy has crimped my sex life, but he's also changed everything, mostly for the better. All the joy he brings me definitely outweighs any difficulty I encounter in being a single dad. And I'm fiercely protective of him.

"How much did Harlow tell you about me?"

She closes her tube of lipstick, kills the light, then flips the visor up. "Not much. I didn't want too many details. Nothing against you, but I didn't want the sex to be an emotional experience. I'm saying that wrong. I just didn't want to get attached."

I get it. Before I met her, before I touched her, I felt the same.

As I race through a yellow light and we roll down Maui's half-empty streets, I realize there's no easy way to say this. "I have a son. And sole custody of him."

Masey's eyes widen. "How old is he?"

"Five months. I'm not trying to be too personal. I'm telling you because my mother was watching him tonight so I could be with you."

"Oh." The ramifications are clearly hitting Masey.

Same here. I'm trying to figure out how I'm going to function for the next few weeks without Makuahine's help. I've got jobs booked, and I need that income.

I'll have to figure that out later.

"I see."

"He's in his playpen now, so he's fairly safe, but—"

"Of course you had to rush over to your mom's. She's hurt. Your son needs you. You don't have to apologize or explain to me."

I suspect she wants to know where my son's mother is and is

simply too polite to ask. It will come up. Maybe Masey won't be surprised or even care. Harlow described me as a man whore. I just don't like the idea of anyone thinking of my son as a burden…and I'm touchy because his own mother felt that way.

"Thanks."

Then there's really nothing left to say as we speed through the evening. The silence is a little awkward—not going to lie. I open my mouth more than once to ask what she's thinking. But I shut it. I've dumped a lot on her in a really short period of time. She said she didn't want emotional, so I can't demand she share her feelings simply to set me at ease.

But there is one other thing… "I should warn you, my mom may try to play matchmaker. She does it all the time."

"She must not be too successful, right?" Masey shrugs. "You're still single."

"Because I don't bring women home to meet her."

"Never?"

"Not since, like, my junior prom. Because my brother was a pro athlete and lived on the mainland, she gave him a pass until he retired and moved home. He literally met Harlow the day he landed on Maui, so she didn't have time to meddle in his life. But I was right here, underfoot, all the time. She tried to set me up with the daughters of every single one of her friends for a decade. She settled for marrying off my younger sister—at least for now."

But if I show the least bit of interest in Masey, I know Makuahine. She'll do everything she can to throw us together.

The fire between Masey and me doesn't need more kindling. We just need a night in the sack.

I have to hope it will fizzle out after that.

"If she's insistent, I'm sure it's only because she wants to see you happy."

I snort. "And because she wants grandkids. And from the moment we accidentally dropped in on Noah and Harlow shortly after they met and it was clear they were…busy, she all but chanted some ancient Hawaiian fertility ritual and prayed daily for Harlow to conceive. When my sister-in-law did, Makuahine was convinced the power of her divine prayer was strong."

Masey smiles. "How do you know it wasn't?"

"Don't encourage her," I warn with a sidelong stare. "Or she'll do everything possible to couple us up. And she won't be happy until we're walking down the aisle and you're announcing you're pregnant."

"You already gave her a grandson."

"And she loves Ranger. But she wants me to have the wife and picket fence, too." I don't know how else to explain it, and I don't have time now that I'm pulling up in front of my mother's house.

I park in the driveway and jump out. The kitchen light shines through the front window.

Of course the front door is unlocked. I keep explaining to my mother that times have changed and she needs to think more about safety, but in this case, her oversight works in my favor.

"Makuahine?" I shout as soon as Masey and I step inside.

"Here." Her voice sounds strained, weak.

Worry grips my throat. She can't die from a broken ankle, but my mother has other health conditions that worry me. And after my father's unexpected death from asthma a few years back, I take nothing for granted.

"The living room is that way," I tell Masey, pointing. "Will you check on Ranger for me? I'll be right there."

She nods and jogs toward the brown-and-blue-checkered playpen while I hustle into the kitchen to find my mom sprawled across the floor. Her usual bun is unusually askew. She's breathing hard. I see the pain on her face.

And her ankle has swollen to three times its normal size.

"Makuahine!"

The moment she sees me, she looks relieved. "I'm so sorry."

"Don't apologize. Of course I was going to come the second you called. I brought a friend of Harlow's with me. Masey is with Ranger now." And I'll need to check on them. My boy is pretty friendly, but like all kids, when he's tired and cranky, he doesn't take well to strangers. "Let's get you off the floor so we can get to the hospital."

After bracing Mom's back against my chest, I reach under her arms and hoist her up. Leaning on me, she hobbles on one foot, looking pale and spent. The pain, still all over her face, deepens.

Suddenly, Masey appears at the edge of the galley kitchen, a sleeping Ranger in her arms.

The sight does something to me. My breath catches. My gut tenses. My goddamn heart flips over.

"Hi, Mrs. Weston. I'm Masey." She smiles, holding my son like he's precious cargo. "A friend of Harlow's visiting from LA. I'd shake your hand but…"

My mother manages a strained smile. "Nice to meet you. Any fuss from him?"

Masey glances at the boy. "A little when I picked him up. But I babysat my way through high school. I'm good with kids. I rocked him for a moment, and he fell right back asleep."

That explains a lot. She looks like a natural.

But I don't have time to dwell on why that makes me happy. "Let's get you in the car, Makuahine. We'll take yours since it has a car seat."

"All right," she sighs.

"Maybe we should get some ice around it to counteract the swelling?" Masey suggests.

"Good idea." I settle my mother in a chair, grab the ice out of the freezer and a clean dish towel from the nearby drawer.

As I move to dump the ice in the terry cloth, Masey stops me. "Wait. It will last longer and be less messy if you put it on a large plastic baggie with a couple of tablespoons of rubbing alcohol." Then she backs away. "Sorry. My mother was a nurse. It's what she did for us as kids, and it always worked."

"Don't apologize." I scramble to find everything, grateful the rubbing alcohol is sitting beside Makuahine's first aid kit in the pantry. Once I do, I assemble the homemade ice pack, wrap it in the towel, and fasten it around my mother's ankle. "Like this?"

Masey nods. "Perfect."

My mother smiles her way. "Thank you."

"Not at all," Masey replies, continuing to bounce and rock my sleeping son.

I try not to be distracted by the sight. "Let's go."

"All right." Makuahine sounds reluctant.

Clearly, she's not looking forward to hobbling out to the carport. I don't blame her. Crawling to her phone and waiting for me to arrive took a lot of her strength. But standing here is only allowing more blood to rush to her ankle, which will make the throbbing worse. And I'm sure she's concerned about falling and risking further injury. I can't let that happen.

"Hold on to me," I tell her as I wrap one of her arms around my neck and brace one of mine behind her back.

"What are you doing?" she shrieks as I lift her against my chest. "I'm not a small woman. You'll hurt yourself!"

"I'm fine. Don't argue," I insist as I head toward the back door, then glance back at Masey. "Ranger's diaper bag should be next to the playpen. Can you grab it and lock the front door, then meet us out back?"

"Got it."

As she spins off with Ranger, I try my best not to jostle Makuahine as I make my way across the grassy yard, past the citrus trees, and to the waiting SUV Noah bought for her a few years ago, even though she insisted she doesn't drive enough to own a car. Funny how that changed once we both had kids. Then she was the first to insist she loves to drive—and needed a good car seat.

Thank goodness I installed it the day she opened the box. I know it's done right.

For now, I ease my mother into the front seat, slide it back as far as it will go, and prop her calf on the dash to elevate her injured ankle. "You okay? Hanging in there?"

"Fine."

She's lying. She sounds winded and exhausted. She looks waxy. I definitely hear more pain in her voice. I'm worried.

"Should I get you some ibuprofen before we go?"

"No. They'll give me something at the hospital. I don't want any medication to interfere."

As much as I hate to see her in pain, she's probably right. "I'll be right back. Where are your car keys?"

Makuahine presses her lips together. "In the glove box."

Now isn't the time for an argument, but I fish them out with a scowl. "Your car is unlocked, and you leave your keys inside?"

She shrugs. "Old habit."

Shaking my damn head, I start the car. "I've told you it's not safe."

Masey races out of the house and bustles to the parked SUV, a purse on each shoulder and Ranger in her arms. As she approaches, my mother rolls down the window. "I'm guessing

this is your purse, Mrs. Weston, and your insurance card might
be inside."

"You're right. Thank you."

Masey leans in so Makuahine can pluck the bag up and set it
in her lap. "You're welcome." Then she glances my way. "It's
been more than a minute since I secured a baby in a car seat.
Maybe you should remind me?"

She's right. Clearly, I'm not thinking straight.

"Sure." I hop out.

Together, we strap Ranger in. He barely stirs.

"Thanks for all your help tonight. I owe you."

She shakes her head. "I hate to leave you to juggle all this
alone. Why don't I follow you to the hospital in my rental?"

"Ranger shouldn't be at the hospital," Makuahine insists.
"Too many germs there, and it's past his bedtime. We'll take him
to your brother's house first."

"That will take too long, and you need medical attention
now. Besides, the playpen is still in your living room. Where will
Ranger sleep?"

Especially now that he's dangerously close to crawling. Once
he's mobile, watch out, world. I often see my son on his blanket
in the living room lifting himself on his hands and knees,
rocking like he's finding the momentum to take off and attack
life.

"I can watch him at your place," Masey volunteers. "I don't
mean to intrude, but he could be in his own bed and you
wouldn't have to take the time to drive all the way back to Noah
and Harlow's place first. I'm happy to follow you there in my
rental. All you have to do is let me in. I'll handle the rest until
you're home."

"She's smart, keikikāne," my mother says. "If you're not
dating her, you should be."

And there's the Makuahine I know. Not even pain and broken bones can keep her from meddling.

Masey gracefully laughs off the comment like it's a joke. "Thank you, Mrs. Weston, but Harlow just introduced us tonight."

My mother smiles. "You must like him more than a little. Your lips are swollen, so I know he's been kissing you."

I'm sure she can't help it, but Masey blushes.

I sigh. "That's none of your business." Then I turn to Masey. "You really don't mind watching Ranger for a few hours?"

"Not at all. I hadn't planned to film tonight anyway, and while he's sleeping, I can jot down some notes I have floating in my head about future videos. I have some product in my purse I can do a little advance testing on… I'll be fine."

As much as I hate to impose, her idea is the best for both Makuahine and Ranger. "Thanks. I really, really owe you."

Before she can answer, my mother jumps in. "He'll take you to dinner."

Masey raises a brow at me. "Yeah?"

Despite everything, I smile. "If you want, absolutely."

"Sure. That sounds nice."

"Perfect." My mother seems more than pleased. "Now let's get going."

After we ensure Ranger is secure, I hop into the driver's seat again and regard Masey. "I'll drive around the front of the house and you can follow me from there."

My condo is probably a mess, but that's not my biggest worry. I'll tell Masey to ignore the small tornado that came through and wreaked havoc.

We were merely supposed to be spending a night together. Granted, it didn't go as planned, and she probably won't judge me too harshly for my lack of housekeeping skills. But I'd hate to scare her off already.

"Great." Masey nods, then heads down the side yard and out the front gate.

I back out into the alley behind Makuahine's house and come around to the front. As we cruise beside Masey's rental, my mother looks smug. "You like her."

"She's nice. Right now, I'm focused on you. How are you feeling?"

"The pain is awful."

I wince. "Maybe you should have let me give you some—"

"No. Talking about you and Masey helps me take my mind off the hurt."

Of course it does.

I try not to roll my eyes as I pull onto the road. Masey falls in behind me.

"Don't huff. It's time for you to settle down," my mother points out. "You're in your thirties. You have a son now. This frat boy hit-it-and-quit-it mentality is no way for you to date anymore."

I turn to her, mouth agape. "Where did you hear *that* phrase?"

"I have the internet, don't I?"

My mother only gets saucy when she's convinced she's right. Honestly, she probably is.

"I'm a little horrified. We'll talk about this later." When she opens her mouth to argue, I hold up a finger. "Like after we get you X-rayed and find out what's wrong with your ankle."

Makuahine doesn't look pleased, but she nods. "All right."

Thank god for small favors.

I fill the otherwise wordless drive with the oldies station on my mother's car radio. As we approach my house, Foreigner helpfully supplies "Waiting for a Girl Like You."

My mother sends me a knowing look. "See? Even the universe knows you need to settle down with someone like Masey."

I send her a quelling stare, but I can't deny that Lou Gramm isn't completely wrong. I have been waiting too long. But Makuahine doesn't know how true it is that my heart has been hurt before, so this time I don't simply want to be sure, I'm determined to be. When his soulful last phrase croons through her car, begging this woman to come into his life, I'm weirdly moved.

Lord, I must be spending too much time with Maxon's wife, Keeley. She interprets life through song, and it seems to have rubbed off on most of us.

From what I can tell so far, having Masey around more wouldn't be all bad. But I'm getting ahead of myself. I don't know her well. She lives in LA. The pull I felt to her earlier won't last, right?

It seems to take forever, but we finally pull up in front of my condo. The place is nothing special, but it's roomy. I'm on the third floor with a big lanai and a banging view of the beach. And my unit is on the corner, so I only have a neighbor on one side, who's almost never around since it's his vacation home. All in all, it works for me. Well, it did. These days I'm feeling a little squeezed by all of Ranger's gear and toys.

I point Masey into my assigned parking spot, then pull in next to a nearby curb and turn to my mother. "Be right back."

After I hop out, I hoist Ranger's diaper bag onto my shoulder and lift the sleeping little guy into my arms. He fusses for a few moments, then settles again with a happy sigh.

The love I always feel for him washes over me. I kiss the top of his head. "I've missed you, little man."

"Is he all right?" Makuahine asks.

"Fine."

When I turn, Masey approaches, locking her rental with a press of her fob. I let the diaper bag with the rocket-ship print slough off my shoulder. She takes it, and I guide her toward my unit. "Everything he needs for a fresh change should be in this bag, but just in case, there's more in his room. I've got formula pre-bottled in the fridge and a warmer on the counter. Just takes a few minutes. He's a good eater, FYI. He probably won't need help burping, but if he does, getting him to do it is easy. If he needs clean pajamas for any reason, they're in the dresser. And excuse my mess. I wasn't expecting company."

She turns to me with a smile as I let her inside my condo. "I'm not here to judge, just take care of Ranger. I've got everything under control. Hand him to me and go take care of your mother. He and I will be fine."

Maybe it's too domestic, but I can't resist kissing her as I settle Ranger into her arms. He stretches a little, lifting a fist above his head, but he doesn't wake otherwise.

"Thanks again. I'll be back as soon as I can. Oh"—I dash in and fumble for a sticky note and pen on the bar separating the kitchen from the living room—"here's my number. Call me if you have any problems."

"I won't. Go. Bye."

I need to get my mother to the hospital, but I'm reluctant to leave Masey. "His room is the last one on the right down the hall. He needs a change, I think, but he shouldn't wake up again until after I get back. Really…I appreciate this."

She's smiling as I shut the door, dart back to my mother's SUV, and take off for the hospital.

At a little after two in the morning, I slip inside my condo, thanking God that Makuahine's ankle isn't broken, and shut the door with an exhausted sigh. Then I freeze.

Masey is nowhere to be seen...but everything in my living room has been picked up and tucked away. The throw Harlow insisted I "need" on the back of the sofa has been neatly folded and its coordinating pillows arranged artfully at either end. Ranger's toys are back in their box. She's stacked his books, which he chews on more than reads, and wiped all the dried cereal off his exosaucer. She folded the last load of his laundry, which I never got around to, and set everything back in the basket. His baby blankets are neatly organized in the little rocking chair with his name painted in big red letters.

The place looks as close to perfect as I've seen it since I brought Ranger home from the hospital.

"Holy shit," I mutter as I wander into the kitchen, where I find more of the same there. The dishes, even the ones I didn't have time to do after breakfast, are squeaky clean. Most are put away. A few odds and ends are still drying on the rack stacked on the basin, but the place is immaculate. There's even a collection of Ranger's little plastic oatmeal bowls and bottles all lined in a row in a corner of the counter. The stove is spotless.

I'm utterly speechless. She watched my son *and* cleaned up?

I definitely owe her. But where is she?

Heading down the hall, I peek into my bedroom, wondering if she fell asleep. Seeing her in my bed...I wouldn't be mad. Not at all.

But when I open the door, the room looks the same as it did when I left. And she's still nowhere to be found.

I wince and make a mental note to put away all my clean

clothes tomorrow. In the meantime, I toss my dirty garments in the hamper and kick my discarded shoes into my closet. But it's probably too late to impress her. Even if she didn't take a curious peek into my bedroom, she has no illusions that I'm an absent housekeeper at best. Whatever. She didn't agree to spend the night with me because I make a mean bed or mop my kitchen until it gleams.

Since we're not going to have a long-term relationship, I shouldn't sweat her opinion too much.

With a shrug, I tiptoe the rest of the way down the hall, into my son's room. The first thing I see is Ranger all cuddled up with his favorite blue blanket, wearing his monster-truck pajamas. His man-in-the-moon nightlight casts just enough glow on his little form to see that he's breathing deeply and evenly.

Finally, I turn to the glider Britta insisted I need to properly rock an infant. Masey is slouched in it, head propped against the back, fast asleep. On the little table beside the glider, I see an empty baby bottle. She still has a burp cloth draped over one arm.

At the sight, my heart does some sort of flipping, melting thing I know is about more than gratitude. I'm reluctant to put these feelings into words.

No denying, Masey is the kind of woman I should fall for… but love hasn't worked out well for me in the past. I need to give her the amazing romp I promised and step away. Even if Masey would never mean to hurt me, Harlow's bestie hasn't been out of her last relationship for long. She's probably too raw for anything deep. And while she doesn't seem like the type who would be cavalierly cruel…I've been wrong before. Either way, I'm not eager to take a chance on getting my heart broken again.

But I can't leave her in the chair. She'll wake up with a

terrible crook in her neck. And the minute Ranger stirs for his early-morning bottle, he'll wake her.

"Hey." I cup Masey's shoulder and softly shake her.

She comes awake with a gasp and blinks up at me.

Her blue eyes are a gut punch.

"Sorry if I startled you."

She sits up straighter and shakes her head. "You're fine. Is everything okay with your mom?"

"Yeah. Her ankle isn't broken, just sprained. She'll need someone to come stay with her for the next couple of weeks because mobility will be a challenge, but as long as she stays off her feet, she should be fine soon enough."

"Did you take her home already? Who's with her tonight?"

"Noah. I texted him from the hospital. He came and he's staying with her for now. In the morning, he'll pack her up and take her to his place until she recovers."

"There are so many stairs in that house."

And not a single bedroom on the lower level. "I know. Tomorrow, he's going to rent a hospital bed and put it in his downstairs office. But for now, he took her home so she could rest."

"Good idea." She rises to her feet. "I'll, um…get out of your hair and let you get some sleep. Harlow already told me you have a booking tomorrow."

I've been wracking my brain about that—and I still have no idea what to do. Makuahine is in no shape to watch Ranger, and Harlow has commitments. "Yeah. I'm supposed to be at the marina at nine a.m."

"That's in less than seven hours. I'll be gone in two minutes. Just need to remember where I left my purse."

I see it on the floor next to the glider and scoop it up for her. Then I hesitate. By the time she gets back to her rented digs, it will be nearly three a.m. I don't like thinking about her driving home alone so late when she doesn't know her way around. I also dislike thinking about her parking her car out front and walking into her rental alone. There are people on the island who take advantage of tasty tourists like her.

And if I'm being really honest, I'm not keen on her leaving.

"You, um…don't have to go. You're welcome to stay."

"With everything that's happened tonight, I don't have any expectations that we'll…well, you know. You need sleep, and I—"

"Sleep." I should have been clearer. "Just sleep. It would be awfully late before you reached your rental and got into bed. Unless you're jonesing to get back, if all you want to do is sleep comfortably somewhere, there's a vacancy next to me. Your call. I promise you, I'm so wrung out right now, I don't know if I'd have the energy for sex."

That's a lie. I can't be in the room with Masey without wanting her. Still, I'm less than honest so she's able to feel safe and comfortable beside me.

Then she bites that goddamn lip—and raises my blood pressure. "Are you sure?"

"Yeah."

"All right. Thanks. I wouldn't impose, but like I said I'm still not sure where I'm going on this island all the time. It will be harder to figure out in the dark. And…I've really been struggling with the time difference and the unfamiliar surroundings since I got here. I haven't been sleeping that well."

In a roundabout way, she's saying she'll feel safer sleeping next to me. It shouldn't, but her implied admission thrills me. "Then stay."

I may regret this tomorrow, but I'm glad she's staying.

A shy smile breaks out across her face. "All right. Do you, um...have a T-shirt or something I could sleep in?"

If we were lovers, I'd want her to come to bed in nothing but her skin and a come-hither smile. But I can't suggest that tonight or sleep will never happen. And I'll be worthless tomorrow. Besides, she deserves more than the hit-it-and-quit-it Makuahine chastised me about earlier.

"I'll find one." I hold out my hand. "Come on, honey."

When she takes it, I try not to think about how close she'll be to me all night, how much I like being with her, or how domestic it feels as we approach Ranger's crib and watch him breathe peacefully together.

"Good night, little man."

"'Night." Masey caresses the black baby-fine hair at his crown. "Sleep tight."

Her obvious affection for him messes with my head. What if Masey isn't like the one who ripped out my heart? Is there any chance...

No. I have to stop thinking like this. It's late, and I'm tired. I'm not making sense.

With my thoughts in turmoil, I guide her toward my bedroom, glad I cleaned up at least a little.

"My sheets are fresh," I promise. "I just did laundry earlier today. Speaking of which, thanks for folding the last load of Ranger's things in the living room. And for cleaning up the kitchen, too. You didn't have to do that."

"I didn't mind. When you dropped Ranger and me off, he woke up, so I gave him a bath. We played for a bit. OMG, he *loves* that plushy football."

I smile fondly. "He does. Noah gave it to him when he was born, and he swears it's a sign that my son is going to follow in his uncle's footsteps."

Her light laughter fills the space between us as we enter my bedroom—and does that something dangerous to my heart again. "I believe it. He's a big boy, too."

"A chunker, for sure. He's already at the top of the height and weight charts, almost twenty-eight inches long and twenty pounds."

"Wow. That's amazing, but not really a surprise. You and Noah aren't small men, either."

I refrain from a sophomoric size joke. It's on the tip of my tongue, but… "It runs in the family. My mom's people have lived in Hawaii for a few generations but they came originally from Samoa."

"Like the Rock?"

"I guess. They're all big and athletic. My dad was from the mainland, but he played football in high school and college. He probably would have gone on to play pro if his asthma hadn't given him so much hell and he hadn't gotten in a motorcycle accident that tore up his knee."

"Makes sense. I'm sorry it didn't work out."

We pause in the middle of the room. I look at her. She looks back at me. I'm exhausted and I'm worried about my job tomorrow. It's lucrative. It alone will pay half my mortgage this month. I don't want to cancel, so I have to come up with some alternate babysitting situation.

But all I can think about is Masey. I'll be next to her. Remembering everything about her. Wanting to touch her. Smelling her. Desiring her.

Maybe this wasn't such a good idea.

Too late now…

"Thanks. Let's find you that shirt."

I rummage through my dresser and find a black T-shirt that reads HI in white block letters and uses the shape of the islands to dot the i. It's a bit too small for me, so maybe it won't be too comically big on Masey.

She takes it from my grip. "Thanks. I'll, um…use the bathroom in the hall."

It's cleaner than mine, and she probably wants some privacy. "Sure."

When she slips out of my room, I hit the bathroom, head for my bed, then hesitate. I usually sleep naked. I don't own a pair of pajama pants; most of the year, it's too hot in Hawaii for that. I debate what to do, then decide to change into a pair of basketball shorts. The rest she's already seen.

After setting my alarm, I'm climbing between the sheets when she ducks back into my room shyly with her hair piled on top of her head and her face scrubbed clean. If she's wearing anything other than the shirt I gave her, it doesn't show. She's definitely taken off her bra, and immediately memories of her soft breasts and hard nipples barrage me.

I clear my throat and pull the sheet back for her.

She slides in beside me almost gingerly. "Thanks."

"No, thank you. It's the least I can do." I roll away and turn off my bedside lamp. "If I snore too loud, just elbow me."

Her laugh is stiff, but I appreciate her working with me to cut through the awkward. "If I hog the blankets, just tell me to let go."

"You got it." I settle onto my pillow with a sigh and wonder if I'll sleep a wink tonight. I can't see her, but I feel the dip of her in the bed next to me. I'm so aware that she's inches away.

She roots around for a comfortable position. Silence ensues. Minutes pass. I'm pretty sure that, like me, she's got no chance of falling asleep anytime soon.

"You okay?" I ask. "Are you too uncomfortable? I can go sleep on the sofa."

"I'm fine. I guess I'm just trying to take it all in."

"The fact that nothing went as planned tonight? Or that I'm a single dad?"

"Both," she admits. "I hope your mom rests well tonight. I sprained my ankle a few months ago playing volleyball. It really does hurt."

"They gave her some pain pills."

"Good."

But there's something else on her mind. I can feel it.

"What's wrong, Masey?"

"Just thinking about Ranger. He's so precious. I can't imagine why a woman would give up custody of him. It's none of my business—"

"The short version is that she was a bitch who thought Ranger was a burden, so he's all mine now." It's a sore subject with me.

"Oh, my gosh. That's horrible. He's just a baby."

"And a really good one. But her loss is my gain."

"Absolutely. Were you together long?"

I hesitate. "A night."

At my admission, she falls silent. I get it. What is she supposed to say? She probably sees a man whore careless enough to nail a random girl and get her pregnant. And what sucks is that she's not altogether wrong.

"I met her at an after-party following Noah's last Super Bowl win." I may as well put the truth out there since it seems like I'll be seeing Masey another time or two. "By the time she came in…I was drunk. She hit on me, thinking I was my brother."

"I can see that. You look a lot alike."

"We hear that all the time. Anyway, I don't remember what happened exactly. Honestly, the next day I thought I'd just had a really vivid dream. But a few months later, she went public and claimed Noah had fathered her baby."

"Oh, I remember Harlow calling me about this. She believed that woman at first."

"Most people did. It was only after a pre-birth paternity test revealed that Noah wasn't the father but someone related that we put two and two together. When Ranger's mother realized I wasn't famous or worth millions and that I wasn't her gravy train, she asked me if I wanted custody. If not, she was going to terminate the pregnancy."

"Oh, my god. At least she asked you."

"I'm grateful every day she did. I hired a lawyer and had the papers drawn up. She signed them an hour after Ranger was born. I told her she's welcome to call and ask about him. I said I'd be willing to share pictures or give her updates if she wanted them. She's never reached out. I hear she's following an NBA team these days."

I try not to sound cynical or bitter. I'm better off without Mercedes Fleet in my life. But I know I'll have to explain all this to my son someday. Granted, not for a while. But I have no idea how I'll keep him from feeling unwanted and unloved by the very woman who gave him life. How will that affect his heart? His psyche? His beliefs about women and love and commitment?

It worries me, but I know I can't solve this problem tonight.

"That's horrible. She doesn't know what she's missing."

"You're right. Ranger is such a good baby and—"

"I meant you," she says softly, cupping my shoulder gently in the dark. "You're wonderful."

I feel her touch through every part of my body. My blood races. My heart revs. My cock, which I finally managed to rein in, stands tall again. But sleep isn't happening, so I roll to face her.

"I'm just trying to be decent. Becoming a single dad hasn't been easy. If it hadn't been for all the family support, especially my mother and Harlow's sister-in-law, Britta, I don't know how I would have made it. I knew almost nothing about babies when I walked out of the hospital with Ranger. I was terrified I'd fuck up."

"I'm in awe. You've done great."

I need to lighten the mood and stop looking into her eyes or I'm going to forget that I promised to keep my hands off her tonight. "Thanks. I've done my best. So...you're here until the eighteenth?"

"Yeah. I have an option to rent the villa for another two weeks, and it's a nice place. But at some point, I have to go home, right?"

Part of me wants to ask what it would take to make her stay. The other part of me knows it's ridiculously premature and none of my business. Besides, where the hell do I think anything between us could possibly lead? Still, that doesn't stop me from wanting to get closer, kiss her, something...

Finally, I say what I hope will help. "Maybe not. Do what makes you happiest."

"Yeah. I just need to figure out what that is," she murmurs. "Hey, I was thinking...who's watching Ranger tomorrow while you're working?"

I wince, but she probably can't see me in the dark. "I'll figure that out in the morning."

"Why don't you let me?"

"I can't impose—"

"It's not an imposition," she argues. "I'm happy to do it. I love kids, and your little guy made me smile tonight. And in case you haven't noticed from looking at my skin, I have a lot in common with a vampire. Neither of us do well in the sun."

"You're really pale."

"And I burn horribly. I probably would never have come to Hawaii if my best friend wasn't here," she murmurs. "Anyway, if you need a babysitter, I'm free."

That would be a godsend. I feel guilty...but I don't have many alternatives. "It's just until about six tomorrow evening."

"That's perfect. I usually start filming between eight and nine, so that gives me plenty of time to get back and set up."

"Before you go, I could feed you dinner. And...maybe after you're done filming, we could finish what we started?"

CHAPTER FIVE

About half past six the next evening, I make it back to my condo. I texted Masey as soon as I docked an hour ago. She hasn't answered. I called, too. Nothing.

Maybe I'm overreacting, but I'm a little panicked. I hope she and my son are okay.

I sling my mother's SUV into a spare parking spot. Masey's car is still where she left it last night. That's a good sign.

But my adrenaline is still chugging as I run to my front door, key in hand, and burst inside my condo. Frantically, I scan the cool interior—and see everything is absolutely perfect.

Ranger is on a blanket in the living room, lying on his belly and gurgling happily as he drools on a teething ring. Masey, still in the nightshirt I lent her and engulfed in a pair of my shorts, stands in the kitchen. She's sautéing something at the stove and bopping to Justin Timberlake, who croons that he can't stop the feeling. The savory scent of Italian spices fills the air as her shoulders sway and her hips shake to the beat.

I can't resist smiling as I ease the door shut.

When Ranger catches sight of me and lets out a delighted cry, Masey glances away from whatever she's cooking and leans around the corner to look at my little man. "What's up? You have such a cute smile. You're going to be a heartbreaker, like your daddy, aren't you?"

"I'm a heartbreaker, huh?"

At my unexpected drawl, she gasps and whirls, pressing a hand to her chest. "Jeez, you startled me."

"Sorry." As I step closer, I notice Masey is even paler than usual. No, wait. She has something smeared all over her face. "What's on your skin?"

Her eyes flare wide. "Dang it, I forgot! Stir that." She shoves a wooden spoon into my hand and gestures toward the sauté pan of marinara sauce bubbling on the stove. "I'll be back."

I watch her race down the hall with a shake of my head, then look down at Ranger. "You doing good, buddy?"

My son makes a happy little coo.

"Good." I nod his way, then stick the spoon in the pan and give it a stir. The heavenly smell makes my stomach rumble. "I'm glad she didn't scare you off."

Just then, she jogs back down the hall, yanking the overlarge shorts up as they threaten to slide down her hips. I can't help but laugh.

"Stop," she protests. "You must think I'm a train wreck. First, I forget to rinse off the face masque I was testing, then I can't keep my pants up."

"You mean my pants."

Masey gives me a saucy cock of her head. "Since I'm wearing them, they're my pants right now."

"Point taken. I called and texted earlier."

"Sorry." She winces. "I was jotting notes and watching some

footage back on my phone. When I do, it's a habit to turn on my *Do Not Disturb*."

"No problem. I just worried—"

"I'm sure you did. I'm sorry. We're good. In fact, we had a great day." She crouches down and skims her palm over Ranger's downy hair. "Didn't we?"

He gives another little cheerful cry and looks up at her like she hung the moon.

Okay, that *really* does something to my heart. When I liked her and she seemed merely sexy and sweet, that was one thing. But now that my son seems smitten?

I clear my throat. "What did you get up to besides masque testing?"

"Well, he didn't want a nap after breakfast, so I found his stroller and the shady trail through the middle of your complex, and we went for a little run. I took some pictures of him at that park in the back, down by the beach. I'll show you during dinner. He's really photogenic."

She noticed that? I smile. "Isn't he? And my little ham loves the camera."

"He really does. He giggled the whole time I was snapping shots of him." Masey picks him up and cuddles him against her chest. "Then we had some lunch and he took a good nap. He woke up hungry, so I called my mom just to double-check with a medical professional. Since he ate his oatmeal with breakfast really well, she said I could safely try him on some banana. I hope that's okay."

"Did he eat it? He likes it in jar form, but…"

"He *loved* it. I cut him off after half because I didn't want him to get sick, but I think it made his day. We rocked and played a little more, then he took another catnap. He just woke up again about thirty minutes ago."

"Sounds like you two had a nice day. Really, I can't thank you enough…"

"We had a great day, and you don't have to. I hope you're hungry. I cooked, not knowing…"

"Starved, honey." I take my son from her arms and hand her the sauce spoon. Without even thinking, I lean in to kiss her. The whole scene seems so domestic I freeze.

"Good." She frowns. "You okay?"

Do I tell her I'm weirded out…in a good way? Like I wouldn't hate coming home to this every day? "Fine. You didn't have to cook, but I'm grateful. Do I have time for a shower?"

"Yeah. This should be ready in twenty."

"I'll be out to set the table in ten. I'm surprised I had enough food in the house to cook." I meant to hit the grocery store yesterday, but I ran out of time.

"You didn't. I had some stuff delivered, so we're all good now."

"Wow, thanks again. I owe you so many favors at this point…" I shake my head, then lean in and whisper in her ear. "I hope you don't mind if I repay you in orgasms."

Her breath catches. "Not at all."

"Glad to hear it." I step away to set Ranger back on his blanket with his toys. If I don't, I'm going to forget she's cooking and that I'm too grimy for all the dirty thoughts running through my head. "Be right back."

As I head down the hall, I wonder… Does Masey have any idea how much I'm aching to touch her?

Quickly, I shower. As I search for a clean change of clothes, I'm not that surprised to find that she made the bed and hung up all my clean laundry.

Was she bored? Is she simply meticulous? Or is she hoping I

notice her domesticity? I'm not as uncomfortable with the last possibility as I thought I'd be.

As I'm shaving, I set my phone on the counter, launch YouTube, and search for her. Hundreds of videos pop up. Holy shit, she really has been dedicated to building this channel. Her number of followers staggers me. I want to see her in action.

Pressing on her most recent upload, I find myself mesmerized and smiling as she welcomes everyone back to her channel and chats through an upbeat intro about the fact she's packing to head to Hawaii, but she'll still be keeping her upload schedule, even on vacation. Then she launches into a full-face tutorial of new products from some brand that's obviously not from the drugstore. I've never heard of it; she even admits it's bougie. She states the price of each product as she displays it, opens it, and begins to apply it.

Now she gets serious and very straightforward about how it feels, smells, and works. She says she's not in a position to wear the full face and film her experience that night, but she will update the description box with her feelings about the products' performance. I pause while dragging my razor over the day's stubble on my jaw and hit the arrow to open whatever comments she added later. Sure enough, she indicated that some products wore great. Others not so much. At the end, she typed that she would wear them again before the month was over, then wrap up her thoughts in her upcoming "April Favorites-or-Forget-Its," which she would post somewhere around May first. A glance back reveals that she does, in fact, do a wrap-up of the previous month's products at the beginning of the following month. She uses and reviews dozens, maybe hundreds of products every few weeks. First of all, who knew there were that many beauty products on the market? Second, how does she keep everything straight? It must take an amazing amount of organization.

I scroll through some of the user comments in the current video. Viewers love her. One points out that she's so glad that Masey is seemingly herself again after her horrible breakup and she knew Thom was a prick from the way he behaved on camera.

That just raises more questions in my head as I scrape the razor across the last of my shaving cream and scrub my face with my towel.

"Trace?" she calls down the hall. "Dinner is ready if you are."

I cut off the video and darken my phone. "Be right there."

Tossing on a clean pair of shorts and a T-shirt that says THAT'S A HORRIBLE IDEA. WHAT TIME?, I run down the hall. She's already set the table and is plating the food. She opens a bottle of red wine and pours us each a glass.

"Didn't mean to rush you," she says by way of apology.

"Are you kidding? Do you know how rare it is that anyone cooks for me? I even have to beg my mother these days. This is a treat."

"It's just spaghetti."

"Um, with homemade sauce, salad, and garlic bread that smells awesome."

She laughs. "Well, I like to cook. I grew up doing it since my dad really couldn't and my mom, as a nurse, worked weird hours. And I decided if the makeup gig ever falls through, I can start another channel about organizing, cooking, and shopping hacks. I love that kind of stuff."

The woman was meant to be some lucky man's wife and have his equally lucky kids. She'll take amazing care of her family someday. Despite cooking, she still managed to set the table and wrangle Ranger into his high chair with a bottle and some Cheerios.

I don't know who will be fortunate enough to be Masey's husband someday...but weirdly, I'm already a little jealous.

And I feel stupid. I owe her a night of sex. That's all she wants from me. It would be better for us both if I don't get stupid thoughts in my head about wanting more.

"Clearly, you're great at it. By the way, your skin after that masque looks pretty amazing."

It's bright and smooth with a healthy glow. Her cheeks appear slightly rosy and her lips have a glossy sheen. Her look now is really different from the vamp in the bar last night, but in a way, I like this version better. This version is real.

"Thanks. Frankly, it should since it's two hundred dollars a tube."

"What?" I can't fathom that. "People pay that much for a masque?"

"Some, but I'm already mentally drafting an email to this brand to tell them that, while I think their product is great, it's definitely not worth the price. I can think of three others off the top of my head that are half the price, work just as well, and don't smell nearly as terrible when you first put it on. They may not care. It's supposed to launch next month. I just don't get it. And I'll be clear when I tell people that in my video." She shrugs. "It's a popular brand, so the people who support it will still drop their money and use the masque—"

"Seriously? Even though there are cheaper and better alternatives?"

"Yeah. That's how brand support goes. The owner is a personality, and people really like her. The brand is still relatively new, so people are even more willing to help out..." She winces. "Sorry to ramble. Eat in peace."

"You're not rambling. It's really interesting. I had no idea this industry existed."

"Pretty crazy, right? In high school, I dreamed I could eventually make money off my love of beauty products and skin care. Now I am. My mom is a little disappointed. I think she wanted me to go into nursing, but I don't have the temperament for it. I take loss too hard."

I can picture that. Masey has a soft heart.

"I get it. I think my mom is less than enthusiastic about my career choice, too," I admit. "But man, there's nothing like being out on the water, looking at seemingly endless blue, and realizing how big this world is and how small you are. It's humbling, you know?"

My ravenous stomach answers with an insistent rumble. We both laugh.

"I'm guessing your belly wants you to talk less and eat more."

"Yeah. I forgot my lunch, and this smells great."

We both dig in. I moan through half my meal because, holy shit, this is amazing. My mom is a great cook, but her specialties are Asian food, anything with pork, and banana bread. I haven't had good spaghetti in forever.

"Damn, this is fantastic," I tell her.

Ranger seems to agree with a screech as he pounds his little fist on the tray of his high chair.

We both laugh, and she sends my son a fond smile. "Maybe I'll make it for you when you get a little older, big boy."

She won't be around, and that kind of dims my mood, but it's sweet of her to make small talk with him.

After I clean my plate—and part of hers she couldn't finish—I offer to do the dishes. She shoos me away. "You've been gone all day. Spend time with Ranger before he goes to bed. Looks like he's already getting sleepy."

Chances are, he'll be lights out by eight or so. It's already a little after seven. I hate the days I don't get to spend more than an hour or two with him.

"Thanks. I'll go give him a bath. He likes playtime in the tub."

"Perfect. I'll do the dishes." She sends me a sassy smile. "And don't thank me. It's better this way. I've seen your version of cleaning."

"Yeah…" I rub at the back of my neck. "Guilty. I'm not a fan. But I'm doing better."

Masey raises an arched brow. "I would have hated to see your place before your 'improvement.'"

She doesn't mince words, and it makes me laugh. "Notice that I didn't say I was great."

"At least you know your shortcomings."

"I do." I saunter in her direction and stop resisting the temptation to slide my arms around her and put my hands wherever I find skin. "I also know my strengths. Want to guess what I'm good at?"

Our eyes meet. Her breath catches. "I think I know…but I wouldn't mind finding out for sure."

"I'll be happy to show you. What time will you finish filming?"

"I'm going to skip work tonight."

I smile her way. "Let's get the little guy in bed. Then…"

"You're on." She brushes her cheek against mine and breathes into my ear.

My body erupts in goose bumps. I actually fucking tingle.

Last night, sleeping next to her without being able to touch her was torture. Tonight, I'm anticipating, will end very differently.

I kiss her slowly and linger. I don't dare go deeper or the dishes will sit undone and Ranger will get cranky because he's not in bed. Then I back away because...adult responsibilities.

Twenty minutes later, Masey wanders down the hall and finds me in Ranger's room, securing a fresh diaper and tucking him into train-themed pajamas. I tickle his ribs, and he giggles for me. Then I reach for his little baby brush and arrange his clean hair in place. Not that it will matter after he's slept.

"Hey, handsome." She pats his back gently.

Ranger lunges for Masey and gives an excited coo when she picks him up.

"So you didn't mean me, huh?" I tease as I finish combing my son's hair.

"I'll get to you shortly. For now, I'm kind of digging this little guy." She bounces him against her chest. "Isn't that right?"

I tsk and bend down in front of my son. "I see how you are, checking out on your old man for the first pretty girl who tells you you're hot. I know. I know... We all get suckered by a pretty face at some point."

She laughs at me as she sets him back on his changing table. "This boy is way too smart for that, just like his dad, I'm sure."

I wish that was true, but Masey is wrong.

Suddenly, I'm standing on the dock of my houseboat with another woman, in another time, having my heart crushed under her dainty heel. My throat closes up.

But Masey doesn't notice, simply kisses my son's downy little head. "Sleep good, baby man." Then she turns to go, casting me a seductive gaze over her shoulder as she breezes out of the room. "I'll be waiting..."

For me to fuck her.

That's what she wants from me. *All* she wants from me.

I don't reply. I can't. My head is a goddamn tangle.

As she disappears into my bedroom, I scowl. I've been playing "house" with Masey all evening. It's dangerous. She's not my woman. She's a fling. A one-night stand. My stupid yearnings have made me consider that we could have more. But she's been clear that she wants me for the experience I can show her. For the orgasms I can give her.

It's not the first time I've been put in my place.

Why would I want to marry *you? No offense, but you're no one. And you really thought...? Sorry. But no.*

Clutching my son, I grit my teeth. That happened four fucking awful years ago, and she was a horrible human being. I'm glad she turned me down so coldly...most days. But there are other days I wonder what would have happened if she'd been the woman I believed and she'd said yes.

You're really great in bed. Stellar. Best ever, honestly. You should stick to what you're good at, babe.

I slam the door on that memory. I won't go down that mental path. In the past, it's caused me to pick up a bottle of whiskey, drink until I black out, and suffer a colossal hangover the next day. I won't give her that kind of power over me again.

Ranger plants his hands on either side of my face and blinks at me. He's smart and he's happy and he's never known the cruelty of others. I'm going to do my damnedest to shield him from all that for as long as possible. I want him to know his worth and believe he can have anything he wants if he works hard enough for it. I hope life never crushes him.

And if it does, I hope he recovers far better than I did.

With a sigh, I kiss my son, rock him for a few minutes, focusing on his baby smell and the weight of him against my chest as his legs stop kicking and his body slowly relaxes.

Soon after that, he's out. I know I'm not supposed to rock him to sleep, and I don't very often. But it gives me a few minutes. I can't get naked with Masey while all these memories are weighing on me like an albatross.

On the other hand, I owe her. And not just a little but a night of one dazzling orgasm after another. Not only has she helped me tremendously in the last twenty-four hours, but I want her to bounce back from Thom's callous breakup, bigger and better than ever.

I want to give her the confidence and reassurance no one gave me after my heartbreak.

But I can't do that until I clear my head. The easiest way is to remember that she merely wants my cock.

And she has no interest in my heart.

With a last kiss on Ranger's head, I set him in his crib, cover him with a light blanket, kill the overhead light...and head down the hall to find Masey. Time to finish what I started.

Slowly, I approach the bedroom. Even though the memories rolling through my head are ugly and I'm only having a fling with Masey, I'm ridiculously eager to get naked with her. I want that woman so fucking bad—more than I've wanted anyone in years. Maybe ever.

After our meet and greet at the bar last night, I went to her place and murmured all the right encouraging words. If my mother hadn't injured herself, I would have followed through on my promise to give her a confidence boost via multiple orgasms. I liked Masey then. And it would have sucked to fuck her a few times, then say sayonara, head home, and never see her again. As the weeks and months slid past, I would have thought about her occasionally. Fondly. Maybe even tenderly. But soon enough, she would have become another of the many. My "number" is too high to count, so I stopped trying. I probably would have forgotten Masey eventually.

Now? Something has shifted. I can't merely focus on her body or giving her a good time. There's a feeling brewing inside me—between us—that's not strictly about the pleasure she asked for. It's way more about her sweet, sassy, sexy personality. And that fucking mouth. It's haunted me all day.

No, might as well not bullshit myself. *She* did.

At the bedroom, I stop in the doorway. She's standing in the middle of the room awkwardly, like she's not sure what to do, wearing my T-shirt and a pair of my athletic socks. I don't see a shred of makeup on her wholesome face. There's not a single tease or curl in her hair. She's not at all trying to be sexy.

Yet the sight of her leaves me struggling to breathe.

"Hi," she whispers.

I stare, wrestle with myself…and I lose. It's clear I'm not going to get my motherfucking head together anytime soon, so I just need to get tonight over with.

"We're finally alone. Let's get to it. Tell me how you want me to fuck you so I make sure you get what you came for."

Masey flinches and rears back, stepping away from me, mouth agape. She wraps her arms protectively around her middle.

That expression, like I slapped her…

Fuck.

I called Thom all kinds of asshole for the way he treated her. And even if I didn't mean to, I piled right on. Why? Because I have emotional, boo-hoo baggage.

Oh, cry a fucking river, dipshit.

She's done absolutely nothing to hurt me. I have no excuse for my behavior. I feel horrible.

"Masey, I'm so—"

"Never mind. I wanted to know what genuine pleasure feels like with someone who liked me at least a little...but I think I'm asking too much of you right now. You've got your hands full and you've worked all day. You'd probably like to call your mom and kick back..." She shrugs, her shoulders lingering somewhere near her ears as she tries to appear like me bailing on her is no big deal. "It's fine. I won't take any more of your time. Good to meet you." She pulls off my socks and lays them across my bed. "I'll, um, wash your shirt and give it back to Harlow. I hope your mom recovers soon. Bye."

She lowers her head, brushes past me, and makes a beeline for the door.

But I can see her face. I know I hurt her.

That makes something in my chest ache. I fucking talked to her the way I would talk to—

Nope. Not thinking about *her* anymore. I will not give that bitch another opportunity to shred my heart. And I damn well won't let her ghost prod me into bruising someone else's.

"Honey." I wrap an arm around her middle before she can escape and pull her back against me.

She's stiff and resistant, shaking her head and pushing at me desperately. "Let go."

I can't. And the tears falling down her cheeks twist my insides again.

"I'm sorry." I cup her face and stare down into her wounded eyes. "I didn't mean to sound snide."

Yeah, you did. You felt like shit and you wanted her to feel the same. Congratulations on your success.

Jesus, I can't remember ever being so torn or confused. One

second, I want distance between Masey and me. The next I can't stand not being near her. I'm taking my anger out on her because—somehow—she has the power to mess with my head. And right now, I want to fall to my knees because I'm afraid she'll leave and I'll never see her again.

What the hell is wrong with me?

You're just not husband material, Trace. Face it.

I shutter that destructive voice in my head. "Let me try this again, Masey. Tell me how I can make you feel good."

She shakes her head. "Don't worry about it. Now clearly isn't a good time for my silly problems. I understand."

But she doesn't. "They're not silly. I—"

She settles a finger over my lips to stop me from talking as her eyes well with more tears. "When I was with Thom, he made me feel like spending time with me was a burden, something he did simply to appease me. When he left, I promised I'd never let myself be in that position again. So let go. I'll get my things and be gone. You won't have to deal with me anymore."

Her words wrench me. I promised to boost her confidence and give her pleasure. Instead, I've both treated her like a piece of ass and made her feel unwanted. She's done everything in the past twenty-four hours to show me she's here for me. And I just shit on her.

She deserves better. She deserves to have everything she wants and needs. Hell, she deserves to be happy. I probably can't give her that, but I owe her whatever I am capable of giving her tonight.

"I'm not Thom, and you're anything but a burden, honey." I cup her face. "Tell me what you need from me. Please."

"Nothing, Trace. You know, maybe I should take this as a sign that I need to work on myself more. In a month or two, hopefully I'll be ready to try sex with someone else, maybe my neighbor or—"

"No." *Fuck no.* I grip her tighter. "Don't walk away. I messed up and I'm sorry."

"I'm sorry, too. I just don't think I'm ready to handle your kind of sex."

"My kind of sex?" Intense? Passionate? Pleasurable?

"Impersonal. Maybe flings aren't my thing after all."

"But you seemed ready last night."

"When you were just a hot guy determined to make me feel good for a night, I thought so. But since I've gotten to know you some…it changed things for me."

My gut tenses. "What are you saying?"

She huffs and shakes her head. "I feel like an idiot. I guess I get attached too easily. Or maybe I'm just in a weird mental place. I don't know. You just don't seem like you're into this tonight, and I can't do the one-sided thing again. It would just be better for us both if I left. We'll tell Harlow that we decided we weren't compatible and—"

"No. *We* didn't decide that at all. Masey, things changed for me, too." Admitting that out loud makes my heart thump uncontrollably. My hands feel sweaty. I might puke.

"What do you mean?"

"Straight up? You're smart. You're kind. You're"—*the type of girl I'd be looking for if I was in the market for a wife*—"nice. You're not like anyone I've ever been with. I…like you. A lot."

"And? What are you saying?"

"If you want to experience pleasure, I'll give you all you can handle. And I promise, nothing between us will feel one-sided. Not one single thing. Say yes, honey. Stay with me tonight."

CHAPTER SIX

*M*asey hesitates, then finally sighs. "All right."

It's not the raving hell yes I would have liked, but she feels uncertain. I get it. I have to put a lid on my resentment that she's using me for a good time when I agreed to let her. She doesn't know a damn thing about my past and she doesn't have to. Tonight is for Masey. I need to make it her best ever.

I'll deal with the fallout tomorrow.

"You won't regret it," I promise.

She blinks at me with big eyes. I brush my thumb across her cheek, then lower my head and stroke her lips with my own. She's stiff. Because she's not sure of my sincerity? Or of her own appeal? Whatever her hang-up is, I need to make her feel so good she forgets it. So I fasten my mouth over hers and delve inside like I have forever to give her this one single kiss.

Cajoling her is an entirely novel experience. By now, the women I hook up with are usually eager to drop their clothes and get busy. But I like focusing on Masey, really connecting with her for a slow seduction.

She opens to me gradually. Her soft welcome jolts my libido. One kiss, and I'm hot for her. Determined. Almost fucking desperate.

Damn, how does the woman have this effect on me?

I tug her closer and tilt her face so I can better eat at her sweet, dizzying mouth. There's some flavor on her tongue, just out of reach… I have to taste it, take it for myself. Own it the way I own her lips. No other man has ever kissed her so thoroughly. That turns me on.

So does knowing that, until the sun comes up, Masey is utterly, completely mine.

I sink deeper. She draws in a rough breath and shudders. This thing between us…she's feeling it, too, right?

I break the kiss and study her face. The signs are there. Her cheeks are flushed and hot. Her ocean-blue eyes are dilated. She's clinging to me. Zing zips through my body and burns lightning through my veins.

With a little whine, Masey winds her arms around my neck, slants her lips under mine, and fuses our mouths together again. The fire between us flares hotter. She steals my breath. I wrap my fingers around her nape with a growl and nudge her open wider for me. It's a move I've made a thousand times…but I've never felt like I'll fucking die if she doesn't give in to me. And when she finally does? I've never strained toward someone the way I am for her now.

What the hell is happening?

I lose my head in the kiss. Thoughts evaporate. Instinct takes over. I barge deeper, determined to earn her surrender. I won't be satisfied until she's weeping and wailing for me in pleasure.

Ruthlessly, I take total possession of her mouth. She doesn't resist, thank god. Instead, her breath catches, and she surrenders more of herself with each heartbeat. I haul her against my body, splay my palms across her back, eliminating any hint of air or light between us…and work down until I'm cupping her ass.

Once her lush backside fills my palms, I rock my aching cock against her pussy. She whimpers and digs her fingers into me as if she'll never let me go.

Masey's need drives mine higher. She's so fucking potent. I kiss her again. Again. And again. I can't stop. Every time I fill her mouth and take more of her flavor, desire jolts me. But there's something bigger and sharper between us that's destroying my composure and crumbling my defenses…

I tear my lips away. Our stares meet. We're both panting and stunned.

But I couldn't stop this now if my life depended on it.

"Tell me you're still with me," I demand.

"Yes."

"Tell me you want me."

"Yes, but I need you to be honest. When we were in the bar, I know you said you wanted me, but if you're only with me now because Harlow asked you to and you feel sorry for me—"

"No. Nothing like that, honey. I want to be all over you. I want to be inside you." Right now, I want to own every inch of her, too, even if that makes no sense.

"A few minutes ago, I told myself to walk away. I meant to. And then you kissed me and now I"—she bites her lip—"don't think I can."

"We're both beyond that. What are you wearing under my shirt? Show me." When she hesitates, I lean closer and breathe in her ear, "I dare you."

She gasps. "That's low."

Because she's not good at resisting a challenge.

"C'mon, honey. Pull my shirt over your head and show me everything underneath."

Masey hesitates, still nibbling that lip. "If I do?"

"I'll make you glad you did."

Silence. Masey doesn't move. I don't breathe. An expectant moment stretches between us.

Finally, she crosses her arms at her waist, grabs handfuls of my overlarge shirt, and begins drawing it up her body. My breath catches as she slowly reveals sleek thighs, lush hips, and the pink thong I barely glimpsed last night. It's lacy, tight, and more transparent than not. The little-girl bow at the top nearly makes me swallow my tongue.

But she keeps going, flat stomach, sharp indentation of her waist, and a mysterious innie of a naval. Then she pauses.

I can't take it. She's too slow. This is torture. It's all I can do not to wrest the goddamn cotton from her hands and rip the T-shirt off her body.

But Masey doesn't have my experience. She's been through a lot. As much as it kills me, she needs to do this at her pace.

"Keep going," I encourage. "More."

"If I don't?" I hear the sudden tease in her tone.

She's toying with me. Does she know that's dangerous?

"I'll do it for you." My eyes narrow. "Before I put my mouth all over you."

Masey hesitates again. My impatience ratchets up. My need flares. Finally, she drags my T-shirt higher, revealing the lacy band at the bottom of her bra. Underwires and decorative supports hold up breasts even more generous than yesterday's red dress suggested. They're damn near spilling out of the cups.

I ogle and gape as she finally tugs the shirt over her head and, with a toss of her dark hair, drops it to the floor. I stare at her, skin gleaming like a pearl in the shadowy bedroom, her curves calling my name.

Oh, holy fuck. I hit the jackpot.

"Trace?" With a classic nibble on her lip, she wraps her arms around herself. "Say something."

"I hope you're ready for what's about to happen." Because I'm going to spend all night making her scream for me.

"I think I am."

She probably does. But hell, I'm not even sure *I'm* ready for this. It's going to be intense.

"It's your turn," she murmurs.

I raise a brow at her. "To take my shirt off?"

A smile creeps across her swollen mouth. "For starters."

I don't hesitate. I'd rather peel every stitch off and pounce on her, but I have to downshift. She needs a slow-burn seduction. She already knows what it's like to be rushed. But to be driven to the edge of her sanity by a pleasure she can't deny or control? She has no clue, and that's what I want to give her.

At least I'm good for that.

I reach behind my head, fist my T-shirt, then pull it off, tossing it somewhere near my closet door. Masey steps closer, her stare fused to me. Then she lifts a hand to the middle of my chest. Her fingers are a barely there touch over my heart.

Her caress reverberates through my whole body. I suck in a breath. And as she lifts her other hand, feathers both palms up my chest, then wraps her fingers around my shoulders, it's all I can do not to shudder at the unexpected pleasure.

She searches my face but says nothing.

I need to know what's rolling through her head. "Honey?"

Masey frowns. "Kiss me."

She's...something. Nervous now that we're going to have sex? Or afraid of how she'll feel once we do?

If it's the latter, we're in the same place.

"Sure." Despite everything, I'm dying to.

Bending to Masey, I slide my hand around her nape, working my fingers into her hair, and contemplate her mouth. Her grip on me tightens. She bites her lip again.

It drives me fucking crazy.

I swipe at her swollen pout with my thumb. "Give that to me."

Masey nods, seemingly half-dazed, and lifts onto her tiptoes. She tilts her head and positions her lips under mine.

My hand at the back of her head tightens as I pull her against me and lay my lips over hers. Soft. So soft. I sink down onto her mouth, and she's like a pillow cushioning me as I deepen the kiss.

This time, I don't have to prompt her to open for me. It's as automatic as breathing.

I can't hold in a groan as I slide inside her mouth. Then I fall down a rabbit hole of sensation and submerge into heaven all at once. There's no escape—not that I want to. But one second I'm standing in the middle of my bedroom with her, present and in control. The next, she has me floating, spinning, falling... She's my only anchor, and I grab her desperately.

Before I plunge deeper into her.

Masey welcomes me, lures me, hungry and moaning as she addicts me to the opium sweetness of her mouth.

As I back her against the nearest wall and wedge her against me, she slides her hands over my shoulders, strokes down my chest, then trails over my abs. Another jerk of pleasure rattles me.

She breathes into our kiss. Every sense I possess is attuned to her, heightened and sharpened by her nearness. But I need to be closer. I need more.

I fit my thumb under her bra strap and lower it until it hugs her arm. I have to taste the flesh I just exposed, so I kiss my way down to her collarbones and nip across to her shoulder.

And as I work my lips over her skin, her grip on me tightens. Her breathing picks up pace. "Trace…"

Her sigh tells me she's every bit as blown away by our chemistry as I am.

I curl a hand around her waist and feel my way up her rib cage until I'm cradling her breast. The weight of it falls perfectly into my palm. But the wires and lace and bows have to go. I need her skin on mine.

I flick at her other bra strap until it falls. "I want to take this off."

"Yes."

"I want your nipples in my mouth."

"Yes."

"I want you bare and in my bed."

"Oh…yes."

That's usually enough to make me happy. Not with Masey.

I grip her chin and hold her gaze. "I want you with me, every moment, every breath, every moan…all night."

She swallows. "Yes."

Her eyes are earnest. Her mouth purses softly under mine. I can't stay away. I can't resist. So I crush her lips under my own, lift her off her feet, and pull her against my chest.

"Trace!"

"Wrap your legs around me and hold on."

She does, and I rush to my bed, then lay her across the mattress. Wordlessly, she watches me, clinging to me. And she's so fucking beautiful as the moonlight shines on her.

"Why does everything feel so different with you?" she murmurs.

Isn't that a good question? The easy explanation is that I'm not Thom, that I'm focused not on what's convenient for me but what feels best for her. But I think her question is deeper. Mine is. Why *does* everything with her feel so different? Why does Masey stand out from all the women I've shared a few hours, a few laughs, and a few orgasms with?

True I don't engage in random sex the way I used to, and being a father has changed my priorities. But that doesn't explain why everything I'm feeling with Masey is so new. Why *she* makes me feel things I've never felt.

Is there any chance you're starting to fall for her?

Yeah. Is there any chance she could fall for you, too?

That notion burns excitement straight to my cock. It's not likely. She's into me for sex, for the experience I can give her. But the idea that she might want more than a fuck or two turns me on. Even if it's a stupid delusion, I might let myself believe it just for tonight.

With a rough exhalation, I crawl onto the bed and hover over her, watching her face. She reaches up for me, and I can't resist wrapping my arms around her, bringing her closer, and capturing her lips again.

Instantly, I lose myself in her flavor, her scent, her softness. I wanted to control tonight and show her everything she's been missing. I certainly never intended to lose my head. I know the consequences too fucking well. But here I am, losing all control and diving so deep into her kiss that I don't care where she ends and I begin. I've known for a while she'd need connection to really experience passion. She won't settle for superficial.

With her, neither will I.

Beneath me, Masey clings. For a girl who had never been well kissed before yesterday, she definitely has the hang of it now. Every soft catch of her breath and her every desperate, pleading touch ramps me up and tunes me into her even more. The thick lust swirling between us bowls me over. It's intense. Dizzying. Mind-blowing.

But feeling actual feelings with Masey? That's new. That's terrifying. That's something I have zero defenses against.

I tilt my head and kiss her wildly, going at her mouth like she's the answer to every desire I've ever felt. She pulls me down, urging me to cover her body with mine completely. I settle on top of her. So much of her bare skin meets mine. We both groan at the contact.

As I kiss my way across her face and down her neck, I fist the clasps of her bra in the middle of her back and squeeze, working each apart with insistent fingers. The band goes slack. The cups lift from her breasts. I strip the garment from her body and toss it away.

And I stare.

"You might have the most beautiful tits I've ever seen," I mutter.

I'm not lying, either. Natural, symmetrical, heavy and round. Her dark areolas frame flushed, upturned nipples that beckon me.

Her laugh cuts through my tension. "Is that your version of a compliment?"

"Not to sound like a complete douche, but yeah." I cup one of her breasts with a sigh. "Oh, fuck, honey."

And there she goes, biting her lip again. Then she shocks me by cupping her breasts and offering them up to me. "Want them?"

Is she kidding? "Fuck yeah. The only thing I want more is the rest of you."

Every inch of her is so kissable it's hard to know where to focus. Her lips, which somehow look plumper and sweeter? Her skin, which shimmers and tempts me in the silvery light? Or her breasts, taut and perfect and looking as if they're straight out of my fantasies?

I don't give her a chance to reply, just like I don't choose between all the perfect places to lay my mouth. I start again with her lips because they keep drawing me back. She's waiting, soft and parted, kissing me like she's ripe and eager to show me how much she wants me, too.

After taking her mouth thoroughly, I ease back, skim my lips over her neck, and nip at her shoulder before working down to the swells of her breasts and laving a wet trail to her nipples.

Before I even reach one, she arches up to me. Hungrily, I close my mouth around the nearest tip, suck it deep, and torment it with my tongue. She cries out, her legs moving restlessly beneath me while I prime the other with my fingers. She digs her nails into me gratifyingly deep, wraps one of her legs around me, and drags me closer.

I draw back on the first peak, circle my tongue around it, toy and lick. Then I assail her other nipple. The instant I fill my mouth with it, she grabs me and holds me against her breast, hissing as if the contact sizzles.

"Talk to me."

"Trace..." she pants.

"You like it?"

"Yes. I don't know why. I don't understand..."

Why it feels different than anything Thom did to her? I get it. She's here for a point of comparison. I'd rather have her simply be into me, but it is what it is.

And if you want more from her, you have to go after it.

I shelve the thought for now. Tonight is about Masey.

"Because you're more aroused?"

She nods. "My skin feels like it's on fire. I can hear my heart racing in my ears."

I smile as I take her sensitive bead in my mouth again and draw long and hard until she keens. "Ever felt that way before?"

She shakes her head—and guides me back to her first breast.

"Want me to suck on it again?" But I know the answer.

"Please."

"I love it when you're polite about wanting something dirty," I murmur as I lower my head and draw on her hard crest until she's clutching at my hair and panting. Then I move back to the other.

Beneath me, it's not just her legs that are restless anymore. Her hips have joined the action, wriggling and lifting, silently begging me to ease her ache.

I skate a hand down her body and palm the curve of her hip —before sliding my thumb under the waistband of her thong and tugging gently.

"I want this off, honey." I look up from her breasts to gage her reaction…but I can't keep my tongue off her. "I want your pussy."

When I drag my mouth over her velvety breasts then suck her darkening nipples in deep again, she arches off the bed, onto her elbows, head tossed back. In between the hard rise and fall of her chest, she nods. "Yes. Whatever you want."

Dangerous words.

I grab her hair and give it a tug, forcing her to look at me. "There are a lot of things I want. We might not get to them all in the next hour."

"H-hour? You could do this for an hour?"

Do what, arouse her? Make her mindless and desperate? Make her utterly surrender? "Honey, I could do this all night.

And to get to everything I want from you, it might take that long."

Or even longer, because I don't see myself being finished with her anytime soon.

I'll worry about that later.

"Trace?"

There's something so intimate about the way she's curled her hand around my jaw and stares directly into my eyes like I'm the only man on earth. "Yeah?"

"Hurry. I want you inside me."

It's where I want to be, but… "Not yet."

She frowns. "Why? I'm ready. I'm wet. I'm—"

"Still thinking too much. And I haven't finished exploring you. Let me, okay?"

"Okay." Her trembling voice sounds like something on the edge of a whine.

But she's trusting me with her body, her experience. Her psyche.

I kiss my way down her body, lips lingering over her stomach. She's so damn soft everywhere. Shadows play peekaboo with her curves and give my tongue places to taste and linger. I slide my lips along the valley of her waist, then up her hip, easing her thong down with me. My hands are definitely on autopilot as I peel the garment off her legs and toss it aside because my stare is fixed on her pussy, shrouded in darkness.

I curse. Why didn't I turn on some damn lights when I came into the room? I can't *see* Masey the way I want to, but what I can discern has fresh lust broiling my veins. She has gorgeous thighs. I see the faint outline of color where she recently tried— and failed—to tan. A dusting of downy dark hair shields everything in between. I suspect her folds are engorged, deep pink, and glossy with her arousal. That's what I'm picturing, but I'd kill for details.

As I wend my way back up her body, my palms glide up her legs, easing them apart to get closer. But it's not enough.

"I want to turn on some lights, honey."

She hesitates. "I've never…"

"Made love with the lights on?"

"No."

"What about during the day?"

"Never."

What the absolute hell? It's a wonder Thom could even find his own dick.

"Another reason to let me." Everything about my night with her has to be different. "Okay?"

"It will be weird to be totally naked in front of you with the lights on." She bites her damn lip. "But okay."

Quickly, I roll to the left and snap on my bedside lamp. It only puts off enough light to set my alarm clock and do a little reading, but that's enough to make me catch my breath.

Masey is even more stunning than I thought, all pale and pink and gleaming and flushed. And so wet.

It's all I can do not to lick my lips.

Suddenly, she uses an arm to cover her breasts and her other hand to shield her pussy. "Trace?"

I can't stop staring. "Yeah?"

"I don't know what that expression means, but it looks like you want to eat me alive."

"That seems like a good place to start," I murmur as I position myself between her legs, gather her thighs in my grip, ignore her squeals of surprise, and open my mouth over her slick flesh.

Heaven. That's the first word that zips through my brain. This is the earthiest, most female part of her. And after one taste, I don't know how I'll get enough. She's like honey—sweet and flowing. Abundant. Gleefully, I run my tongue between her smoothest flesh and wrap my lips around the hardest part.

The worry and protest I saw forming on her face before I buried my mouth in her pussy? Replaced by little gasps and whimpers, long moans, shudders, and rolling hips.

She likes it.

If I were to add up all the hours I've spent eating pussy, I'd probably be embarrassed by the grand total. But I know how to give Masey a pleasure that's all for her. She doesn't have to work or worry or participate. She just has to enjoy it.

Her fingers thrust into my hair, slide along my scalp. As I suck on her clit, she tenses and tugs.

"Feel good, honey?" I glance up her body.

Her cheeks have gone pinker. She closes her eyes as if she's melting into the mattress. "Oh, my god. What are you doing to me?"

In answer, I draw her into my mouth again, flicking her tip with my tongue. She arches and spreads her legs apart in an unconscious offering that's so gorgeous I can't resist tucking my hands under her lush backside and lifting her up to my mouth.

"I want to make you come," I say as I eat at her.

She writhes in my hands and plucks at her nipples. "It's so much. Too much. I don't know how to…"

"Handle it?" I swipe a thumb across her clit, then swirl a lazy circle.

Her whole body tenses. She's clenching and clamping as she clutches me desperately. My scalp tingles and burns—and I love it. Masey is usually so put together and controlled. I might have a long track record when it comes to sex, but it's serving me well now as I unravel her.

"I can't."

A niggling something pings at my brain. "Have you ever had an orgasm you haven't given yourself?"

She hesitates. Because she's sifting back through her past and trying to recall an instance? Maybe, but it also might be because I'm licking at her most sensitive spot while I'm wedging two fingers inside her.

Masey tugs on my hair again as her body bows. "Trace!"

"You want to come?"

"Yes," she pants.

"You ready?"

"Yes!"

"All you have to do is answer my question."

"What?" she shrieks.

"Did Thom ever make you come?"

"I think so."

But she doesn't sound sure. And frankly, if she's not…the answer is no.

Holy shit.

I'm going to fix that. I'm going to spend all night fixing it. I'll fix it again in the morning if she'll let me. Because a woman as sexy as Masey not being properly pleasured is just wrong. I'm all too happy to show her what she's been missing.

If you do…well, she stayed with Thom for ten years. Would she be willing to stay with you if you make her feel good?

It's an intriguing question.

With a new sense of purpose, I bend my head to her again and lavish all my attention where she needs it most. I drag my tongue across her clit over and over, while swishing my fingers inside her, searching for that smooth, sensitive spot that will make her—

"*Trace!*" Masey's eyes flare wide as saucers.

Come. There it is…

I'm fascinated by the way her body bucks, her skin turns the sweetest shade of pink, her pussy engorges a gorgeous red, and she gives herself over to passion so honestly. Her eyes slam shut, and her *O* face is real—not something she practiced in a mirror to impress anyone. And I'm convinced it's a face Thom never saw because this climax seems everlasting. Sure, I'm dragging it out by heaping all the pleasure on her I can, but she's tightening and gyrating as if she's never known a sensation like this.

God, Masey is stunning, and I can't wait to be inside her.

Slowly, she starts to whimper, and I back away. Her breaths return, hard and sawing, and she opens her eyes, blinking directly at me, still perched between her legs. Her expression is a cross between worship and panic.

"You okay?" I prompt.

"Oh, my god. What did you do to me?"

Slowly, I sit up and raise a brow. "You didn't like it?"

"I *loved* it. Now I know what I've been missing."

That makes me smile. "Let's make sure you get more, then."

"Yes. Please. Now." Masey lunges for my shorts and tugs.

"You really want them off, huh?" I can't resist teasing her.

She gives me the cutest little embarrassed grin, complete with a dimple. "Too eager? Sorry. I wanted to…you know, make sure you were ready before we…"

"I don't mind eager," I say to reassure her, but it takes me a hot minute to translate the rest. I can only come up with one meaning—and it's a WTF. Her ex expected head to be "ready" for sex? "But as much as I'd like your mouth now, I don't expect you to go down on me tonight."

That clearly confuses her. "You sure you can—"

"Perform? Oh, honey, I'll have no problem."

She winces. "Sorry. I shouldn't have assumed… Thom and I got into a routine—"

"That clearly wasn't doing it for either of you. Now let's stop talking about him, huh?"

Masey closes her eyes. "Absolutely. I just realized… I'm so sorry. I didn't mean to imply that you'd have problems, um…"

"I don't, but you're cute."

She sits back on her heels and covers her face. "I'm embarrassed."

I take her by the wrists and gently pry her palms from her cheeks. "No, you're gorgeous. Let me inside you so I can make you feel good again."

Masey nods. "That sounds great."

I smile as I climb off the bed and grab a condom from the nightstand, then pull my shorts off before kicking them to the far side of the room. When I turn back, her eyes go wide.

"Oh, my…wow."

I laugh. "I'm just a normal guy."

"I used to attend naked frat parties, so I've seen a lot of penises. That's not normal."

"Naked frat parties? Sounds like I missed out by not going to college."

"Well, they started as swim parties, but…" She stares at me some more. "I lost my train of thought."

"Come here," I encourage as I saunter closer. "How about you let me kiss you again?"

It's important because I think, once I get my hands on her, this is going to go fast.

Still on her knees, she edges forward on the mattress and lifts her hand. "Can I?"

"Honey, you can touch me anywhere. I just want to be clear that I don't expect you to do anything except feel good."

"I already do." She smiles softly.

Then she places her palm on my chest and feels her way down, down until she's gripping my shaft. I suck in a breath as her curious fingers stroke me from base to tip.

I close my eyes and groan. "You don't know how good it feels to have someone else's hand on me."

"H-has it been a while?"

"Since I brought Ranger home from the hospital. Been too busy..."

"You've already made me feel so good, let me—"

"It's not about tit for tat." And if Thom made her feel that way, I'm going to be hard-pressed not to hunt this asshole down and punch him in the face. "I want to be *with* you, okay?"

"I want that, too."

I lift her hand from my cock and press a kiss to her palm before wrapping my arm around her, bringing her against me, and kissing her slowly. "I want this to be right for you."

"I appreciate that, but what about you?" She stops me with a hand at my chest. "Are you okay now?"

It takes me a minute to realize she's circling back to my stupid-ass swipe earlier. "Yeah. I really am sorry."

"I just didn't want to be in your way after you've had an eventful twenty-four hours. I wouldn't have had any hard feelings—"

"You're not in my way, and I don't want you to go." I take her hand in mine and lay my lips over hers so I can get her off this topic.

Masey doesn't protest or try to ask more questions, and I'm grateful. Except...when have I ever been with anyone who really gave a damn about my feelings?

Honestly? Never.

Then again, I never hooked up with girls because they were

kind or sweet or caring. I've usually pursued women who wore short skirts with high heels, had an aversion to boundaries, and loved sex.

That isn't Masey…yet she's flipping my switch.

I need more. I need to taste her, feel her, take her.

I don't know if a night will be enough.

The kiss I laid on Masey to misdirect her ends up distracting me. A hint of coconut fills my nose, but now it's combined with the scent of her pussy. Suddenly, I can't resist sliding my palms down her back, grabbing a handful of her ass, and hauling her closer.

Masey melts against me and wriggles her slick, swollen folds against my cock. My blood ignites. My need surges, ripping away the vestiges of my control. I wanted to take this slow, make her ache before I finally gave in and filled her with every inch of my cock. Now?

Waiting isn't an option.

With a growl, I lift her against me and follow her back to the mattress. On top now, I slant my mouth over hers again, sinking inside her sweetness.

It's still not enough.

"Oh, honey…"

She tightens her arms around me, her lips burning a path over my shoulder and up my neck. "This is crazy."

"This?" I can't keep my mouth off her, either. I sweep across her jawline, urge her head back until I'm laving at her vulnerable throat, then tongue my way down to the dainty hollow below.

"This desire. I didn't know I could feel anything this intense. After the climax you gave me—which made me realize I've never actually had one—I thought I'd be sated and ready to focus on you feeling good. But…"

"You want more." A dirty grin spreads across my face.

She nods. "You don't seem surprised."

"Not even a little. I don't want you satisfied yet." I sit back on my knees just long enough to tear the condom wrapper open and roll it down my length. "I want to be deep inside you, driving your pleasure, when you're satisfied."

Her straight white teeth nip into that pouting lower lip. Is she trying to test my control?

Once the condom is in place, I lower myself back over her body, cock in hand, and fit the head against her opening. Masey is already holding her breath, body taut. I stroke her hair back from her forehead. "Don't be nervous. I got you."

She shakes her head. "I'm excited. This feels…right."

Hell yeah, it does. And nothing is going to stop me now.

Bracing my hands on either side of her head, I nudge my way forward. She's so slick that submerging into her is like a slide through melted butter. She's warm and silken around me. Tight, yes. Dear god, is she. I close my eyes and groan as I keep plunging down and deeper.

Surprise fills her gasp, which quickly turns into a throaty moan. "Oh, Trace…"

I know exactly the shock she's responding to. I expected being inside her to feel good. To tingle. To burn. But this isn't like that. It isn't like any pleasure I've ever felt. It's bone-deep and hot. As I bury myself in her snug clasp all the way to the hilt, what I feel is sharp and urgent. It won't be denied, put off, or controlled. This choke hold of desire is shutting off my brain, ramping up my respiration, and attuning my every receptor to Masey's scent, body, flavor, and need.

I grind into her, trying desperately to get deeper. Her shocked stare locks onto me. Her nails claw into my back. Her legs wrap around me tightly, like she intends to keep me from withdrawing from her honeyed depths.

As if I'd leave now.

"Honey…" Gently, I withdraw enough to feel the mind-blowing tug and clasp of her flesh cling to me. But even that distance between us feels like too much, so I widen my palms on the mattress and use my leverage to thrust even deeper. "Jesus."

Ecstasy rips the word from my throat. Masey whimpers out more of her need, then rocks with me, up to me, accommodating another inch of me. But it's enough to make me sweat, groan again, and hold her tight.

What the fuck is going on between us? I've never felt anything like this.

"Yes." She pants out before her plea turns high-pitched and sharp. "Yes."

Fuck yes.

I brace my knees on the bed, palm one of her hips and lift it up, then ease back again, only to shove inside her with even more force and find my way a little deeper still.

What's happening is stunning. A revelation. A fast-rising imperative. A fucking addiction.

"Too slow. More. Faster," she pleads.

I'm not saying no to that, not when it's something I need, too. "Hold on."

She does—and not just with her hands but her whole body. Her fingers grip my shoulders. Her teeth nip into my neck. Her thighs tighten on me. Her pussy clenches around me.

It's insane, but in this moment, I swear that if I could have only one woman for the rest of my life, I'd choose this one.

Imagining that Masey belongs to me rips away all hint of restraint. Suddenly, I'm naked and facing an oncoming train of desire. I'm happy to let it run me over.

Gnashing my teeth, I growl as I pull back, then push into Masey, slowly enough so that she feels every ridge and vein of my cock but still quickly enough to make her catch her breath. Then I do it again. And again. And then…I don't stop.

My head feels light. I get dizzy. Nothing registers except the staggering bliss gushing through my body and demanding more of Masey.

I drop a ravenous kiss onto her mouth, plunging deep inside and taking her tongue as I turn up the speed and force of my thrusts. She's right there, flesh burning hotter, getting tighter. She rocks and scratches at me. Reluctantly, I pause the kiss to suck air into my starved lungs. Pleas and praise fall from her lips.

Fuck. My orgasm is coming, barreling down on me like an unstoppable storm. I'm praying like hell she's with me. She has to be. I *need* her to be. I don't want to do this without her.

"Open your eyes," I demand.

Her lashes flutter up. Her eyes glint so blue, framed by the thick black fringe and her arousal-stained cheeks. They lure and beg me.

I squeeze her hip with one hand and tug her hair with the other. I know she can barely move. I'm being rough and possessive. I can't stop myself. Merely having my dick inside her when this climax blows off the top of my head won't satisfy me. I'm desperate to drown in her—submerged in her eyes, her thoughts, her veins. I want to be more than a memory.

I need to be in her heart.

"Trace. Trace." She chants my name as she gasps for air. "Trace…"

Her pussy tightens. Her fingers cling. When her eyes start to slide shut, I tug on her hair again. "No. Look at me. You going to come?"

"Yes. Already. I don't know how. I don't…" Her shuddering inhalation sounds more like a whine. "Please."

Fuck, I can't stop this. Fuck, I need this. Fuck, I'm toast.

I shove my way deeper into her body faster, faster. *Bang. Bang. Bang.* My headboard smacks the bedroom wall in a hard, consistent rhythm. If my next-door neighbor was around, I'd apologize later. If my son weren't a heavy sleeper, I'd worry about waking him.

But nothing and no one is going to stop me now.

"Yes." I plunge inside her harder, faster, aware of nothing but her blue, blue eyes and the way she surrounds me as ecstasy rises up to assail me.

"Oh, my…" Her body tenses and bows as she cries out in a hoarse, breathless cry. *"Trace!"*

Under me, she begins to shudder and pulse.

I lose myself in the shock of her stare as I follow her into an abyss of startling, strangling pleasure. I plunge in, strokes shorter, faster, more furious than before. Moments later, a wave of something washes over me—sweltering, dizzying, disorienting. It flattens me. It rips the guts out of me.

And as I pour myself into Masey, it changes me—once and for all.

CHAPTER SEVEN

*W*ith a deep, sated sigh, I settle back into bed beside Masey after making love to her a third time tonight. And I can't remember ever feeling this sated—and complete.

After the first rush of passion, we dozed for an hour, then awoke, my chest plastered to her back, mutually hungry for each other. I barely had the patience to nudge her to her hands and knees and roll a condom on before gripping her hips and surging as deep inside her as I could. With my mouth on her neck and my fingers biting into her shoulders, her screams drove me while I rode her to a gasping climax. Then we dozed again.

This time, we woke facing each other, tangled in the other's arms and stares. Together, we lurched into action. This time, Masey grabbed the condom from the drawer while I positioned her thighs on either side of my hips, straddling me. As soon as I sheathed my cock, I surged inside her. I spent the slow, sensual ride hypnotized by her flushed cheeks, her bouncing breasts, and her clutching pussy. Finally, we both hurtled into another explosive climax.

And damn if I don't already want more of her. What the fuck, am I seventeen again?

I glance at the clock. Three fifty-four a.m.

Will she let me make love to her one more time before Ranger wakes up and I'm forced to pay attention to something besides her body and our pleasure? I really hope so because sex may be the best—and only—tool I have to persuade Masey to stay long enough to see if this fling could lead to more.

I sound like I'm out of my mind. But I'm totally, completely serious.

As I slide against her, she welcomes me with open arms, pressing reverent kisses across my chest before she lays her head there with a satisfied sigh. "Wow."

"Wow," I second.

"I'm exhausted and sore, but my body feels so alive."

Just what I wanted to hear. I roll her to her back and hover over her with a smile. "Not regretting tonight so far?"

She shakes her head, her stare solemn and honest. "No. I thought I would. I thought I would feel as if I'd done something rash or unwise or… I don't know. I'm all for a woman having sex with whomever she wants if it makes her feel good. I can't stand slut shaming. But I never saw myself being with anyone but Thom and I worried—"

"You'd wish you hadn't?"

"Yeah." She glides a hand over my shoulder and kisses me. "But now I'm kicking myself for not taking Harlow's advice sooner and coming to meet you."

Her admission hits my brain. "You came to meet *me*?"

"Yeah. I wanted to see Harlow, and I needed some time away to get a fresh perspective. But—"

"Because the breakup was too new?"

"You'd think so, right? But no. I kept seeing them, Thom and Betsy—"

"That's his new girlfriend, Betsy?"

"Yeah. I kept seeing them around town and I thought I'd feel something. Jealousy? Sadness? Anger?" She shakes her head. "Nothing except regret that I'd wasted ten years on a man who didn't really understand me—and didn't try to."

I hold her closer. "I'm sorry, honey. He's a douche, and you deserve more."

"Don't apologize. It's not your fault; it's mine."

"If I could have been there to save you from all that, I would."

"I'm not sure I would have listened. I needed to go through the crap and the breakup, you know? And once the shock wore off, all I felt was numb. Doing my job seemed normal. So did spending time with my mom. But everything else felt like a void. I spent months thinking I was...broken or something. The day we split, I cried, mostly because losing him was like losing a fixture in my life. Well, and my dad had died the week before."

"I heard. What a prick," I mutter like a curse. "Thom, not your dad."

She nods. "But I haven't cried since. I didn't know why... until you pointed out that I'd probably never really loved him in the first place. I'd just gotten used to him. I feel stupid that I didn't recognize it sooner."

"Not stupid. Loyal. And there's no reason to be ashamed of that. I just hope you've learned to make your happiness a priority."

"I'm trying. But I thought having sex with someone else would feel weird, foreign, wrong. Something." A big smile transforms her lush mouth into something beautiful. "But it was amazing."

I can't resist kissing her—and prying for more information. "What if I'm not done with you yet?"

She giggles. "I won't be upset. Who needs sleep? Unless you have to work later. Then not sleeping will suck but—"

"I don't have to work."

"I should, but I'll squeeze in a nap or two once I get back to my rental."

She thinks I'm going to just let her go? Not if I can help it. If I can keep her another day or two, somehow parlay that into a week or two, is there any chance she'll fall for me for real? Maybe, but my inner bachelor warns that I could fall, too.

But I'm worried it's already too late to save myself.

"Or you could take the day off," I suggest.

She traces her fingertip across my jaw with a teasing flick. "And do what?"

"I'm pretty sure I could come up"—I rock my erection against her hip—"with something."

"Doesn't that thing ever get tired?" Her giggle tells me she's not at all upset.

"Not when you're around."

"Well, since I'm here and you're here and we just happen to be naked…"

"And in my bed with my cock screaming for more of you… Are you too sore, honey?"

"I'm sure I'll manage."

"That's what I like to hear." I reach into the drawer for another condom.

At the rate we're going through them, I'm going to need a trip to the drugstore by noon.

Masey sighs. "I can't remember ever feeling this happy with Thom."

"Yeah?" I palm the little foil wrapper. "Let me see if I can make you even happier."

In seconds, we're protected, and I'm gripping her thighs, pulling them apart, and easing my way inside her again.

Fuck, it's as good as the first time. No, better. She's swollen and gripping me and wetter than hell, yes. But she's more dialed into me. She seeks my mouth, insistent that I kiss her. She wraps her legs around me and moves with me, determined that I fill her. I never told her how much I like her digging into my shoulders, but she must have figured it out, because she gives me exactly what I crave.

I tear my mouth away to let out a groan, and she plants her lips near my ear, panting and sending shivers down my spine. She probably figured out how much I like that, too. Then she does the one thing designed to utterly undo me.

She talks to me.

"Every time I think you can't get any deeper inside me, you do. I feel you…"

"I fucking feel you, too, honey."

"Every bump and ridge scrapes—" She gasps, then sinks her teeth not into her lip for once but into my shoulder as her nails rake my back again. "I'm going to come. How?"

Already, that's what she means. Because we're fucking good together.

Because we belong together?

That isn't logical, but I can't find any other explanation why, whenever I get inside Masey, it's even better than the last time. And why else would I feel joined to her in a way that's not merely about our bodies? I need more. It's a turn-on that I've taught her something about her pleasure and a thrill that she seems determined to mark me. But I love that being with her feels special.

What makes it even better? I've figured her out, too. I know what will send her over—and I don't feel bad about using it mercilessly.

Sliding my hands under her ass, I tilt and lift her so my every stroke rubs friction over the nerve-rich spot inside her. Her eyes flare wide. After a couple of thrusts, she's clinging and whimpering. A few more…and fuck, she's coming apart for me again, clamping down and crying out. Her voice bounces off the ceiling. Her arms and legs hold tight, like she'll never let me go. And when her stare fuses itself to me through the last of her shudders, she unleashes something wild inside me. I lunge into her, filling her depths, and let go.

The climax is so intense I can't divert any energy to breathing. Black spots dance at the edges of my vision, and I groan so long and low my throat feels like I've gargled gravel.

Masey presses kisses to my shoulders, face, and mouth as I come down from the dark, euphoric high.

The second I catch my breath, I capture her mouth. I've never had a fucking orgasm like that. I've never cursed the limits of my body because, after a whole night of sex, I don't feel remotely sated. Physically, I need a goddamn nap, a meal, and a shower before I can take her again. Realistically, I don't have any assurance that she won't simply hop up from my bed, stretch that lithe little body that drives me crazy, then head back to her dazzling vacation villa to spend another ten days without me. Or worse, test her chemistry with someone else.

She pulls free from my mouth with a tired sigh. "You have to let me sleep at some point, you know?"

I pull her closer. "Close your eyes."

Masey does. Almost instantly, she drops off.

Normally I'd do the same. My body is exhausted. But my mind won't rest.

How do I persuade her to stay longer and give us a real chance?

I've already thought of a dozen ideas and discarded each as colossally stupid when my phone buzzes on my nightstand. I jerk around and stare at the device.

Nia Cook, one of Harlow's sisters-in-law. Why is she calling before five in the morning?

Something is wrong.

I jackknife up and snatch the device, giving a low hiss into it. "Nia?"

"I need your help. I didn't know who else to call." She sounds panicked.

"What is it?"

"Evan flew out yesterday to London for some meetings tomorrow," she says of her husband. "Amanda Lund and her son were going to stay the week with me so I'd have some company. But people found her. A mob gathered in my front yard. Someone even broke into the house. I called the police."

Holy shit. "Are they there yet? Are you all okay?"

"Yeah. Fine, just shaken. The trespassers are gone now. But Amanda can't stay here."

"You're right. You have to think about your safety." Nia is too pregnant to be dealing with a gang of people out for blood.

"I feel horrible, but…yeah. We both agree."

"Tell me how I can help. I can be there in less than thirty."

"You don't have to come. Evan says he'll fly home as soon as he can. Stephen will be here the moment he's free, but I need to help him figure out where Amanda can safely stay. Anyway, I remember you telling me you met a guy recently. Um…a firearms instructor, I think."

"Tanner Kirk, yeah."

"Any good?"

"From reputation, one of the best."

"He ever do any bodyguarding work?"

I don't know for sure, but… "Probably."

He seems like the sort.

"Amanda wants to hire him. Today."

Because she's afraid. I already know from extended family gossip that this isn't the first time she's been hunted and terrorized for her past. She's endured death threats. Some have even threatened her son, who hasn't had his first birthday yet. *Assholes.*

"Yeah. Sure. I'll reach out to him now." I sigh. "What the fuck is wrong with people?"

"I don't know. She's terrified."

So is Nia, but she's doing her best to be strong.

"How long will it take Stephen to get there?"

"A while. He's at the hospital. Skye is spotting and having contractions. The baby isn't due until October. They're worried. In the meantime, Harlow is on her way to help Amanda pack up—"

"Harlow?" But not Noah?

My brother is probably taking care of their son…and our mom. He's got his hands full.

"Yeah. She insisted. She suggested I call you, too."

Twenty bucks says my crafty sister-in-law is up to something. "Tell Stephen to stay with his wife. And Evan doesn't need to fly home. I got this."

If Tanner is free, he'll chip in. He's a good guy. He won't let this shit keep happening to Amanda. I'll work with him to make sure it doesn't.

"Thank you." Nia sounds relieved.

"Happy to help." I'm not thrilled about leaving Masey right now, but if I persuade her to watch Ranger, she'll still be here when I get back.

"I really hate to impose, but I appreciate it."

"You're not imposing." I won't dump this problem in the lap of a woman thirty weeks pregnant. "I'll be right there."

When I end the call and turn to wake Masey, I find her rubbing her eyes and frowning. "What's going on?"

Reluctantly, I climb out of bed. "Sorry to do this. Could you watch Ranger again for a few hours? That was Nia."

"Evan's wife, right? I haven't met her yet."

"She's fantastic. But she's got a situation. She has Amanda Lund staying with her and—"

"The one who got pregnant by Harlow's dad?"

"She's one of them, yeah."

"She's younger than me."

"Yeah." Barclay Reed was an absolute scumbag before his unsurprisingly violent end. "I know she had an affair with a vile human being, but she came to Maui to get away from the press and the mob 'justice.' They just keep finding her."

Masey looks concerned. "Why? Does she know anything?"

"They all assume she does because she was Barclay's last mistress. She was with him when he was embezzling most of his clients' funds. But Harlow and all her siblings insist their father wouldn't have told her anything. Bethany was working for him as his right hand, and he never said a peep to her. Why would he tell the girl he was screwing?"

"Wow." Masey looks bowled over. "My hat is off to all of Barclay's kids. Despite the fact their dad cheated on their mom with a girl younger than his daughters, they're doing their best to help Amanda. It's admirable."

"Yeah, but her son is also their brother. In the last year or two, the siblings have really come together, even the illegitimate ones, to form a true family. They're not going to let resentment keep them from having Oliver in their lives."

Masey nods. "Sure. And I agree. He's just a kid…"

"Exactly. Can you stay and watch Ranger?"

"Sure. We'll hang and have fun. No problem."

Just like that, our night together is officially over. I don't know if I have the right to do this anymore, but I'm going to act like I do until Masey tells me otherwise, so I lean in and kiss her. "Thanks, honey."

Then I dash to the shower, clean up, grab a protein bar, take the travel cup of coffee she thrusts into my hand, then hop into her car—she insisted—and leave her the keys to my mom's SUV in case she wants to go anywhere with my son.

"I won't be any longer than I have to," I assure as I pull out of my parking spot.

"No worries. Ranger and I will be happy."

I leave to the sight of her smiling and looking gorgeous in the pre-dawn light. Thankfully, traffic is nonexistent. On my way, I dial Tanner Kirk. I don't expect him to pick up before five a.m. on a Sunday, but since I know he likes to fish early, I'm not totally surprised when he answers. "Hey, Trace. Good to hear from you. Looking for a fishing buddy this morning?"

"I wish. I have a prospective client who wants to meet you, like now."

I hear a scuffle on his end. There's a pause. Then he's totally dialed in. "Fishing gear away. What's up?"

"I'm calling on behalf of a family friend," I say for simplicity's sake. "Amanda is twenty-six. Single mother to a boy about to turn one. The father of her baby is…notorious."

"Sounds like you're putting it nicely. Is she worried he's coming back for her?"

"No, thank God he's not violent, just dead. But all his enemies are after her, and they want blood."

He hesitates. "I'm happy to do what I can, but I have to be honest. I haven't done any bodyguarding in a while."

"And I know you're just getting settled on the island. I wouldn't ask…but they're also threatening her kid's life. Could you protect her, just for a bit?"

"Fine. A few days. While I'm finding her someone more competent, I'll teach her how to defend herself."

In the long run, that would probably be best for her. "Perfect. Thanks, man. I owe you."

"No problem."

I give him Nia and Evan's address, then drive into the morning with the sun slanting through my side window. I reach their awesome beachside place in record time. Outside, Nia stands, hands on her hips, talking to a pair of cops. Her white silken robe accentuates her pregnant belly and makes her umber skin gleam. She's a beautiful woman, and on paper, she and Evan shouldn't work since they're total opposites. But somehow, they're perfect together.

Beside her stands a waif with a long, pale braid that swings as she shakes her head stoically at the officer questioning her and stares with haunted blue eyes. She cradles her sleeping son against her chest—and looks ready to rip the head off of anyone who dares to touch him.

I haven't met her before, but she must be Amanda.

I hop out of Masey's car. The police turn, ready to spring into action.

Nia calls them down. "He's family. He's fine."

I raise a hand. "Hi. Trace Weston. I'm Noah's brother."

I hate dropping my famous sibling's pro-quarterback name on the island, but it's a quick shortcut to goodwill.

The officers shake my hand, all smiles, then turn their attention back to Barclay's final mistress.

Nia gives me a once-over and whispers, "Looks like a rough night. Or, based on the love bites decorating your neck, a really good one."

The best. "You called me here for something other than gossip."

"Yeah." She sobers. "Did you get ahold of Tanner?"

I nod. "He's on his way."

"Great. His arrival will be a relief."

"What happened?"

Before Nia can answer, the officers nod, hand Amanda a card, then depart. As they pull away from the curb, Evan's wife leads us into the house. "A shit show. There were about a dozen assholes. I've got a broken window." She gestures where someone clearly tossed a rock into her living room. "And some cleaning up to do. The police got here before it really got out of control, but one guy...he was super unhinged. He was heavily armed, and if he was acquainted with sanity, it was only in passing."

"That's not good." I turn to Amanda, who looks drawn into herself, like her defenses are made of steel. But I'd bet anything it's a facade. "Hi, Amanda. I'm Trace."

She exhales, letting her guard down the tiniest bit. "Thank you for coming."

"No problem. You okay?"

"This isn't the first time something like this has happened. I hoped when I left California, where most of Barclay's clients lived, that it would be the last. But some of these people are so determined, and now they've hunted me down here."

"That's what Nia said. I'm sorry. I've called a buddy here to help you. Tanner Kirk should be here any minute."

"I appreciate that." She seems to withdraw into herself again. "I'm going to check on Oliver in his playpen. Excuse me."

We both watch her go, then I turn back to Nia with a shake of my head. "She's rattled."

"She's pissed. These idiots need to leave her alone. She doesn't know anything. Barclay used her and left her holding the bag. Well, the baby."

"From what I hear, he did that a lot."

"Yeah." Nia leads me into the kitchen. "Coffee?"

"I'm good for now. I had a cup in the car."

"I'd kill for caffeine," she says glumly. "But I can't. It makes my little monster crazy."

When she glides a hand over her swelling belly with a smile, I do my best to bury my envy. Evan gets to see his wife round, his child form. He gets to go to doctor visits, study sonograms, hear his baby's heartbeat. I missed all of that with Ranger. I'm thrilled I have him now—don't get me wrong. But if I had a do-over, I would have insisted Mercedes not shut me out during the pregnancy. And if I ever find myself in the position of becoming a father again, I'm going to be with my woman every step of the way.

Out of nowhere, an image of Masey pregnant and stroking her belly careens through my brain. In my head, a diamond glints on her left hand, and I come up behind her, drop a kiss on her shoulder, and give her bump an affectionate rub.

Holy shit. It's *way* too early to think about that.

But is it? Last night was beyond amazing. I definitely want more. A lot more. And if it leads someplace serious...I wouldn't mind that.

Actually, I'm really into it.

"Is she going to be okay?" I head bob toward the other side of the house, where Amanda presumably disappeared.

"Once this shit stops, yeah. Until then? No. Your friend can't get here soon enough."

"Tanner won't be long," I assure. "How did, um, she get mixed up with Barclay? I know she worked for him and she'd known him most of her life but…"

"I'm sure like all the others. He hired her young, just out of school. He paid her well, said all the right things, and gave her attention. Barclay was a son of a bitch, but a handsome one. And apparently good enough in bed to persuade a long line of his assistants to sleep with him."

"Yeah. I hear he did it for decades."

"It seems. Bethany was born only four months after Maxon. My husband was born three days before Harlow."

"And yet…don't you think it's odd that he supposedly managed to go twenty-five years without getting even a single one of his assistants pregnant?"

Nia frowns. "One of them a few years back had an abortion."

"Even so…"

"Yeah, that's always bugged me, too. A leopard doesn't just change his spots."

"Nope."

Her frown deepens. "Barclay left Evan to be a ward of the state after his mother died. He was five, and his biological father didn't give a shit what horrors might await him in foster care."

"The world is a better place without Barclay. I don't know exactly what he did to Harlow, but Noah has said more than once if he ever saw the son of a bitch again, he'd kill him."

"I'm not surprised. But Evan and I have wondered… Does the man have other children out there? If so, where are they? What are they suffering?"

It's a logical, perfectly terrible question. "It's a possibility worth exploring."

"Actually, we have been. Evan's siblings keep hoping that all the skeletons are out of Barclay's closet now that he's dead and buried."

"I wouldn't count on it."

"I'm not." She drops her voice. "We have a lead on one possibility. He's a junior at UCLA. His mother worked for Reed Senior not long before he was born. She was broke, then suddenly had both money and a new job. His middle name is Barclay. By all accounts, he's an absolute prick. And other than the eyes, he's a dead ringer for Griff."

I wince. "Sounds like you've got a candidate."

"Unfortunately, yes. We're looking into a few others, too."

"Holy shit, didn't this guy believe in birth control or care about the kids he was fathering?"

I'm a fine one to talk since I don't remember conceiving Ranger at all. I doubt I wore a condom. I'd taken one with me to the party, just in case. And I'd already used it earlier with a sultry blonde eager for a good time. I've been tested since Ranger's birth. I'm clean, but still... I take my responsibility seriously. I can't imagine indiscriminately having kids and not caring what happens to them.

"Apparently, he took pride in impregnating his assistants. He got some dirty thrill out of knocking them up in the office."

"What a scumbag."

"You must be talking about dear old Dad," Harlow suddenly quips from the archway leading into the kitchen.

She looks cool and sporty this morning, long hair in a ponytail and wearing a pair of shorts that show off her tanned legs.

"How'd you guess?" Nia grimaces. "Coffee?"

"Not while I'm breastfeeding, but thanks."

"Make your little guy jumpy, too?"

"Unfortunately. You okay?" She glances back at the shattered glass in the living room. "What can I do to help?"

Nia shakes her head. "Cleaning up the house can wait. Let me check on Amanda and put on some clothes. I'll be quick. Then we'll sort it all out."

"No rush. Noah has daddy and dutiful-son duty today."

As Nia leaves, I see my sister-in-law eyeing me with speculation, so I seize the conversation first. "How's Makuahine?"

"Fine." She looks me up and down with a whistle. "Tell me about your night. You look like Masey wrung you out and ran you over."

I send Harlow a stern stare. I'm not saying shit about Masey's personal business, even to her best friend. "I'm good."

She scowls. And it occurs to me that if I'm serious about wanting to see if there's anything more between Masey and me, Harlow would be a hell of an ally.

"And?" she demands, dark brow raised.

"I want to talk to you about her."

"Uh-oh. What happened? She didn't freeze up or suddenly decide she misses Thom, did she?"

"No." Not at all, thank god. "She was"—I filter through a whole bunch of ways to describe Masey before I finally settle on one that says a lot without saying too much—"perfect."

Harlow claps her hands. "So glad my bestie got over the 'hump' of humping someone else."

"Aren't you funny?"

"Okay, so it's almost as bad as a dad joke, which your brother is getting too good at. I'm going to have to smack him."

I laugh at her because I know better. "I'm serious. I need to talk to you about Masey."

"I'm all ears." She sets her purse on the white marble

counter, then walks past me to grab a glass of water. As she heads back, she yanks up the back of my shirt. "Holy shit."

I don't know what my back looks like, but based on where Masey's fingernails spent most of the night, not to mention the stinging and tingling when I showered, I can guess.

I shrug away from my sister-in-law. "Do you mind?"

"Oh my god, thank you. Masey *needed* good sex. I don't think she'd ever had any."

"I'm happy to have helped. Thank you for introducing us. We really...clicked." Now I have to be honest. "And the truth is, I'm not ready for it to be over."

Harlow shrugs. "I'm sure she'd be down for another hot and steamy night with you."

"I was thinking more."

"A week? Two?"

I shake my head. "More serious than that."

"Like...making her your girlfriend?"

"Yeah, and seeing if we have any kind of future."

My sister-in-law rears back. "You, thinking relationship?"

"Why not?"

"That's not going to happen."

"Because?"

She sighs. "Well, for starters, she doesn't live on Maui. But... you were just supposed to help her with the sex, buddy. That's it."

Of course I was.

"'Cause that's what I'm good for." I grit my teeth and try not to be hurt that my sister-in-law just told me in not so many words that I'm not good enough for her bestie. "Got it. I'll figure it out alone."

I don't want to be around her right now and know she's watching me with a pitying stare, so I push away from the counter, haul ass across the kitchen, then head toward the front door. After I pull the heavy decorative slab of wood open, I make to slam it shut behind me. It never hits the threshold.

On the front walkway, I whirl around. Harlow is marching out after me, hands on hips. "Hold up. I never said you were only good enough to fuck her. I'd be happy as hell if two people I love fell for each other. But I have to be honest. Masey just spent *ten years* with someone. She wants to be alone—probably for a long while—before she attempts the romance thing again. I'm trying to save you a broken heart."

I stop and glare at Harlow. "How do you know I can't change her mind?"

"I don't...but I don't want you to get hurt."

"That's my problem. She's here for another ten days, right?"

"Yes, but—"

"If you can get me enough time with her, I might have a shot."

My sister-in-law looks at me like I'm crazy, but shrugs. "It's your heart. What did you have in mind?"

"I have an idea." But it's crazy, and she'll probably tell me that. Still, I've got nothing else.

Before I can spill it, a classic red Mustang pulls up, motor purring, and screeches to a halt. Old-school grunge music rattles the windows until the engine falls silent. A familiar figure steps out and whips off a pair of aviators. His hair is just a shade too light to be called brown. He's dressed in khaki shorts and a tight black tank that shows off a physique that clearly indicates he has a more than passing knowledge of fitness.

"Hey, Tanner," I call.

"How you doing?" he asks as he locks his car, then greets me with a handshake and a shoulder bump.

"Okay. Thanks for coming so early and on such short notice."

"No problem. I'm not okay with a mob threatening women and children." He glances at my sister-in-law. "You Amanda?"

"No, I'm Harlow."

"She's my brother's wife," I supply.

"Nice to meet you." He shakes her hand. "Where's Amanda?"

Nia joins us on the front walkway and answers for me. "Inside. Oliver is cranky since his sleep has been disrupted. She's trying to get him back down. I'm Nia Cook."

Tanner nods her way as they shake. "Nice to meet you. Can I go in and talk to her, start getting a feel for how I can best help?"

"Sure. She's at the back of the house, down the hall, first door on the left."

"Thanks." Tanner glances my way. "Catch up with you later?"

"Yeah. I'll figure out a location and call you. Good to see you, man."

"You, too." Then he disappears inside.

"He came quick," Nia remarks.

"He'll take care of Amanda," I promise.

"That's a load off my mind. Now if I could just figure out a place for her to stay, I would feel better. And in case you were thinking of volunteering your house"—she sends a direct stare at Harlow—"she's already sworn she won't go anywhere someone else's baby might be in danger."

"Probably just as well right now. As of last night, we also have my mother-in-law for a couple of weeks." Harlow explains my mother's injury. "So we've got a lot going on. But there's got to be somewhere…"

"As I was just explaining to Harlow," I say, "I have an idea."

It's a little after eight a.m. when I pull up in front of my condo again, nerves rattling. I wonder what Masey will say when I tell her what I'm thinking.

A glance across the parking lot reveals that my mom's SUV is here, but now in a different parking spot. Apparently, she and my little guy have already been out and come back.

My hands are damp, so I wipe them on my shorts, blow out a breath, and decide to go for broke.

I let myself into the house and stop short at the sight of Masey bouncing all twenty pounds of Ranger on her thigh like she's giving him a horsey ride. Neither of them sees me, and a smile crawls across my face as I watch her bouncing and smiling, encouraging my son. And I hear his sweet giggle.

It's not a sound I hear a lot. My little man is a tough customer when it comes to being outright giddy. I can calm him when he's fussy. I entertain him when he's bored. But getting him to laugh so absolutely has always been a rare feat.

Watching them together does my heart good. Masey might think she wants time alone to contemplate her ten-year disaster with Thom, but when I think of the way she filled my arms last night and I see her with my son, I'm hard-pressed to believe she couldn't develop some feelings for us over time.

Pfft. You thought that about her, *too. Where did that get you?*

Why won't that fucking voice in my head shut up?

"I'm back," I announce.

"Whee!" Masey sends Ranger sliding down her leg, earning another baby laugh. "That's good timing. I think he's about ready for a change and a nap."

"I'll take him. Thanks again."

"Everything okay at Nia's?"

"For now, yeah." I take my boy from her arms and kiss his

soft little cheek. Absently, I notice he's drooling more today than yesterday. It fits. I figured he'd start teething soon.

"Good. If you don't mind, I'd love a shower. Then I'll, um… get out of your hair."

"Could I talk to you first?"

She frowns. "Sure. What's up?"

Ranger fidgets, sticks his fist in his mouth, and starts fussing. I see his eyes drooping. He rubs at one in a gesture so cute I wish I had my phone handy to record it.

"Why don't you grab that shower? I'll put my man here in his crib. Then we can talk, okay?"

"Sure." She turns to go, but her eyes cling to me. I see it. I feel it.

That stare means something, right? But I'm only good at deciphering females when they're thinking about sex. I'm totally horrible when it comes to grasping emotion.

Finally, Masey looks away and heads down the hall. I can't let her go like that.

"Wait." With my free hand, I grasp her wrist to stay her.

She turns to me again. "What?"

I have no idea what she'll say or how she'll receive this, but…nothing ventured, nothing gained.

With a gentle tug, I bring her body against mine, dip my head, and cover her mouth. She doesn't resist me at all. Instead, her lips pucker and soften beneath mine, welcoming me even when I nudge her open and slip inside, tasting her in a long, slow melding of tongues.

Like last night, she's perfect. She smells like the sex we had. She tastes like a hint of something both minty and sweet. She feels like absolute paradise against me.

I'm making the right choice. I just hope she agrees.

When Ranger lets loose an irritable screech in my ear, I reluctantly pull away. "Sorry."

"Don't be."

For Ranger screeching? Or for kissing her? "All right, I won't. Besides, I don't think it's possible for me to regret kissing you, honey."

"I don't want you to. But I meant your squealing little guy. He's so cute he can make all the sounds he wants and I'll still tell him he's a handsome devil." She rubs his cheek fondly. "Just like his daddy."

I smile at Masey. "Meet you back here in ten?"

"Sure."

Reluctantly, I watch her disappear into the bedroom and head off to Ranger's nursery on the opposite side of the hall. Absently, I wonder…if he goes straight down for his nap, will Masey still be in the shower? Would she want company—and an orgasm?

It's worth a fantasy, but Ranger has other ideas, howling and throwing a fit when I change his diaper and try to wrestle him into a clean onesie.

"Buddy, you're not making this easy. There's a girl in the next room. I think you like her, too. How about you cut me some slack?"

He just gives me another high-pitched wail, little fists balled, and pumps his arms and legs.

"C'mon," I cajole. "Just this once…"

Finally, Ranger calms enough for me to finish snapping him into the garment. I lift him off the changing table, kiss his forehead, and set him in his crib. When I grab his stuffed football and his pacifier, shove the former in his hands and the latter in his mouth, he calms right down.

I send a glance upward. "Thank You."

By the time I back away from the crib and hit the threshold of his doorway, I can already hear his deep, even breathing.

Heaving a sigh of relief, I head into my bedroom just in time to see Masey step out of my bathroom wearing nothing but my robe.

I've had no sleep, one protein bar, and four orgasms in the last nine hours. And the instant I lay eyes on her looking so fresh and squeaky clean, a hundred lascivious ideas about how to dirty her up race through my head. My cock is totally on board.

And I need to shut that shit down, at least long enough to talk to Masey. Then, if she agrees? I'm eager to take her back to bed.

"You look great," I blurt.

She laughs. "You're being nice. I look like a drowned rat."

"Nope." Rats don't have straight, shiny hair that flows to their shoulders and clings wetly to their breasts, making me wish my damn bathrobe was transparent. "Not even a little bit."

A pleased smile crawls across her face. "Thanks."

I clear my throat before sex overtakes my brain. "We should talk in the living room."

Masey glances around with a confused frown. "We can't talk here?"

"Honey, if you don't put some clothes on and get me out of this room, we'll end up in bed and we won't be doing much talking."

She gives me a little shrug. "I'm game if you are."

Fuck. She has no idea how game I am—or how much game I've still got. "I am. Absolutely. But this conversation is important. I'd put it off for an hour or two if I could, but everyone is waiting on a phone call from me...once I talk to you."

"Oh, I didn't realize. I'm not sure how much I can help her, but I'm happy to try. Are they okay over there?"

"Fine, just rattled." I take Masey by the hand. She so sweet—not just to look at or taste—but she's so kind that it messes with something in the middle of my chest I'd rather not identify right now. I half walk and half drag her to the living room, then maneuver her onto the sofa before I sit in my usual recliner. "Great. Here's what we're hoping, and I know it's asking a lot, but it would help more than one person if you're okay with it."

"I'm listening."

"Would you be willing to let Amanda stay in your vacation rental for a few days? She can't stay with Nia, who's home alone and thirty weeks pregnant. She can't stay with Noah and Harlow. They've already got their own son and now my mother to deal with. Amanda's brother has his hands full, too, like the rest of Harlow's siblings. I'd give up my place, but I don't have a way to take care of Ranger anywhere else the way I do at home and—"

"I don't have a problem with her being there. But what if the mob finds her?"

I shake my head. "We think they found Amanda at Nia's because the loons following her know they're related by marriage. Guessing she'd be there wasn't a huge stretch. But you are in no way affiliated with Amanda. The rental is in your name. There's no reason for anyone to imagine she would be there."

"That's a good point. But I don't know that there's any place to put a baby there."

"Harlow hit up the rest of her siblings and gathered enough stuff to put together a makeshift nursery. Griff and Britta had an extra crib since their oldest son outgrew his and they won't need it again for a while."

"But you think they'll need it?"

I nod. "They think no one can tell Britta is pregnant again."

"Didn't she just have a baby?"

"In January."

"Wow, they didn't waste time."

"They didn't. And I won't be surprised if Maxon and Keeley have another one soon. They both seem over the moon with their daughter."

Masey smiles, but I can tell something has dimmed her happiness. Is she…envious?

Interesting thought.

"She can stay with me, I guess. Sure. The place only has two bedrooms, so she and the baby will have to share—"

"Actually, I was thinking she could just have the place and you could…stay with me."

"Here?"

Does she hate that idea? "If that's okay, yeah. You'd be helping me out a lot, too. Since my mom is laid up and she usually watches Ranger, and I've got jobs booked…"

And what else? What are you offering her? She's already had the sex. What if she doesn't care if you two have more? Or she wants something more platonic going forward?

That would suck.

"And I could use your help. I'm willing to help you in return," I assure her.

"With what?" She scowls.

That expression tells me to tread carefully. "Whatever you want."

"I have to work some while I'm on the island."

"I have an office at the end of the hall. I don't use it much, but you're welcome to it. It gets lots of natural light if that means anything. I can help you set up a studio in there. It's quiet in this corner of the complex most of the time…"

"What if I want you to be in a video or two?"

I don't know why, but… "Sure. What do you need me to do?"

"I don't know yet. I've got a couple of video ideas I'm batting around. Can I let you know?"

"If you'll come stay here, then yeah."

"Where will I sleep?"

"Wherever you want. You can have the bedroom, and I can find a blow-up mattress to set up in Ranger's nursery."

"You'd do that?"

I shrug. "Sure. You're doing me a huge favor. That's the least I can do."

"And what if I want a repeat of last night?" She bites her lip.

My heart stops. My cock jolts. I grin. "Honey, I'm happy to give it to you. Just say the word."

CHAPTER EIGHT

By midday, we're back at Masey's vacation rental. After I call for roadside service to change the flat tire I got Friday night, she insists on packing up her studio and camera equipment first. As we do, Ranger seems blessedly content to lie on his activity mat, batting at the colorful, musical toys dangling from the rainbow arch above his head while he kicks at buttons that make random noises with his feet. Ten minutes later, the video and lighting stuff is packed, along with her laptop, but the room is still crowded with stacks of boxes.

"What's this other stuff?" I frown.

"Products I haven't tested yet."

Is she serious? "You only have one face."

She laughs, and it does something crazy to my heart. "Which is why I need to get busy putting this goop on and giving the people of YouTube my opinion. I'm hoping to film a few videos tonight."

And I was hoping we'd be doing something else, but I can't get in the way of her work when she's agreed to help me make sure I get to mine. "Once we get your equipment set up at my condo, I'll keep Ranger quiet for you."

"Thanks."

Except for my son's play noises, silence falls between us. And I find myself wanting to know everything about her. "Do you ever see yourself doing anything else?"

"Right now, no. In five years?" She shrugs. "Who can say? I've been asked if I'd like to work at a style magazine or for various cosmetic companies on their development team. They're flattering offers with decent money, but I like making my own hours, deciding what I want to talk about, and not being beholden to anyone so I can give my unbiased, unvarnished opinion."

For all that Masey was insanely loyal to Thom for a decade, she has an independent streak. I like it. She and Harlow are both mavericks in their own way, not prone to girl group-think or pack mentality. Probably why they're such good friends.

"I respect that," I murmur. "And I can't tell you how much I appreciate this. I know you're giving up this insanely gorgeous rental and this secluded beach—"

"Actually, it's not that much of a hardship. One of my viewers recommended the place, and the pictures looked great…"

"But?" She doesn't like it.

"It's not very homey. It's blandly white and looks like something out of a magazine. And"—she hesitates like she hates to admit what's rolling through her mind—"I've sat on rocks that are more comfortable than that sofa."

I laugh. "It doesn't look super cushy."

"The one time I turned on the TV, I ended up sitting on the floor because the throw rug had more give."

"Well, you're in luck. My couch is insanely comfortable. I can vouch for it since I've taken many a nap there lately, usually when Ranger gives out."

"I'm not surprised. He's a high-energy boy."

I nod emphatically. "Right? A bottle of over-the-counter pills comes with a warning. May cause dizziness, vomiting, drowsiness...whatever. Kids should come with a warning, too. May cause sleeplessness, irritability, anxiety, and eventual insanity."

"You're not insane—yet," she assures me with a musical laugh.

"Good to know I have something to look forward to. And he hasn't even started the terrible twos, puberty, or adolescence. What was I thinking in tackling this single-dad thing?"

"I don't know, but you're a brave man."

"Or a stupid one."

She swats my arm playfully. "Definitely not stupid."

I grunt and start stacking some of the boxes lining the wall so I can haul them out to the car. "Good thing I still have Makuahine's SUV. Otherwise, we'd have to rent a truck to get this stuff to my place."

"I forwarded my mail temporarily to Harlow. I didn't realize how many boxes would be waiting." Masey winces as she looks at the cardboard overload around us.

Suddenly, Ranger squeals, and she turns her attention to him. When she makes faces at him and plays peekaboo, he gurgles with delight.

Ranger likes her—and he doesn't like everyone. And Masey seems to like Ranger, too. Sure, it's good for our temporary living arrangement, and my boy will be in good hands when I'm working. But I'm thinking beyond that. I'm focused on the future.

If Masey and I end up together, will she agree to raise him as if he's her son?

It's probably too early to think about that kind of commitment. And I hear Harlow's warning about Masey not wanting another relationship in my head. But my mother has told me over and over I shouldn't date anyone who wouldn't love Ranger like a mother. I get her logic. Why waste time and romantic capital on someone who ultimately won't accept my son?

"You okay?"

Her concern means something to me. I should probably stop staring. "Fine. Be right back."

I cart the boxes and stash them in the back of the SUV, trying to make as much room as possible for more. As I duck out to retrieve more inside the house, Tanner pulls up to the curb in his classic red Mustang. He exits and leans into the back seat, then straightens up again with a baby. Well, nearly a toddler. Oliver has wavy light brown hair and the signature Reed green eyes. He takes one look at Tanner and starts to fuss.

My buddy looks near the end of his patience.

I rush over. "Need help?"

"Pointers, maybe. I've never been around kids."

"Ever?"

He shakes his head. "I'm an only child. But more importantly, I need my hands free...just in case."

Someone violent is lying in wait. "Masey and I have been here for a bit. We haven't seen anyone."

Amanda climbs out of the car and runs around to claim her son. She's all of five foot two, and Oliver is a big, strapping boy who already looks half her size. She sends Tanner an apologetic glance. "Sorry. He's still behind on his sleep."

"It's no problem," he assures.

Even Amanda isn't buying it, but she lets it go and glances

my way. "Hi, Trace. Do you know where I can lay my son down?"

"I don't. I've only been here a few minutes, but Masey is inside. Since she knows her way around this place, she'll help you."

"Thanks." She grabs her diaper bag from inside the muscle car, soothes her fussy son with a soft whisper and a smoothing of his hair, then shoots Tanner a sidelong stare before she disappears inside.

"How's that going?" I ask.

He takes a hot minute answering, seemingly too busy watching her walk away to form words, before he turns to me. "Um...interesting."

"That doesn't sound good. Shit. Sorry, man. I'll pay you for your time and headache."

"No." He waves me away. "She's doing it. We've worked something out."

It's not what Tanner says—but what he doesn't—that tells me there's a problem. "But?"

"She's...wary."

"Of you?" I'm not sure why. He's a great guy. Smart, good sense of humor... What's not to like?

"Until just now, I didn't know if it was me or men in general. But she doesn't have a problem with you." He sounds perturbed.

"What do you think is going on with her?"

"I have some theories."

So do I. They're attracted to each other. Amanda is gun-shy, and Tanner doesn't like unprofessional feelings messing with his duty. But they're stuck with one another for now.

Maybe I should feel guilty that I cooked this situation up to be closer to Masey. But I don't. Amanda needs safety; Tanner will give it to her. The rest? That's up to them.

"Got any luggage?"

"Yeah." He nods. "I could use a hand."

I help him in with a duffel and a rolling suitcase that must be Oliver's, given the race-car motif. He handles Amanda's enormous bag and what's clearly his gun case.

By the time we stroll inside and find the women, they've settled Oliver in the out-of-the-way walk-in closet on his blanket, surrounded by pillows. Amanda is moving her things into the bedroom and bathroom since Masey managed to pack up her stuff in the last few minutes and wheel her suitcase into the hall.

"Need anything else?" Masey asks the blonde.

"Did you find a grocery store nearby? Or a delivery service?"

Masey fills the other woman in, then we take a few more trips with her boxes out to the SUV. The back is piled high when roadside assistance arrives, tosses the spare on my vehicle, and leaves with my signature. Finally, we put the rest of Masey's things in the back of my truck, then head inside to collect Ranger.

I stop short when I find Amanda backed against the wall in the hallway while Tanner stands over her, palm flat just above her head. Their eyes lock. He leans closer. She lifts her chin. They're breathing hard. I can't tell whether they're going to argue…or kiss.

I clear my throat. "We just…um, need to grab Ranger and his gear from the office."

They jump apart like a pair of scalded dogs.

"Sure." Tanner gestures me into the office at the end of the hall, trying not to look guilty.

Amanda puts as much distance between them as she can. "I think I'll just...get some water."

With a passing nod to them both, I lift my son from the office floor. Masey is right behind me, arms outstretched.

So this is what it's like to have another pair of hands who can make these little tasks easier. I've envied my brother. Harlow is a great mom, always concerned with Nolan's happiness and welfare. She and Noah are a parenting team, while I've been flying solo and wondering if I'm bound to be fifty percent worse because I'm alone.

"Thanks," I murmur as I set him in her arms.

Ranger goes happily, and Masey smiles down at him in a gesture that makes my heart flip. "I got the good part. You can carry his stuff."

Her quip makes me chuckle. Even Ranger grins at Masey. Then we're out the door with a wave and heading back to my place.

Once we arrive, we drop off all the boxes. I deliver Masey's suitcases to my bedroom while she heats up a bottle for Ranger. When he's done eating, I change him and give him a pacifier. The moment Masey picks him up again, he's out cold.

"Damn," I mutter.

"What? Not nap time?"

I glance at my phone. "No, it is. But it's already after noon. I'm starved."

"Me, too. I can cook."

"No. If you have to work most of the evening, I'm not making you cook, too. Let's grab a bite out."

"What about Ranger?"

"He'll sleep on the road. We'll have to drive through somewhere and eat in the car unless we want to deal with pissed-off little boy."

Masey smiles. "That's fine."

A few minutes later, we're sitting in my mom's SUV, unwrapping fast-food burgers, and sitting under a shady tree in the parking lot.

"I take you to all the best places, don't I, honey?" I tease.

Her lilting laugh fills my ears again. "As hungry as I am, this will probably taste like the most amazing burger ever."

I unwrap my own, take a bite—and groan. "You're right. Damn, that's good."

"Totally," she moans as she takes another bite, then reaches for the SUV's stereo system. "Is this okay?"

"Sure."

She turns it on. Some old song I've never heard that has a bouncy melody punctuated by a guitar and—is that a flute?—blares through the speakers. We both bust out laughing.

"What the heck is that?"

"I don't know. Some seventies music. This is Makuahine's car, and she loves this stuff."

Then some dude starts singing. And in fifteen words, he fucks with my head. Is it even possible Masey is the woman I've always dreamed of? I never thought such a female existed. But I can't deny that as soon as I saw her face…something changed for me. Something I don't understand. Something I'm still grappling with.

The musical interlude is laughably old-fashioned, and I'm about to write it off when that guy starts singing truths again. Masey does have this certain way of sending my senses reeling every time she smiles. I've never experienced that before. I've thought girls were pretty, sure. I've been sexually attracted to many. But before Masey, did I ever care about spending time out of bed with them?

One. And it was an unmitigated disaster.

"I have no idea what that was." Masey is still laughing.

"Me, either. Something that passed for music in the seventies, I guess." I try to smile, but too many things are barraging my brain.

We finish up our lunch, and when I reach for the stereo dial to turn it to something else, Masey touches my arms. "Don't. Now I'm curious. My parents are children of the eighties, and I can sing you lots of Bon Jovi—"

"Can you?" I back out of the parking spot, then cast a challenging glance her way. "Are you a cowboy?"

"On a steel horse I ride," she quips.

I laugh. "Nice."

After some deejay chatter, the next song starts with a gently lilting guitar. It's going to be some sappy ballad, I guess. I sip at my soda as the male vocalist sings that he's going to grab his baby and hold her tight. He goes on to croon that he's going to grab some afternoon delight. I almost spit out my Coke.

Beside me, Masey's jaw drops. "Are they singing about... what I think they're singing about?"

I listen for a moment longer. Rubbing sticks and stones together and sparks igniting that lead to skyrockets in flight pretty much answers the question.

"Oh, my god. They are!" She bursts out laughing.

I have to chuckle, too. The song is such a thinly veiled reference to sex it's ridiculous. The steel guitar solo in the middle makes it kind of a shit show...but it's also weirdly catchy.

"Yep. I think I heard this song in a movie once."

"Seriously? It had to be a comedy."

"It was," I assure her as I pull onto the road and into traffic.

When the song ends, she turns the music off. "I don't know if I can take any more seventies' flashbacks."

I grin. "Same."

But the car falls silent. All I can think about is grabbing some afternoon delight with Masey. I wonder if she's thinking it, too.

At a stoplight, I glance her way. She looks back. I see awareness in her eyes.

Yeah, it's crossed her mind—and parked there.

Fuck, how soon can we get back to my place?

Thankfully, the answer is three minutes. When I pull into my assigned spot, we both bail out of the car. I grab Ranger. She snatches up his diaper bag. We both practically run for the door to my condo. Inside, we race to get my son settled, and he falls into his crib with a deep sigh, sucks on his pacifier, and instantly melts into his mattress.

"He okay?" Masey asks from the door.

"Yeah," I whisper, touched that she cares so much.

Then I turn to her. She's already shed her shoes, ditched her lightweight cardigan, and unwound her hair from the loose bun she shoved it in earlier.

Heart pounding and harder than hell, I make my way across the room and crowd her back into the hall. "I've been thinking… Do you have to set up this afternoon for tonight's filming?"

She bites her lip. "I should."

I nod because I understand. My overeager dick doesn't, but it may have to wait. She's doing me a favor by being here, and I shouldn't get in her way.

Still, I can't resist. "Do you have to do it now?"

"Oh, to hell with it," she mutters as she lunges against me and lays her lips over mine.

Excitement spikes. My blood pumps. I shove her against the nearest wall and drown in everything Masey—her pillowy mouth, her coconut scent, her little catches of breath, and her lush breasts pressed against my chest as I dive deep in her mouth and explore her with my kiss.

When we finally pull away long moments later, she's panting as she blinks up at me. "Show me just how comfortable your couch is."

She wants me. I can't stop smiling. Masey can kid herself, but she isn't the kind of woman to get physical without any emotions being involved. So I don't think she would initiate sex unless being with me meant something.

"My pleasure." I pull her down the hall.

"Just to be clear, I was thinking less napping and more skyrockets in flight."

"Yeah?"

"Yeah."

When we reach the living room, she yanks my shirt up my torso and over my head. I lift her sundress and jerk down her panties. Her skirt is still swishing around her thighs when I tug at the tie fastening the top of her dress around her neck. It tumbles down to reveal the fact she wasn't wearing a bra, and she still has the most gorgeous tits I've ever seen, topped with hard, well-loved nipples. "Oh, honey, I'm definitely thinking afternoon delight."

I shove my shorts down and find the condom I hopefully tucked into my pocket earlier, just in case. I roll it on, plop onto the sofa, then lift her onto my lap.

"It's like you read my mind," she gasps as she splays her knees on either side of my hips and sinks down onto me slowly.

"Yeah…" I groan. "Let's rub our sticks and stones together."

She giggles and moves rhythmically over me. "We already are, and it feels ahhhmazing."

"I'm going to go out on a limb and say the sparks are already ignited." But to make sure, I tell her to rub at her clit while I take one of her bobbing nipples in my mouth.

Twenty minutes and three screaming orgasms from Masey

later, I finally let go and sink into the sofa with a long, satisfied sigh. "Damn."

"That was so good."

It was. And honestly, it just keeps getting better between us.

"I believe you now," she murmurs sleepily.

Believe me? "About what?"

"This *is* the most comfortable couch ever."

After a shower and a catnap, we awake refreshed in each other's arms—to the sound of Ranger crying.

"Someone's up," I mutter.

"And clearly not thrilled about it."

I roll over and brush a kiss across Masey's mouth. And I can't help but linger.

Jesus, I'm so fucking happy, especially when she kisses me back as if she has no other agenda than to shower me with her affection.

But another wail from Ranger has us jumping apart.

I curse. "Coming, buddy."

My voice quiets my son a little.

On the other side of the bed, Masey rises and stretches. "I'm behind, so I need to start the studio setup and edit a video I filmed my first day here before I start on others."

"Behind? Already? You've only been here a few days."

"I pre-filmed some of my videos before I arrived, but my video card corrupted one of them, so I have to record one more than I planned. And Harlow signed for a package the day I flew here. It's a launch from a major brand. Time-sensitive, so I'll have to make that video tonight, then edit and upload by tomorrow." She grimaces. "Sorry."

"Hey, duty calls."

When Ranger wails again, she nods. "It does."

"I'll get him settled and come help you with the studio."

"Thanks."

We go our respective ways, and as I'm changing Ranger and loving on my little man, I hear the faint strains of happy pop music. I can't identify the song...but it's nice to have other sounds in my condo. It hits me it makes the place feel full. Complete. Like a home.

I like having Masey here. And if I want to keep her, I need to get smart. I'm not much of a plan-ahead sort of guy, but I need to decide how the hell to make the most of the ten days she has left in Hawaii. If I do this right, maybe she'll agree to stay with me.

Do you really think that's possible? She *had days and days of you before she walked away and never looked back.*

I wish that voice in my head would shut the fuck up.

After meandering to the kitchen, I warm a bottle for Ranger. Once he's eating, curiosity lures me down the hall again. The strains of "Shape of You" fill the room. Ed Sheeran isn't shy about his feelings for the girl he's met. He just puts them out there. My bedsheets totally smell like Masey, and I am discovering something new about her every day that I like. I'm definitely in love with the shape of her body, but my heart seems to be falling, too.

I have to show her how we could fit together in each other's lives...somehow.

That scares the hell out of me. What if I can't convince her?

I take a deep breath. One day at a time. I'll figure it out...I hope.

When I peek my head inside my largely empty office, she's already plopped her laptop on my desk and started setting up her background and props for filming. As Ed Sheeran's final notes fade away, he's replaced by something definitely more down home. It's some country band. They're popular. The name escapes me.

I'm only half listening when I hear the male vocalist sing something I should keep in mind. Something profound. If it's meant to be, it will be. Masey just needs to ride with me and see how this thing goes.

Her hips are swaying as she starts tearing into boxes, checking the contents, then sorting them into three piles.

"Need help?"

She gasps in a startled breath and whirls, hand pressed to her chest. "You scared me."

"Sorry."

She waves me away. "Not your fault I was off in my own world. He good?"

When she glances Ranger's way, I stroll over closer. This isn't just about seeing if she can fall for me but for my boy, too. We're a package deal.

She smiles as we approach, then drops a kiss to his forehead. He coos happily, little legs pumping.

Her affection does something for me. It's not sexual exactly…but I'd be lying if I said I wasn't interested in another round.

"He's fine. I'll bet I could give him some toys on a blanket and he'd be happy if you need me to lend a hand."

"That would be great. I'm struggling with the lighting. Every room is just a little different, and I'm so used to my studio at home…"

"Sure." A few minutes later, I've got Ranger in a jumpy seat with some teething toys and his stuffed football. He seems content to watch what's going on around him. And after a few minutes of adjusting the angle and brightness of the lights, Masey sighs.

"I don't know if this will work. I'm going to run some test footage. Can you start the video when I say go?"

"Sure."

She settles into my office chair, wheels herself under the desk, which she moved away from the wall, then nods. "Go."

I press the button. Masey looks up at the camera and mocks her usual greeting, grabs for the first items beside her, and starts describing. "This is the Matte Fabulous Flawless Foundation by...crap, I can't remember." She reads the bottle and rattles off the name of a company I've never heard of. "They're a small indie brand based out of Denver and..."

After a few minutes and a few products, she signals me to cut off the camera.

"Now what?"

She looks at her phone, then her eyes pop wide. "Is it really almost five o'clock?"

"Yeah."

"Damn it!" Then winces as she casts Ranger a glance. "Sorry."

I shake my head. "That will start mattering around his birth-day, I guess. It doesn't yet."

"Whew. I need to find some clothes to wear and"—she looks around at the stacks of boxes—"in one of these should be my hand mirror. If I'm going to put on a face in front of the camera, I need that."

"I'll find it. You grab some clothes." I drop my voice. "But if it was up to me, you wouldn't need any."

"I wish, but I'd get banned for that." She laughs as she races out the door.

I find the mirror in the second box, wrapped in tissue paper, and set it on her desk. Some of the boxes in the room are mine, paperwork and some high school shit I keep packed away. Those I stow in the closet.

She dashes back into the room then, wearing a bright T-shirt with a scooped neck and capped sleeves, along with pretty mother-of-pearl jewelry. She's fluffed and sprayed her hair, too. From the waist up, she looks really put together. From the waist down, she's wearing a pair of my basketball shorts rolled up around her waist. Her bare toes wiggle against the tile.

I laugh. "Nice outfit. Fetching."

She shrugs. "Typical for filming. The magic of the camera is that they don't see anything I don't let them. Will you do me one more favor while I dig up the rest of the products I need for this video?"

"Name it."

"Can you please take the camera out to the kitchen or living room—somewhere not in this lighting—and compare the brightness of the footage we just took and the brightness of the footage I've shot recently at home? I'm trying to get this right so I won't have to refilm."

"You got it."

She hands me the camera, and I reach down to lift Ranger into my arms. Masey shakes her head. "You can leave him here. I like this guy."

When she winks at him, my son giggles again.

Yeah, he's as smitten as you are…

"Picking favorites already, huh?" I tease. "Fine. I'm out."

As I head down the hall, I hear her riffling through more boxes. I sink into my recliner, rewind the footage we just shot, and study it critically. She's a natural in front of the camera. She seems really comfortable running a one-sided dialogue, yet she makes viewers feel as if she's engaging in a cozy chat for two. But she asked me to check out the lighting.

For comparison, I pull my phone from my pocket and launch YouTube. Her past videos now appear in my recommendations. The first one that pops up is entitled "We Broke Up." The thumbnail image shows Masey sitting in a plush chair that doesn't appear in her usual beauty studio. She's pressed her hand over her mouth and looks as if she's holding back tears. A cat is curled up beside her, seemingly without a care in the world.

The video has nearly thirty million views. Holy shit.

I tiptoe into my bedroom and search my nightstand for my earbuds. I feel a little guilty, as if I'm somehow spying on Masey, but she put this out there for the public to see. I'm the public, too.

Yeah, but the rest of the public isn't sleeping with her.

I silence the voice, stick the buds in my ears, and launch the video, dated June twelfth of last year.

Instantly, I can tell she's struggling to keep it together.

"What's up, everyone? Welcome back." The greeting that sounded chipper in her test shot now sounds just shy of mournful. "As you can probably tell from the title of this video, Thom and I decided to call it quits over the weekend."

She pauses and draws in a shaky breath, seeming to grapple for control.

A fresh urge to beat the shit out of her ex for hurting her assails me. I know enough about Masey to know she isn't dramatic. She doesn't do angst. Most often, it seems like she tries to see the best in people and situations. Do I think she's got a dark side under her pretty skin that I haven't seen yet? It's possible. But she's also not the kind of girl to crumple easily.

When she wipes away a tear that falls from her eye, she sniffles and puts on a brave smile. "The split was amicable. And we'll remain friends. But I need a little time away to rest and rejuvenate.

"As many of you know, I also recently buried my dad. My mom needs me more than ever, and I think this is a good time to step back. I have a few videos pre-recorded, so I'll be releasing one a week for the next six weeks. After that, I plan to return to filming and get back on track. So don't worry. You haven't seen the last of me."

Beside her, the cat stands, stretches, walks in a circle, and plops again, this time planting its aristocratic chin on Masey's thigh. She lets out a watery laugh and strokes the gray tabby's back. "Even Harry needs a break. As you can see, he's desperately overworked. He also likes to remind me that he's the most important man in my life."

She pauses to rub the feline's head again. His purr is so loud it's audible through her microphone.

After another little laugh that sounds a bit more forced than the last, she addresses the camera again. Her eyes fill with tears once more, but she blinks them away. Her nose is a shade redder, and her lips are stiff. But she pushes on. "I can't thank you all enough for your support, words of encouragement, cards, DMs... It means so much to know you're thinking of me and keeping my family in your prayers.

"I know many of you are wondering about the palette challenge video review I teamed up with Lali Eastbrook to do a few weeks ago. It's filmed, and she's edited her part. I'm sorry I haven't finished mine, but Lali has been incredibly kind and supportive. Our videos will be released simultaneously once I've had the chance to make it upload-ready. I appreciate everyone's patience. I promise it's at the top of my list. Other than that...I just hope you all understand that I need a few weeks to take care of me. Thom and I would both be grateful for privacy. As always, I'm so humbled by your continuing support and love. I promise I'll be back soon. Until then, hugs and lipstick to you all!"

Then the video fades to a graphic of a heart with her first name scrawled in pink script over it.

I pause before a different video starts and scroll down to the comments. They are many, varied, and shocking. Over eighty thousand of them. I won't be able to read them all, but I can't resist reading some.

A group of hardcore fans banded together to send cards, gifts, handmade candles, and other things meant to cheer Masey up. Some people recount their own breakup experiences. One viewer tries to cheer her up by saying that, while it must hurt, at least Thom didn't leave her at the altar as her boyfriend did. Some others try to give post-relationship advice about being good to herself, healing at her own pace, and crying if she needs to. The vast majority are incredibly supportive of her decision to step away and heal.

And a healthy handful of them loathe Thom.

Quite a few of those say they all knew he was a douche when he refused to participate in the Boyfriend-Does-My-Makeup Challenge because appearing in something so "silly" damaged him professionally. Some others piled on and agreed, saying they knew Thom sucked as a person because he seemingly didn't care that his refusal hurt her. Still others wrote that when he reluctantly played along with the Boyfriend-Chooses-My-Makeup Challenge but refused to allow any shots of him except from the back that he was a self-important prick.

I can't disagree.

But a small, vocal minority of the commenters seem viciously determined to tear Masey apart while she's down. They claim she's ugly. That she's a hag. That she's getting what she deserves because she's stuck-up now that she's found success. That she has all the sexiness of shoe leather, so she shouldn't be surprised that she lost her man to an internet star with better tits. That she's getting what she deserves. That other beauty influencers— multiple names provided—are prettier and Masey should fuck off. That they hope she rots in hell. That they hope she dies.

I clutch my phone and gape. What the fuck is wrong with these people? Fury boils my blood. I'm not violent, and I was taught never to raise a hand to a woman. But I'm not even sure they pass as human beings. At the time of this filming, she had lost both her father and the man she'd spent a decade with, and that's the compassion these people show? Even if I didn't know Masey, I'd want to reach through the screen and throttle them. I want to tell every one of these mean-spirited halfwits to eat shit.

Above all, I want to protect her.

Even as I fight the urge to log in right now and go all keyboard warrior, I know she wouldn't want me to.

Goddamn it. I hate feeling impotent. I'm a dude who takes action and sorts shit out later. But all of this happened ten months ago. If I do anything now, am I just reviving old wounds?

"What do you think?" Masey peeks down the hall. "Is the lighting in here all right or too dark?"

I have no idea since the video I watched wasn't set in her studio, and I didn't pay a fucking lick of attention to the lighting.

How does she continue to post video after video, knowing there are people out there who hate her enough to wish her dead?

Masey may seem like she's on the quiet side. She may seem polite, even compliant. But I know damn well she's got layers.

And now it's clear that, under her sweetness, she has balls of steel.

"Um...still trying to figure it out. It's hard to tell. Give me a few more minutes?"

"Do you need help?" She starts to approach me.

Quickly, I close her breakup video and launch one about a new drugstore makeup haul she uploaded just before flying to Maui. "Nope. Just want to do a few more comparisons."

She shoots me a saucy glare, hand on hip. "Look, if you need eyeshadow pointers, don't be shy. You can come right out and say it. I won't judge."

"I don't." I scowl. "Have you done a man's makeup?"

"Sure." She shrugs like it's commonplace. "I have some beauty influencer friends who are guys. They're amazing. We swap tips sometimes."

I'm not surprised that men wear makeup. But I have a burning question... "Do they shave first? I would think putting that stuff you spread across your face—"

"Foundation?" She sounds amused by my lack of makeup knowledge.

"I guess that's what it's called. Wouldn't that be hard with stubble?"

She grins. "It adds a little challenge, but I like being tested. Last spring, I surprised a subscriber who had been in a fire as a kid. Someone had asked her to prom, and her sister wrote me and begged me to come do her makeup. This girl wanted to look her best. She watched my videos but never felt good enough to show anyone her efforts. The whole thing broke my heart. She agreed to star in a video so I could talk about working with scarring and texture for the best face possible. I think I cried through most of that day. She was so sweet and appreciative. It only cost me a few hours and some gas to make her prom one of the most special days of her life. We keep in touch all the time."

Despite the way some of these people talk to her in the comments section, she put all the negativity aside to help someone else. Because she could. Because she wanted to. Because she's an amazing woman.

Why didn't you fall for this one to start with, brainiac? No, you let your dick choose her, *and she fucked you up. Good job.*

God, I hate that nasty voice in my head.

"I'd like to see that."

She wrinkles her face and shakes her head. "I doubt that. You're a macho kind of guy."

"I'm serious, honey. I want to know all the things about you."

Masey waves me away like she doesn't completely believe me, but she also flushes and smiles. "Later. I'll start editing until you figure out the lighting situation."

"Sounds good. I won't be long."

When she leaves, I shove my earbuds back in and listen to her talk about all the exciting new releases at the drugstore. Some brands are really stepping up…and some are surprisingly disappointing, but she'll break down which is which if I stay tuned.

Trying to clear my mind and focus, I compare the lighting in the test shot on her camera with the video on my phone. Honestly, it looks spot on. I'm not surprised. Masey clearly knows what she's doing. But to be sure, I launch a few other recent videos and watch a minute or two—one about a big Sephora sale, one about an amazing new palette, and yet another about the best long-lasting liquid lipsticks. In all of them, the lighting looks similar to the test.

I should get up and tell her she's good to film. After all, the longer it takes for her to get started, the longer it will be before I can peel off everything she's wearing, kiss all over her body, and leave her with a satisfied smile. But...I want to see whatever I can of Thom. I want to know for myself what the ex was like and how much she put up with.

Blah, blah, blah. Stop lying to yourself. You want to see how you stack up against the competition.

Okay, that, too.

It takes a little searching. Masey took down her Boyfriend-Chooses-My-Makeup video, but others have archived it, so with a little searching and stealth, I finally hunt it down and launch it. There's not much to see. Thom is obviously wearing a suit. He's got a decent set of shoulders. Probably goes to the gym.

He seems impatient and spends about two minutes on camera before he tells Masey he has to go. No goodbye. No kiss. No *see you later* or *I love you*. The douchebag just leaves.

She carries on with what I now recognize as a fake smile. The rest doesn't matter much, so I cut it off with every intention of hauling ass down the hall and letting her know she's good to film. I'll see if I can help. It's probably reactive, but I want her to know I'm on her side and I love that she's succeeding.

But another video pops up as a new recommendation from a channel called Juiciest Tea, titled "What You NEED to Know About Masey Gee's Humiliating Split." It's got twenty million views.

It's probably all tripe and stupid, made-up nonsense, but I'd like to know what the rest of the beauty community thinks happened between her and Thom. She said very little about the split or the reasons for it, so it's no surprise that shit starters and drama freaks would create a narrative of their own. After all, they're after those money-making clicks.

I hate supporting this shit by giving these fucking gossips

the view they want, but if I don't, I won't know what Masey has faced.

A man and a woman in their early twenties sit in front of a background of spilled tea with smirks on their faces. Oh, they try to pretend sympathy and shock, but I can see the glee in their eyes.

"Hey, juicy tea drinkers!" the female greets. "We've got a scoop for you… In case you've been living under a rock, Masey G., one of the it-girls of the beauty world, has just split with her longtime boyfriend, Thom Jordan."

"Yeah." The dude wearing a skullcap and fake lashes jumps in. "According to both, the split was amicable and something that evolved over time. But…hold up. She's lying—to you, to me, to everyone."

"Makes you wonder what else she's lying about, doesn't it?" The girl with the messy purple pixie cut and the plaid shirt casts a doubtful stare at the camera, brows raised, finger pressed to her lips.

"How do we know she's lying?" the guy pipes up again. "Welllll, a month before the split, Thom is seen coming out of this high-dollar strip club in LA at two a.m. As you can see, he's not alone."

An image of a man, supposedly Thom, with his arm slung around a blonde coming out of the back of a building and emerging into an alley appears on screen.

"He's with a woman named Betsy Main."

"But you probably know her better as Candy Kitty." The screen fills with an image of a woman with straight hair down past her fake boobs, pursing her utterly fake lips. She's got on a ton of makeup, and the photo shows her more naked than not. "She's known all over the internet for showing all the women out there how to better self-love."

The purple-haired woman snickers. "And giving all the straight men something new to put in their spank banks. Because we know who her subscribers *really* are."

"Oh, girl, I totally know. My brother *floves* her and thinks Thom must be the luckiest dick on the planet."

From what Masey said, Thom wasn't very good with his dick. So how did he get this woman who makes a living getting off?

"So, check this." The woman cuts in as if she has more scoop. "Sources tell us that Thom and Candy have been getting it on for months. And he's complained—loudly—that Masey G. is a terrible lay."

"Dead fish." The guy gives a superior nod. "But, in her defense, Candy is probably just one of the best."

"Oh, yeah." Ms. Pixie Cut nods. "I'd do her."

"Even I might. Rawr." The dude rakes his hand through the air like a claw.

Together, they laugh. I want to puke. No, I want to punch them both for being terrible human beings who make a living off of broadcasting speculation about other people's pain.

The woman holds up a hand that assures the viewer there's even more. "And now I hear that the ring Masey G. waited ten years for—"

"*Ten!*"

"Crazy... But I hear that ring might be going on Candy's finger soon."

"Oh, snap!"

"Right?"

He nods. "We'll have to see how all this unfolds, but as of right now...looks like it sucks to be Masey G."

Together they laugh. There's still another three minutes on the video, but I can't watch. I can't stand what they've said about her or the way they've dragged her personal life through the mud. Most of all, I can't stand that they've hurt her and that they're utterly wrong.

Since I can't go fight an internet war, I need to help Masey in some other way. I'm just not sure what.

Slowly, I rise and meander down the hall.

CHAPTER NINE

When I reach my office, I see Masey in my chair with a pair of Beats headphones over her ears, frowning as she watches the replay of a video she clearly shot at home. Nearby, Ranger gives a happy squeal, and she turns to him with a big grin and a peekaboo that makes him laugh.

Then she catches sight of me and sets the headphones aside. "Got a verdict?"

I nod, trying to swallow back my fury on her behalf. "You're good to go. There's more natural light in this room than in your studio, I'm guessing."

"Definitely."

"So if you're going to film at night, you'll have to up the light factor a bit."

"For sure." She rises, concern filling her expression. "What's wrong?"

I'm not in a hurry to tell her I was snooping. But more importantly, I don't want Masey to think for one second that I'm with her merely because I feel sorry for her. And I'd rather not open her healing wounds over old shit I can't change. "I made the mistake of looking at the news."

"What's going on?"

"Oh, you know. Crime, hate, terror, greed, disease, and destruction." I shrug sarcastically. "The usual."

She rolls her eyes. "Nifty. I try not to think about that while I'm working or I won't get anything done."

"Another reason I appreciate having the ocean as my office."

She nods. "Now I'm just jealous."

I struggle for something to say. I can't blurt what's blaring across my brain. *Thom is a dick. You're great in bed. People online suck. I think I'm falling in love with you.* None of those things are going to fix the situation or ensure that I get to spend more than ten days with her. Now not only do I have to figure out how to persuade Masey to accept me beyond a fling and coax her into staying longer, I have to hope all of these toxic people who thought nothing about ruining her life haven't hurt her so much she'll never open her heart again.

From what my sister-in-law told me, I may be hoping in vain.

But I refuse to give up.

"Before we met, Harlow was telling me that Thom refused to appear in your videos." It's not entirely true, but I'm hoping to both help Masey and get closer to her. "If you still need someone with a Y chromosome in a video, I'll volunteer."

She looks surprised—in a good way. Then she seems to think better of it. "That trend passed. No one cares about the hashtag anymore. I always wanted to do it, but…you might not want the exposure or questions that come with it."

"What do you mean?"

"It's the Boyfriend-Does-My-Makeup Challenge. Thom hated the whole idea. Honestly, it wasn't a necessity, but it would have been nice back then... To me, those videos were always cute and funny, and you could see how in love some couples were." She waves away the idea. "But we'd have to tell people you're my new boyfriend."

"I don't mind. Besides, being your boyfriend comes with some awesome benefits." I wink to lighten the mood.

"But I don't want to lie to my viewers. I can't break their trust."

"Then consider me your ten-day boyfriend." But I'm hoping by then she'll remove the expiration date on our relationship and want to stay.

"We'd have to act really smitten."

"Not a problem."

"And strangers might dig into your life. It could turn into a whole thing."

I'm a big boy. I also don't have a lot of social media, so anyone looking for dirt on me won't come up with much. Besides, it seems like a small price to pay if I can persuade Masey to stay with me beyond ten days. "I appreciate the warning, but I don't care. I want to do this with you."

"Are you sure? Eventually, we'd have to publicly break up."

"If you feel you owe these people an explanation about your romantic life, you could eventually tell them I was the rebound guy or that we live in different states...or whatever works." But I'm hoping she doesn't have to say anything.

"You would do that for me?"

"Sure."

"Why?"

She can't guess at all?

"Would it make you happy, honey?"

Masey nibbles on her lip. "Yeah. It probably sounds silly

since it's not a trending hashtag anymore. But I never got to participate and…"

She felt left out, sure. More than anything, she felt as if Thom didn't love her. Probably because he didn't.

"You wanted to. So that's why I'm volunteering to do it."

"Just because you want me to be happy?" She looks as if she can't decide whether that should make her smile or cry.

That expression reaches right into my chest and squeezes my heart. "Yeah."

Finally, she smiles. "How much do you know about makeup application?"

"Almost nothing."

"Perfect. It will be a complete train wreck."

And she sounds thrilled about it. Is that the point?

"More than likely, yes."

"When do you work next?"

"Wednesday night. Sunset cruise. A regular of mine is going to propose to his girlfriend."

"That sounds really romantic." A wistful note fills her voice for just a moment before she's all business again. "Mind if we film Tuesday, then?"

"Works for me."

"Fabulous." She saves the video she's working on, then closes the laptop lid and sets the device aside. "I want to get two videos filmed this evening, so I need to get busy. This product release has to come first." She picks up a sleek silver rectangle. The packaging is shiny and looks as if the manufacturer spent some money on it. "I also received some other recently or soon-to-be-launched items, so I'll make this a new products first impressions video. Let me make sure I've got everything ready. Products are here…" She looks around at the pile of makeup in front of her. "Yes, I have everything for a full face. Clean brushes, check. Bottle of water, check. Damp sponge, check. Lighting is good. SD card is empty. Microphone is on stand-by..." She looks my way. "Anything else?"

I shake my head. "Not that I know of, but you're the expert here."

She shrugs. "I do my best."

"You want me to take my little guy and go?"

She bites her lip. "I'd love to have you both stay. But you can be unexpectedly loud," she coos at Ranger, who grins at her. "Yes, I'm talking about you, handsome." Then she glances at me. The hint of mischief in her eyes kick-starts my libido. "And you're distracting."

"You mean you don't want me to get comfortable"—I peel off my shirt, stretching and flexing to give her the best view —"and hang around to watch how sexy you are?"

Masey covers her eyes with her hand...and peeks at me through her parted fingers. "Personally, I would love that. But it would lead to other things, and I'd never get any filming done."

"We could always film that." I raise a brow at her.

"I can't film us having sex and post that online." She tsks at me.

"Who said anything about sex?" I play innocent. "I meant you gawking at me. But your mind went right to the gutter, honey. Whose fault is that?"

She picks up some powder puff thing and throws it at me with a laugh. "Yours. I never thought about sex until you."

"Never?"

"Not really." She gets quiet and frowns. "No."

She's already admitted that her heart wasn't wholly in the relationship. Maybe it knew Thom was an asshat and a half, just like her body seemed to. Her loyal streak and schoolgirl romantic fantasies tangled her mind. But instinctually…she knew her ex wasn't the man for her.

I wonder how she's feeling about me?

"Are you thinking about more than sex now?"

"More?" Masey goes stiff. She looks decidedly nervous as she gives me a jerky shake of her head. "I promised I wouldn't be a clinging vine. We're together because I wanted experience, and the sex is beyond amazing. Everything I thought it would be—and then some. But that's all. I don't expect anything else."

A snappy response sits on the tip of my tongue. *More than the sex could be amazing if you'd let me into your heart.* But she's not. Because she's not feeling it? Or because she's afraid I'll reject her?

I have to believe the latter or I'm fucked. And I can't risk spooking her yet by saying I think about more than sex between us a lot. I need to let this play out, be with her longer than a day or two so she can experience how good we can be together.

"Don't be afraid to expect more. Maybe you should." After draping my shirt over my arm, I turn to Ranger and lift him up in his jumpy seat. "We'll leave you to it. Holler if you need anything."

She nods, but I see the shock on her face. She can't decide what to make of my words. I'm not staying to explain. She'll figure it out.

With a wave, I shut the door. I don't hear any movement inside the office or a hint of her voice for long minutes.

Finally, Ranger seems bored by hanging out in the hall and starts demanding out of his jumpy seat. I hustle him down the hall and find his stroller, then wrestle into my shoes. "How about a run, big guy?"

When he sees his stroller, he gets practically giggly. He loves the outdoors. He's definitely my boy.

Soon, we're out the door, and I'm pushing the stroller as I run a few laps around my condo complex. When I round the final corner and jog on the sidewalk at the perimeter of the parking lot, heading toward my unit, I see a sporty blue convertible pull up.

What shitty luck. Caitlyn Everson is the last person I want to see.

But she seems all too eager to park, hop out, and smile my way. Even from a distance, I see the invitation in her eyes. And the question. I haven't seen her—let's be honest, fucked her—since shortly before Ranger was born. She knocked on my door a couple of months back. I would have...but my son needed a bottle, and I didn't feel like explaining to a woman I only know sexually that I had recently become a father.

Still, I have to jog right past her. I can't exactly do that without saying hi. And now that she's seen the stroller, she's bound to have questions.

"Hey there." She flirts as she approaches, wearing a chic black jumpsuit with a plunging V-neck and ridiculously high heels. She bats her lashes at me, flashing a pageant smile. "I haven't seen you in a while, Trace. You look...really good. Doing all right?"

I am not flirting in return. Zero interest. In fact, I'm not sure what I ever saw in her.

Sex. A lot of no-strings sex.

"I'm great, Caitlyn. How about you?"

"Busy. Work is a zoo. But I'm not too busy to spend a few hours with you. I'm free this evening..." Her eyes eat me up as she comes closer, licking her lips before she notices the stroller and frowns. "You babysitting or something?"

"No. I have a son now. We were just out getting some exercise."

She frowns. "Do you suddenly have a wife, too?"

"No. His birth mother gave me sole custody. His name is—"

"When did that happen?"

She doesn't care what his name is, how old he is—nothing. Hell, she doesn't even try to peek in the stroller.

I do my best not to look as annoyed as I feel. "Last November, the day he was born."

"Oh. Well, if you can get a babysitter or want to call me after he's down for the night, I would love to come over." Her frown turns up to a coy smile as she flips her fluffy blond hair over her shoulder. "It's been too long since we made each other feel good."

She's straight-up offering me a booty call. Not because she likes me as a person or wants to start a relationship, just because she enjoys the way I once touched her.

Now I know why we never talked much. Her hair is a lot bigger than her heart.

Still, I know Caitlyn. She's a pharmaceutical sales rep. She's a shark. If I turn her down flat, she may take it as a challenge, and I'll never see the end of her.

Instead, I lie. "He can be a really fussy baby. Teething and all. He isn't sleeping through the night. Maybe in a few months when he settles"—or never—"but right now—"

"I don't mind a quickie. Or two. Or more." She sidles closer and lifts a hand to me, sliding her fingertips over my sweat-slick chest. "I've thought about you a lot."

I ease back. "Have you?"

If she has actual feelings for me, then I've read her all wrong. And I certainly never meant to use or hurt her. But when we spent time together in the past, she talked a lot about wanting to marry a surgeon. In fact, I heard recently that she was dating one.

"Absolutely."

"What about Dr. Brain Surgeon?" His name escapes me. "Aren't you dating him?"

"He's nice. And he's well respected in the medical community. He has a great sense of humor." Her stare travels down my naked chest and dips between my legs. "But no one has a cock like you. And no one knows how to use theirs better. Want to remind me?"

So she *is* dating the brain surgeon. She just wants me to be her something on the side.

She can go fuck herself.

I'm already crafting the most permanent way to tell her to get lost as she leans closer. Instead of whispering something in my ear, she unexpectedly plants her lips onto my pec and licks up the rivulets of sweat rolling down my skin.

In the middle of the parking lot. In broad daylight. Without giving a shit who can see us. When she has a boyfriend.

What. The. Fuck?

Suddenly, I hear the sound of something shattering behind me.

I whirl to find Masey standing there, still wearing her T-shirt, jewelry, and my shorts. Her mouth gapes open. At her feet, her phone lays broken, the screen smashed into a thousand pieces. Her expression tells me she's crushed.

Dread gouges out my belly. I know exactly what she's thinking.

With a sound that's more cry than gasp, she turns and runs toward my condo as if her life depends on it.

"Fuck." I pluck what's left of her phone off the sidewalk and grab the handle of Ranger's stroller.

"What time should I come over tonight?" Caitlyn asks.

I'm over being subtle. "Never. Don't come. I'll be with my girlfriend."

Then I take off after Masey. I've got to catch her before she reaches my door and slams it between us.

It's a close call, but I catch up to her as she darts inside.

"Excuse me. I'm sorry," she says to someone on her right, then takes off down the hall.

Who the hell is she talking to?

When I make it inside my condo, my brother and my mother are sitting on the sofa, staring wide-eyed into the awkward silence. The office door at the end of the hall slams.

"What happened, bro?" Noah asks.

No time for that now.

I drag Ranger's stroller over the threshold and shut the front door. "Can you watch him?"

"Sure. Is Masey all right?" With a jerk of his head, he motions down the hall.

"I don't think so." And I understand why.

Thom cheated on her. She thinks I'm no better.

I jog down the hall and stop in front of the closed office door. "Honey, can we talk?"

"I have nothing to say."

"Then let me explain."

"Don't bother."

If I want any chance at a future with her, I don't have a choice. "I want to."

"Don't. I'll just leave."

Where does she think she's going to go? "Honey…"

"Don't honey me," she lashes out.

And she sounds furious. On the one hand, that worries me. Is she too pissed off to talk? On the other hand, it's also a good sign. She wouldn't waste her anger if she didn't give a shit.

"Talking through a door is silly, Masey. I'm coming in." And she can't stop me because the door doesn't have a lock.

I barge inside and stop short when I find her standing in the middle of the room, arms crossed over her chest, glaring my way with the fire of hell in her eyes, silently daring me to take even a single step closer.

Yeah, she's definitely pissed. But she's even more hurt. Tears roll down her face, making two silvery paths through her otherwise perfect face makeup.

The sight rips at my heart.

Swallowing, I shut the door behind me. I can only imagine what my brother and my mother are thinking, but they aren't my problem right now.

Masey is.

"Get the fuck away from me."

Softly, I shake my head. "You're mad. I understand."

"No, you don't. I'm mad at myself." She tsks. "I should have known."

"I'm not Thom."

"So you know what he did?" she demands.

"Cheated? Yeah."

"Did Harlow tell you that, too?"

"Does it matter?"

"Nope. But I'm not going to give you the chance to lie to me like he did." Her laugh sounds mocking. "I should thank you. It was years before he slipped up enough for me to realize he was cheating. It only took you an hour after becoming my 'boyfriend'"—she holds up air quotes—"for you to show me what you're really like."

"Masey—"

"What were you going to do, give her your 'special' tour of the couch while I filmed in your office?"

Ouch. "No. I had zero intention of seeing Caitlyn beyond our run-in in the parking lot. And zero interest."

"Right…" She nods skeptically. "Look me in the eye and tell me you've never fucked her."

"I'm not going to lie to you. I have. Ask me how long ago that was."

"I don't care."

"Oh, I think you do." I charge closer and grab her arms. "You care enough to start an argument about it."

"I'm not arguing. I'm leaving. I'll ask Noah to have Harlow come collect my stuff later."

She tries to rush past me. I grab her and hold her firmly in place.

"Let's get a couple of things straight first. If you want to leave after that, I can't stop you." I also won't stop pursuing her, but since that will just start another argument, I keep that to myself.

"I don't care."

"That's a lie. You care. I care. Neither of us would be having this conversation if we didn't. So let's try being honest. I'll start. I haven't seen Caitlyn in at least six months. She all but jumped on me when you walked up."

"That's a good one. Almost as good as Thom's excuse for why he was spending time with Betsy. He'd hired her to teach him how to be better for me in bed, you see. Fool me once, shame on you. Fool me twice—"

"I'm fucking not Thom!" I clasp her arms tighter and pull her closer. "She wanted to come over tonight, and I told her no. I told her never to come over again. I told her I would be with my girlfriend."

"We're not actually dating." She tries to wrest free.

There's no way I'm letting her go. "Let's talk about that. You want to know something honest? Nia probably could have found somewhere else to park Amanda and Oliver. She has connections on the island. And if she couldn't find a place, I guarantee Keeley would have found somewhere. She knows locals for days. But I volunteered your rental. Wanna know why? So you would stay with me, and I could be with you."

"Pfft. You needed a babysitter."

Damn, she's tenacious when she's pissed off.

Masey probably thinks I'm all chill, but she's about to find out I can be fucking stubborn, too. "No, I wanted you. I wanted any excuse to keep you next to me, in bed with me, talking to me, maybe falling for me. Because I'm falling for you. And I wasn't going to tell you that until I thought you were ready to hear it. I was going to ease you into it and show you how good life with Ranger and me could be. But because you saw a former fling make a move on me, you decided I'm like your asshole ex. It's completely fucking unfair. If I'm good in bed, honey, it's because I went through a long string of women like her who only wanted me for my cock. To them, I wasn't good enough for anything else. Should I lump you in with them like you're lumping me in with Thom?"

"No," she whispers, and I can't tell whether she feels shocked or chastened.

"Is the only thing you like about me the way I fuck you?"

Fresh tears fall down her face. "Of course not. That's horrible."

"Do you feel anything for me besides desire?"

She hesitates for a long moment. Her eyes water, and her face twists like she's trying not to cry. "Yes. And I'm scared."

I can barely hold in my sigh of relief as I pull her closer. I don't care that I'm sweaty or that I'm getting her shirt damp. I don't care that I vaguely hear my son fussing down the hall or that my family has probably heard every word of this conversation.

I only care that Masey is developing feelings for me, too.

"Don't be scared. Just…one day at a time, okay?"

"I don't know if I can do that."

Because trust is hard for her.

You get that. It's taken you four years after her *to trust enough to try the relationship thing again.*

This won't be a quick fix. We'll need to talk, but I've got to deal with a whole bunch of other stuff first.

"Stay here. Give me one minute."

"Trace…"

"One." I hold up a finger as I back toward the door, then open it behind me, slide out, and shut it quietly again.

It will be a miracle if she stays.

I jog down the hall to find Noah helping my mother to the front door with one hand. He's holding Ranger with the other.

"Everything all right, bro?" he asks.

I shrug his question away, then turn my attention to Makuahine. "You okay? How's your ankle?"

She sends me a soft smile that tells me my concern is unnecessary. "Tender, but otherwise fine. Don't worry about me."

"Good." I focus on Noah. "You? Harlow? Nolan?"

"All good. We just came by to visit. Makuahine wanted out of the house. Harlow said Masey was here, but it didn't occur to me she would be filming." Or that we would have a fight. "Sorry."

I shake my head. "It's fine. If you don't need anything from me…"

"No. Why don't you let us take Ranger for the night?" my brother offers.

My mother's face softens. "Focus on your girl, keikikāne."

I'm torn. I love my son, but Masey and I need the alone time right now. If I want to keep her, she's where I need to focus.

"That would be helpful. Thanks."

"No problem," Noah assures. "He's got clothes at Makuahine's place. We'll swing by there since she wanted to check on her plants anyway and pick those up, along with his playpen. Just call us tomorrow when you're free. No rush. We'll bring Ranger back. Until then, we'll have fun." My brother bounces my son in his arm. "Won't we, big guy?"

He looks alert and content, then he lunges for my mother, who happily coos and cuddles him.

I kiss his little head and rub his shoulder. "I'll see you tomorrow, baby man."

Noah nods my way as he helps my mother and my son out the door. Makuahine pauses so I can kiss her cheek. Then they're gone, and I lock the door behind them.

I'm alone with Masey.

I march back down the hall and throw the door open. "They're gone now. It's just us."

But I see she's already got her stuff half packed. "May I borrow your phone? I need to call Harlow to come get me. As soon as Noah gets home—"

"He'll tell her to keep her ass put. They're watching Ranger for the night. She won't come for you."

"Then let me call a taxi."

"Stop. This isn't about what you think you saw me doing with Caitlyn. This is about you licking your wounds and making excuses for not confronting your fears. How's that going to work out? You going to keep running? How long can you do that? A year? Two? Five? A decade? Are you so afraid of taking a chance with me that you'd tuck tail like your ass is on fire and throw us away before we even figure out what we've got?"

"Don't psychoanalyze me. Maybe I'm just not ready to try again."

"Or maybe you just don't care if he wins."

"Wins?" She clenches her fists at her sides and scowls. "It's not a game."

"No, it's your *life*, and ten months after he walked out of it, you're still giving him power over you."

"What do you know about relationships? By your own admission, you've never had one."

"None that lasted, and I learned from my mistake."

"What mistake was that?"

"I blamed myself for everything that went wrong, just like you're doing. You believed you weren't sexy enough or good enough in bed or that you worked too much. And you thought all that because Thom told you so. Just like he told you everything else was your fault. Because you're kind, sensitive, and caring, you took his blame. Then when he fed you excuses about your sex life and how he was spending his time, you swallowed those, too. It was *all* bullshit, honey. You're sexy as fuck and great in bed. Only you know how much your business needs attention, not him. Not me. *You*. Thom was the kind of misogynistic narcissist who believes everything is about him. The only way you move on is to let go of everything he told you and do what makes *you* happy."

Masey doesn't say anything at all for long moments, just stares and blinks. "What do you want from me?"

"Honesty."

She looks away, casting her gaze out the window to the lush grounds beyond the pane. "I'm being honest."

"Not with yourself. You're being scared. I get it. You invested a decade in Thom, and he still hurt you, so why should you trust some guy you've known for a weekend? But don't leave; talk to me. Let's figure this out. You didn't like seeing Caitlyn touch me."

"She wasn't just touching you. She had her *mouth* on you. She was licking you like she had every right to."

"Because she's like Thom, a narcissist to the core. Before you, I had a type: sexually aggressive blondes. I fucked a long line of them, and they seemed all too happy to let me."

Masey's mouth pinches shut as she grabs a box off my desk and pulls it against her chest like armor. "That's it. I'm leaving."

When she tries to march past me, I grip her arm and jerk the box out of her hands, then slam it on the table. "Not until we talk this out. Then, if you want to leave, I'll take you to Harlow myself."

"You don't get to tell me what to do."

"I don't. But let me ask you a question. Can you think of a time Thom fought to keep you two together? Even one?"

She sputters, then falls silent, pressing her lips together mulishly and focusing out the window again.

"That's what I thought." I cup her face, bringing her gaze back to me. "I've spent two days with you. Do I know if this is a forever kind of thing? No. But I think we've got something that's worth exploring."

Actually, I'm almost convinced this fling could lead to something more but...baby steps.

"So special that you needed to tell me about all the blondes you've taken to bed. Why, so you can point out that I'm not your type?"

"No. So I can tell you that this"—I gesture between us—"has taken me by surprise. But I'm rolling with it. I'm telling you that I'm completely into you."

When my confession slips out, my heart starts pounding. Jesus, I'm making myself awfully fucking vulnerable to a woman who's fighting me for everything except sex. Yeah, she banters with me. And she likes my son. But she wanted to meet me for the sex. She probably came to stay with me instead of getting a hotel for more sex. I can't pretend to be disinterested in sex, mostly because I can't be near Masey without wanting her. But it says a lot about what I'm feeling that if I had to choose between spending the next ten days talking to her or fucking her, I would—though begrudgingly—choose the conversation.

Masey is quiet for such a long time, I don't have the faintest clue what she's going to say. "You weren't in any hurry to push that woman away."

"She shocked me. One minute I was telling her about Ranger, who she had no idea existed, and the next she started licking me. After you ran away, I basically told her to fuck off."

Masey's expression doesn't change, but at least she's looking at me. "How do I know that's true?"

I fucking want to beat Thom, plow my fist into his pretty face, and hurt him for hurting her so much. "You don't. All I can give you is my word. I realize Thom gave you his and then lied straight to your face."

"And I stupidly believed him."

Because she wanted to. So now she's afraid to believe me. But that would only scare her if she wants to believe me.

"I get you." I hesitate explaining why. As pasts go, it's the part that's most painful. Humiliating. Emasculating. It was, hands down, the worst day of my life. But telling Masey may be the only way she believes I would never stab her in the back. "Can I tell you something I've never told anyone?"

That gets her attention. "Never?"

"Ever. The night we met, you asked me if I'd ever had any long-term relationships or fiancées along the way and I said no.

That was true…but not the whole story. There was a bitch who ripped my fucking heart out."

"The one you claim you learned from?"

"Yeah. I'll tell you if you want to hear. And I'll explain why I know that, if you want to move on and have any sort of life, trusting someone else is not only fucking hard but vital."

Masey doesn't answer me, just lifts one shoulder in a half shrug.

"I'm not going to push it on you. Tell you what? You decide if you want to hear it, and I'll go take a shower. When I come out—"

"Fine. Tell me."

"Will you really listen?"

"Yeah."

With a nod, I release her. Time to gather my balls. If I tell her and she doesn't care, it will fucking hurt.

But then you'll know you're way more into her than she's into you.

I can't argue with that.

I draw in a deep breath and prepare to slice open my soul.

CHAPTER TEN

"About four years ago, a woman hired me to do a private, two-week sailing for her and her boyfriend. She wanted to go from Maui, around all the islands, with stops at a different island each day, then a stay at a new resort town each night. On the morning the couple was scheduled to arrive, only she—I refuse to say her name—showed up."

"You won't say her name? What is she, Voldemort?"

I try not to crack a smile. "Close. It's a good comparison. Anyway, when she appeared that morning, she was all runny nose and tears. She said her boyfriend had walked out on her without warning. They'd been drifting apart, and she'd hoped this getaway would bring them back together. But since he was gone, she intended to use the trip—which she'd already paid for —to 'soul search' and figure out where to take her life next."

"That's not what happened?"

"Not even close. Her first night on the boat, she told me her poor-little-rich-girl story. She claimed the man she loved left her because he was intimidated by the money she'd been born to and the ills of their relationship were all because he was intent on keeping up and couldn't. By the end of the first night, she cried in my arms until she fell asleep. I felt sorry for her."

"That wasn't all you felt. Don't tell me; let me guess. Hot blonde?"

"Yep. I won't deny it. And I'll spare you the gory details, but over the next couple of days, we fell into bed." And we hardly got back out, but no reason to rub that in Masey's face. "Toward the end of our two weeks, she said her head was so much clearer, her heart had direction, and she knew exactly where she belonged. Since she was nuzzling my face and smiling at me as she said it, I assumed I fit somewhere in that future. I thought I was in love with her. On our last stop, in Honolulu, I told her I had to run an errand. I spent every fucking dime I'd saved—for a down payment on a new boat so I could expand my business —on an engagement ring. I proposed that night."

Masey's blue eyes go wide. "Oh, my god. And she turned you down?"

"Not right away. She said she wanted to think about it overnight, because we'd never been together in the real world and all that. But when we docked in Maui, her pissed-off boyfriend was waiting. She was wearing my ring, and he was furious. They started screaming at each other, and it became really clear that she'd used me in an elaborate scheme to make her billionaire boyfriend—yeah, she lied about him being poor —jealous so he would finally propose to her. Lo and behold, he did. And she accepted—with me standing right there. Then she tossed me a few dismissive words about the fact I'm a 'nobody,' so of course she couldn't marry me, but thanks for the orgasms because I was great in bed. Then she took off with her billionaire fiancé and left me standing with a fortune in engagement ring all by myself. So you're not the only one who's suffered, honey."

She presses a hand over her shocked mouth and stares. I'm not sure what reaction I expected, platitudes? Questions? The brush-off?

In a million years, I never dared to hope that she would throw her arms around me and press herself against my sweat-laden body with such visceral understanding in her touch. "I'm so sorry. I can't imagine how horrible that must have been…"

I should have guessed Masey would respond with compassion.

I slide my arms around her and melt against her small frame. Funny, after only a couple of days with this woman, I feel comforted by her, despite the fact she's doing nothing more than hugging me. Her coconut smell usually strikes me as something between exotic and sultry, but today it's the equivalent of apple pie in the kitchen. It's homey. It's soothing.

Her lips travel gently from my shoulder and up my neck before brushing my ear in a gesture that's more consoling than seductive. "You deserve better."

I cup her face and fuse our stares together. "So do you. And that's my point. She—"

"Voldemort?"

"Yeah. She treated me like I was disposable. Like trash. We only had two weeks together, so I know comparing ten years isn't the same but—"

"What good am I doing myself if I don't stop letting him affect how I feel now that he's long gone?"

"Exactly. The things he convinced you of and the feelings he foisted off on you were convenient for *him*. As long as you were willing to take the blame, he could convince himself he'd done nothing wrong."

Her mouth curls derisively. "You're assuming he's capable of that much self-reflection."

"Voldemort wasn't, either." I brush a thumb across her lips. "I know how much Thom hurt you. It's not just the infidelity but the faithlessness, the way he acted as if your feelings meant nothing. It's hard to recover from that. It's even harder to put it behind you enough to trust again."

She sighs like that task is already so monumental it's weighing her down. "Yeah."

"And I get it. So I can be patient. But can we agree on one thing?"

"What?"

"I'm not Thom, and you're not Voldemort. And I would never go out of my way to hurt you."

Slowly, she nods, then bites her lip. This time, it's not a coy gesture but genuine concern. "We can do that, but I'm only here another ten days. Does any of this matter?"

She's asking about our expiration date. It's time to confront this head on. "Who says we have to be over then?"

"How would that work? I live there, you live here…"

"I don't know. I only know that it works if we put in the work and we want it to work."

Masey nods slowly. "I've always thought that's true about relationships. Thom told me I was looking at the world too simplistically."

"Thom is a douche."

"He had good moments. Great ones, even. But…yeah. I think you're right." She bites her lip again, and this time I can tell it's purely because she's contrite. "I'm sorry about everything."

"Don't be. This isn't how I might have chosen to have this talk—"

"You mean me flying jealously off the handle, marching past your family, tears and door slamming in full force?" She grimaces. "It's so cringe. I wish I had a do-over."

"But it told me I matter to you." I'm afraid to tell her how much I needed to know that.

"You do." She strokes my face.

"Honey, you matter, too. Don't ever doubt that." I kiss the tip of her nose. I want to be closer to her, not just sexually—though I'd love that—but physically and emotionally.

I want to make love to her.

Because I'm pretty sure I'm *in* love with her.

But if I touch her, I can't guarantee that she'll get to finish her filming tonight.

"I should go take a shower." I hoist my thumb in the direction of my bedroom. "And let you get back to filming."

She looks disappointed but nods as she caresses my shoulders—and eats me up with her stare. "Okay."

Shit. I need to get out of this room now…or I'll end up inside her, not caring about anything else.

With a nod, I leave and shut the office door behind me.

In the hall, I let out a long sigh. Sure, we made progress—more than I thought possible. But I want to be with Masey so badly. It's lousy timing that she has to produce this video tonight. Still, I can't stand in her way. Thom did enough of that.

Inside my bathroom, I slide out of my shorts and turn on the faucet. Moments later, I'm stepping inside, grateful for the sluicing of the cool water over my skin. But it doesn't do a damn thing to soothe my restless mind.

Where do Masey and I go from here? I know what I told her about putting in the work if we want it to work, but realistically…she's right. I live here. She lives in Cali. I don't know where that leaves us.

Suddenly, the shower door snaps open. I swipe the water from my eyes long enough to see Masey slip into the stall with me, naked as the day she was born, and sink to her knees.

"What are you doing?" I ask her, my hands automatically sinking into her dampening hair.

She looks up at me with warm blue eyes. "Voldemort and Caitlyn and a whole bunch of other women may have wanted you for the way you make them feel. I'm sorry I wanted to meet you for the same reason. But I'm with you now because you give me a lot more than pleasure."

Her fingertips glide up the backs of my legs as she presses kisses down my abs, over my hips, and across my thighs. Water splashes over my shoulders and gently onto her face, clinging wetly to the lashes that now brush her cheeks. She's completely bare to me—not merely naked, not merely makeup-less. Utterly bare. That barrier I've sensed between us since we met, the soft, awkward uncertainty she's used like a shield to keep me at arm's length so often, is gone. And she's beautiful.

"Masey..."

She cups my balls, grips my shaft, then opens her eyes enough to watch me watching her as she sucks me in deep. I toss my head back and groan.

When she takes her first drag on me, I'm a goner. The heat of her mouth is... *Jesus.* But it's the warmth, the giving of her affection that's doing me in even more. She's not sucking my cock to twist me inside out or as any sort of thank you for the orgasms I've given her. Not even so she can show off her well-practiced skills. I've experienced all those blow jobs in the past. This is different. This is purely because she wants to pleasure me, give another part of herself to me.

Because she wants more with me.

That sinks in as she strokes my cock up and down with her full lips, covering every surface inch of my sensitive shaft she can. But it's her devious little tongue that's undoing me most. It sweeps across my crest with the barest of touches, teasing and lingering as it ignites me.

My fingers burrow deeper into her hair, digging at her scalp as she takes me nearly to the hilt, then sucks out my self-control and my soul slowly, with agonizing efficiency. All my blood rushes to my cock. I'm getting dizzy. I'm on fire. I can't stop pumping my hips to meet her waiting mouth.

I stagger against the shower stall for support, but I still feel as if I'm swimming through ether. My knees start to give out. My heart roars.

She's going to blow the top off of my head in seconds. Normally, I'd be thrilled. Hell, I'd salute her for a job extremely well done. But we've said so much and come so far together today, I don't want this orgasm alone. I need to be with her.

I'm less than gentle when I tug on her hair to detach her mouth from my cock. Masey looks up at me, blinking. Questioning. I don't have the patience for words.

Shoving the shower door open, I haul her to her feet, lift her against my body, and carry her, dripping from the shower, to my bed. I lay her flat, wedge myself between her legs, and thrust my way deeper inside her than I've ever been.

Immediately, she wraps her arms around me and digs her nails into my back. "Trace!"

"I have to fuck you."

"Yes," she breathes.

"I have to be deeper inside you than anyone has been. Ever. God, you feel so fucking good." I slant my lips over hers and penetrate her mouth as wholly as her body.

Under me, she rocks and writhes, clinging, gasping, and giving every bit of herself back to me with every dirty, surrendering moan.

"More," she murmurs mindlessly. "Don't stop. Don't ever stop. I need…"

"To come?" I grab her chin and stare down into her eyes as I bang her body into the mattress. "Is that what you need?"

She nods with a little whine in her throat, and for a moment, I wonder if I've read her all wrong. Did I convince myself of all the warmth and caring behind her touch because I wanted to feel it? Because I wanted to believe I mattered to her?

"But I need you, too. You make me feel alive again." She peppers kisses across my face, then onto my neck, nipping her way down my shoulder. "You make me feel whole."

Oh, fuck. Her words ignite a powder keg of desire inside me. When I thought she merely wanted me to scratch her itch, I had a hard time letting her out of my bed. But hearing her admit that what we have is more than physical, like we might both be falling in love?

That does something to me I can't control.

I reach above Masey's head and across the bed, gripping the side of the mattress so hard I can't feel my fingers. What I can feel? The swelling of my cock as I use my leverage and every bit of my strength to drive even farther inside her. She takes everything I give her with grateful sighs and clings to me desperately for more.

"Trace," she pants my name in my ear like a plea. "Trace. Trace!"

"Scream for me, honey."

She answers with breathless sobs. Her pussy clutches me tightly. I feel her cling to every fucking inch of me in a delicious velvet grip.

"I'm there."

I lift my head to look at her, elbows digging into the mattress, hips surging rapidly. "I know. Come with me."

"Yes." She spreads her lips across my skin again with tiny, fevered presses before she opens her eyes.

Her stare is like a light from heaven shining on me and all my favorite sins from hell all rolled into one.

That and the cries that tear from her bucking body are enough to undo whatever's left of my restraint. I can't help myself; I sink in as deep as I possibly can, bare my teeth, and release inside her for endless, euphoric thrusts.

Holy shit. This isn't an orgasm. I don't know what it is, but I spill everything I have into her. Black spots glimmer and flash at the edge of my vision. A possessive wave overtakes me.

I grab her wet hair and force her eyes open. She has to look at me. I have to put my mouth on her. I have to sink my teeth into her. I have to leave my mark on her.

That's all I can think of as I bite into her shoulder and shudder through the last of a climax so epic I feel as if I should write songs or shout from the rooftops about it.

"Trace..." she whimpers. "Trace."

I finally catch my breath and lift my head. I'm a little embarrassed that I left actual teeth marks in her neck. I'm slightly shocked that I've wound her wet tresses around my fist and tugged so tight I see the strands at her hairline straining. And as I shift to give her room to breathe, I'm stunned to realize that I fucked her without any protection at all.

Instantly, I release her and slide free, staring down at her and trying to find the right words. "I'm sorry."

It's all I can think of.

She frowns. "Why?"

Maybe she doesn't get it yet. "I lost my head. I was rough. I forgot the condom."

"Oh." She frowns, then shakes her head. "It should be all right. I've been on the pill since I was sixteen to help regulate my periods. I missed most of the weekend, but I'll get back on track with them tonight."

I let out the breath I've been holding. It's a good thing she's on the pill. It is. Really…despite the random images bombarding my brain of a pregnant Masey coming to my bed all bare breasts and rounding belly, with her heart in her eyes.

Yeah, I'm an idiot. That's not happening, and I shouldn't want another child right now, especially with another woman who hasn't—and might never—commit to me.

"That's…good. I'll be more careful next time." I get to my feet and tell myself to get over this ridiculous disappointment.

"Whatever you want. But you're clean, and I've never…"

Had sex without a condom? Thom was a germaphobe, I remember. Or maybe that was his excuse for why he gloved up. He was probably getting around a lot. I doubt Candy Kitty was his first piece of ass on the side.

I struggle for something to say when I realize that the shower is still on—and I left the stall door wide open. "Shit!"

I force my rubbery legs to sprint back into the bathroom. Sure enough, a sheen of water covers the floor around the bath mat.

"What?" Masey asks.

"I was too distracted to turn the fucking water off. It's going to be slick as hell. Stay there."

"I'll grab more towels."

Absently I nod and make my way to the stall. The water is freezing. Apparently, I ran through the reserves in the hot water tank while I took Masey to bed. If we want another shower, it's going to have to wait.

As I turn the water off, I start laughing.

"What's so funny?"

"The water is fucking icy. Guess we're waiting or shivering as we clean off."

She giggles and tosses towels my way. "Oops. I'd say I'm sorry for distracting you but..."

"You're not." I toss the terry cloth on the tile, then wipe up the floor enough to motion her in.

She comes to me without hesitation. That hasn't always been the case. I take a mental victory lap at the progress.

"The good news is, I think we'll live without showering again. After all, why bother when we're just going to get dirty once more?"

I cock my head at her. "I like the way you think."

She glances at the clock on my nightstand. "But now it's getting really late, and since you got my shirt dirty and all the foundation I had on dripped off in the shower, I have to start over."

I didn't exactly start the fight...but I ended it with a bang—literally. "I'll help. Just tell me what to do."

Watching Masey work is fascinating. As soon as we cleaned up the bathroom, she dried and fluffed her hair. I've never paid attention to a woman's beauty routine, but hers is precise and specific. Now all the jars and bottles on my bathroom counter make sense. But in front of the camera is where she amazes me.

In no time at all, we adjust the light to accommodate the encroaching darkness, then she gets serious. After giving her traditional greeting and introducing herself with a reminder to like and subscribe, she begins with the products. "Today, I'll be starting with the Luminous Blurring Glow Primer from..."

I watch her describe the product. Hell, I really don't even

know what it's for unless it's like a primer before painting kind of thing. But I swear from her description I know exactly what this product would do to my skin.

Then she moves on to an eye primer—what's with all the priming?—followed by foundation, blush, bronzer, and contour. She'll skip the highlight and come back to it since it's the star of this video. She unwraps a new palette that's launching in a few weeks, but she'll give everyone a sneak preview with a "simple" eye look. Four colors and a lot of blending later, she seems evening ready. She finishes with liner and mascara. No lashes today because this is an "easy spring look." I'd hate to see what she considers complicated.

Finally, she opens the highlighting quad with the fancy-schmancy packaging. Because she's fair-skinned, only two of the shades will really work on her, so she chooses the lightest with a pink-champagne shift, whatever that means. One of the deeper tones she says she'll use as a blush topper. Blush needs to be topped?

I'm confused by the time she brushes the highlight across her face. It doesn't blend well, because even I can see two metallic stripes on the tops of her cheekbones. She tries to buff it out and soften the edges. She even tries to sponge and powder over it. Nothing.

She gives a strained smile. "Beauty influencers, like all of you, have different preferences. The Madeline Mill Strobing Accent Palette would be up your alley if you have a richer skin tone or self-tan regularly and enjoy that strobe-you-can-see-from-outer-space effect. If you're like me, and you prefer something more subtle, this may be something you pass on. As for everything else..."

Masey gives a rundown of the other products she used and her initial thoughts, followed by a promise to use the foundation and the eye-shadow palette more in future videos, especially when she has time to wear the face longer, so she can give her complete feelings about the products.

Then she signs off with a smile, hits the button to stop recording, and sighs. "One down. I need to edit that and get it uploaded. I'd like to finish editing the video I started chopping down earlier, too. But I'm starved!"

I am, too. "Want me to call for a pizza?"

"You'd be my hero…"

"I'm not already?"

"Well, you don't have a white horse or a suit of armor."

"I don't," I say glumly. "There hasn't been a big call for either in the last five hundred years."

She waves me away with a laugh. "Details."

"What do you like on your pie? Hopefully, having food delivered will get me closer to hero status."

After we agree on sausage and mushroom—and that pineapple, no matter how yummy on its own, doesn't belong on pizza —I place the call.

Masey starts reconfiguring my desk, which she's turned into her "beauty space."

When I realize she's sorting all of the products she has with her into different baskets or boxes, I frown. "What are you doing?"

"Prepping." She gives me a sly grin like she's up to something, but doesn't say anything else. Just turns to her computer and finishes editing the video she was working on earlier. I watch as she uploads and sets it to publish later in the week.

Then she opens up the video she just finished filming. "Oh, this turned out pretty good. The lighting really works… I'll have to remember this watermelon-colored shirt does nice things for my skin."

I thought it was hot pink. "Yeah?"

"Yeah. Come peek," she says over her shoulder. "I look…"

Freshly fucked. I don't tell her that, but as a guy, I can see that relaxed expression and sated smile, and I know exactly what it means.

"You look great," I tell her.

"Thanks. I don't know what it is that's different about this shoot—the lighting, maybe?—but I like it."

"We can work on figuring it out and replicating it."

She turns to me, looking touched. "You'd do that just to help me?"

Every day—at least once. Preferably a whole lot more. "Happy to, honey."

She frowns, looks at me, then glances back at the monitor. Then she tsks and bats at me. "I know what you're thinking. Perv!"

"Tell me I'm wrong."

Masey peers at the screen some more, studying it critically, then sighs. "Women won't see that."

"Sure." *If you say so…*

"We're not having this conversation. It's a *makeup* video. I never once mentioned sex."

I wink. "You didn't have to."

With another prim glare, she turns back to her computer and ignores me.

I chuckle as I go in search of napkins and silverware, then place a quick call to my brother to check on Ranger. He assures me all is well.

"Harlow is worried," Noah says. "Anything I can say that will set her at ease?"

Not really. "Masey and I talked. It was a misunderstanding."

"I don't think so, bro. I think she's falling for you, so if that's not what you want—"

"That's exactly what I want. I'm…um, in the same place," I say obliquely so Masey doesn't overhear.

"You're serious about her?"

"Getting there, yeah. But you can probably guess some of the hiccups I'm having."

"I can. You know, you might try being honest. Just tell her how you feel."

Before I can respond to my brother, there's some rustling on the other end, then I hear a decidedly feminine sigh. "No, don't tell her that."

"What?" I blurt. It's the same question Noah asks on the other end.

"Thom was really good with words. He said all the right things. He told her exactly what she wanted to hear, when she wanted to hear it. But none of it was true, and she's leery of pretty speeches. But actions? They will speak way louder to her right now. After all, words are cheap, right?"

"Right."

Which gives me an idea.

After chatting a little more, hearing that Ranger was winding down for the evening, and saying good night to my mother, we hang up. The pizza arrives, so I take it, the utensils, and a bottle of wine to the office.

I serve her a piece, pour her a glass, and smile her way. "How's that going?"

"Really good. I don't have that much to edit. I didn't do a lot of takes on any one part and I didn't flub my words much, so the bits I need to cut are minimal. I'm just going to speed up some of the application process to keep the video under twenty minutes, paste in the intro and outro, then I'm done!"

"That sounds great. Eat first, honey."

She nods and takes a sip of her wine, followed by a bite of her pizza. Her low moan sounds so rife with pleasure I get hard again.

"Oh, my god, that's good."

"You sound like you're enjoying that more than time between the sheets with me." I raise a brow. "Should I be worried? Or offended?"

"No. And no, I'm not enjoying it more than time between the sheets with you. But you knew that. I can't believe you're fishing for compliments."

"Not fishing...but I never mind one from you."

"You already know you're good at that. But I'll tell you that you're great just to make you happy."

"I'll take it." And since she's relaxed and enjoying her time with me, I think it's time to put my idea in motion. "I know we were going to wait until Tuesday to film the I-Can't-Remember-the-Boyfriend-Name Challenge video, but we're on a roll. Maybe we should do it now."

The glance she sends me tells me she's pleasantly surprised. "Really?"

"Yeah."

"Even though it will open you up to public attention?"

The kind Amanda Lund has been dealing with is all negative and all dependent on what the press has said about her, almost all of which has been negative, too. But Masey controls her message. We're not broadcasting via every major news and cable network. This will roll out to one platform with a smaller audience. Thankfully, it's not the same.

"I'm not worried."

"Great. When you're done eating, I'll film you picking out my makeup." She bites her lip. "I was hoping you'd agree to do it now, rather than waiting, so I was already sorting everything."

"You're, um…going to give me pointers, right?"

She grins. "No."

"C'mon. Hints, at least."

Her grin widens. "No."

I take a panoramic sweep of all the products around the room. "I have no idea what I would need to do your makeup."

"Oh, I'm dividing all the product types up so that you'll get one of everything you need. But once you've chosen those, I'm not saying a word. I hope you were paying attention earlier when I walked through my makeup. Remember what I said about the usual order of things? Today wasn't it."

I freeze. I must have some sort of surprised Pikachu face going on because Masey laughs. "Um…"

"This ought to be fun." She sounds gleeful.

Damn. I'm going to fuck this up.

After we finish our pizza, Masey lifts her glass to me and toasts, "Here's to adventure."

"You could call it that," I grumble.

She laughs again as she cleans up the box, dirty napkins, and plates. While she's gone, I stare at all the crap around me and try to recall what she said as she filmed her last video. But it's pretty fuzzy.

I'm doomed.

A few minutes later, she returns fresh-faced. All hint of her previous makeup is gone. She's changed her shirt, and as she strolls back in, she's gliding on some lip balm. She tosses a black shirt at me. "Put this on."

It's a tank top. There's no writing and no graphic design. I can't even remember the last time I wore it.

"Why this? It's kind of boring."

"There's nothing on it that will violate anyone's copyright." She shrugs, then smiles my way. "Besides, you'll look hot."

She's buttering me up, but I'm okay with it, so I jerk the tank on over my head, smooth my hair, then shrug. "All right. Let's do this."

"One second…" She's writing on scraps of paper she's cut up from my printer and labeling each of the little white plastic baskets she pulled out of some box or another. A minute later, she nods at her handiwork. "Can you read my writing?"

"Primer, foundation, concealer, powder…" I don't really know what all of this does, but… "Yeah."

"Fantastic!" She claps like an excited child.

I catch her by the shoulders. "Does this make you happy, honey? I want you to get your hashtag."

Masey nods. "I know it shouldn't be important, but it is."

"If it's important to you, it's important to me." I kiss her forehead. "It always will be."

Girlish excitement softens her face. "I don't know how Caitlyn and Voldemort and all those women never saw the real, wonderful you, but I see."

With my surprise pinging and my heart melting, she kisses me.

There's no way I can hold back.

I grip Masey, bring her in tight, crush her against me, and slide into her mouth like I could stay here forever. I get lost in her sugary taste and her tropical scent. I swear the longer she's in Maui, the more she smells like coconut and the beach. Like home. And the more I want to be with her, stay with her. Keep her.

I'm trying, man. Really trying. We can't fuck this up.

Her kiss is everything I could want—sweet, open, accepting, passionate, tender…

God, is this what actual love feels like? If so, then I've never felt it.

Of course you didn't love someone nicknamed Voldemort. That would be crazy.

My inner asshole is right…but at the time, I thought I would never feel as wild about a woman as I did about *her.*

Now I know I was an idiot. I'm much happier with Masey.

Until she plants her palms against my chest and gives me a gentle nudge. "Trace?"

She wants to stop kissing. I don't. That's a horrible idea. Worst ever. I think she should forget whatever exercise she has planned with this makeup and this camera and let me seduce her.

But I promised, and she's wanted to make this video for years.

Besides, once this is done, I can take her back to bed.

With a sigh, I back off. "Sorry. I got carried away."

But when I glance at her, I'm not sorry. Not only does she still look glowingly sated but now she looks freshly kissed. Her lips are red and just a bit swollen.

Despite the fact she doesn't have on a shred of makeup and she's wearing a prim V-neck blouse in girlish pink, along with another pair of my basketball shorts all curled up at the waist, I can't remember a time she's ever looked more beautiful.

Fuck. I really am in love. Just like that. I didn't even know this woman two days ago. Now I can't imagine my life without her.

I've got to convince her to stay…somehow.

"Usually I like it when you do." She winks. "But work first. Then…"

"Play?" I drawl.

"We have all night," she points out.

"Hell yeah!"

"But you have to do a whole face. A real face. Well, your best attempt, anyway."

"Shit." I shrug. "You asked for it."

She digs out a few more products from the boxes lining the wall, away from the camera, then drops them into their appropriate plastic bins. "There. That's everything I have with me."

"You have more than this?"

"At home? Oh, yeah."

"How much more?" Because this is already a metric shit ton.

"I have a whole beauty room and its closet, plus more in my bathroom, and I keep some overflow in my guest bathroom, too." She shakes her head. "Let's just say my apartment is half makeup and leave it there."

Whoa. Okay, that's a lot, but it's her business. If I can convince her to stay, we're going to need another place to live. She'll need a dedicated studio and office. And I'd love a house with more bedrooms for the—hopefully—brothers and sisters we'll give Ranger someday.

You've lost your mind, buddy. But for once, I'm on board.

"Stop. You're frightening me," I tease her.

She tsks at me and play-swats at my arm. "Stand next to me. I'm going to start the camera. We're going to introduce you to everyone, so be nice. Then I'll let you pick the items you're going to put on my face, one from each bin, got it?"

"Is it too late to back out?"

"Yes." She giggles and reaches for the camera. "Then you'll put it on my face however you think it goes, using whatever tools you think you need—"

"Tools?"

She gestures to the right side of my desk. "Brushes or sponge of your choice. Fingers work, too."

"I do like to use my fingers." I grin, mostly to cover the fact I'm clueless. She's probably going to look like a horror-movie clown when I'm finished.

Masey wags a finger at me. "Nothing below the neck on camera. We covered that. Mostly, smile and do your best, 'k?"

"Sure. I hope you remember your sense of humor when I'm done."

With a light laugh, she reaches over to start the camera, then waves and does her usual intro. "What's up, everyone? Welcome back! Today, I have an extra special treat. I might be a few years late on this, but..." She draws in a deep breath, and her smile lights up my world. "Today, I'll be completing the Boyfriend-Does-My-Makeup Challenge. A lot of you have asked how I'm doing since my split with Thom. Thank you! From the bottom of my heart, your caring means the world to me. If you're a newer subscriber and you're lost, um...welcome. If you want to catch up or you need a refresh to understand what I'm talking about, my ex and I split up ten months ago after a decade. Long, ugly story, but I'll link the breakup video in the description box below. Anyway, you asked when I would start dating again. And...I am. As many of you know, I'm in Maui on vacation. And this is Trace."

I wave. "Aloha, everyone."

It feels really weird talking to an inanimate camera and getting no immediate feedback, but it seems totally normal to Masey, so I play along.

"This is new for both of us, but we're having a good time together while I'm here in his home state. And since he's a great sport, he's agreed to fulfill my wish to complete the Boyfriend-Does-My-Makeup Challenge. And he promises it will be horrible."

"The worst, hands down." I nod. "Epically bad."

"So it will be awesome." She giggles.

Her happiness is so infectious I can't stop myself from leaning in to kiss her softly. "It's nice to know my utter failure will make you happy. You're a strange woman, and yet...I like you."

Her laugh sounds even happier. "Good to know. So, why don't you start by choosing all the makeup?"

I look at the dozen-plus white plastic baskets and rear back. "Are all the things in here the right color?"

"Not necessarily." And she sounds pleased about that.

"Son of a—"

"You can't say that. We're family friendly here."

"Bee sting." I grimace.

She devolves into a fit of giggles, then peers at the camera. "If you could hear what he was saying to me about five minutes before we started filming..."

"You were the one with your mind in the gutter," I point out, then look at the camera, too. "She was. I'm innocent."

Masey snorts. "No one will believe that."

"Yes, they will. They don't know me." I wink.

"Pick your products, goofball."

"Okay. I'm just going to apologize in advance, honey. And to you," I tell the camera.

Then with a shake of my head, I approach the first basket. Primers. I remember she put that on first earlier. But there must be over twenty here. Bottles, squeezy tubes, flat pans. Some are white. Others are pink. Some are straight-up oil. I'm already confused.

I grab a squeezy tube of stuff that says it's infused with roses. That should at least smell nice. But then I read it has hyaluronic acid. Acid? Isn't that bad for your face? I'm not taking a chance, so I set it down. I pick up another that calls itself a camera-ready radiant velvet primer. Okay, we're in front of a camera and velvet is nice, so that should be good.

What the fuck do I know?

The next basket contains foundations. Again, bottles, squeezy tubes, and pans. I'm sensing a theme here... The color of the pigments are all different. Some packaging says the product is full coverage. But Masey doesn't have a lot to hide. I especially wouldn't want to cover up her few freckles. They're totally adorable, so I avoid those items. Does matte mean not shiny in the makeup world? A lot of the bottles say that. Some have SPF, and that seems responsible...but the sun is down now, and she won't need that tonight. Then I see one called Natural Glow Perfecting Liquid. Never heard of the brand, but that's no surprise. I hold the bottle up to her face. I guess that's the right color.

With a shrug, I set it on the table and move to the next basket. Thankfully, the next few choices are much easier. I choose a shade of blush that matches her shirt. Same with her lipstick. I sorta get the purpose of a bronzer, so I pick one that's called South Beach Suntan Glow. It's a little dark, but it seems like they all are. I especially avoid the one that looks oompa-loompa orange.

I'm not sure what to do with contour, so I grab a stick thing that looks less intimidating than the other pans of stuff. I choose a powder in a shade called cool fair, mostly because the packaging is interesting. Masey calls it bougie.

Next, I pluck up an eye primer in a tube and an eye-shadow palette. This last part is the most confounding. So many colors, even neon. People put dayglow yellow on their eyes? That's a hell no for me. I end up choosing a palette called Hawaiian Beach with nice brownish shades. After all, when in Maui... Finally, I choose a mascara and something called a setting spray.

When I finish, I feel a little worn out. "Am I done?"

"Eyeliner." She points to the basket in the corner.

I glance between the pencils and tubes of that stuff and the contour stick in front of me. "They do different things?"

"Very."

I'm so fucked. "Um…"

"Just do your best."

"You're going to laugh at my expense."

"We're going to laugh together because you're cute."

"Flattery will get you everywhere."

"I hope so." She winks.

"Ugh," I growl as I look down at my choices. Finally, I grab a purple pencil eyeliner. She looks good in purple. This should work, right? "Now am I done?"

"Now you get to apply everything."

"Oh, the horrific part." I take a deep breath. "Okay, you asked for it…"

"I'm sure you'll make me beautiful."

I cup her face, utterly forgetting about the camera. "You already are."

The contented smile that curls her lips and makes her eyes sparkle is one I'd love to put there every day. She purses her mouth at me for an air kiss.

I'm not getting out of this, clearly. So I pick up the primer and scan the bottle. Directions are nonexistent. "How much of this should I use?"

"Just give me your best guess."

With a shrug, I squeeze a half-dollar size into my palm and start spreading it across her face. But it's white and gives her a ghostly sheen. It's a little sticky. And it's not soaking in. Did I use too much?

I grab the sponge and wipe some off. The rest I drag around

her face until it finally seems to set in.

"Tell everyone what you just did and why."

"This is primer. I just squirted some in my hand. When I rubbed it in, it seemed too white, so I took some off with the spongie thing and tried to rub in the rest."

"What does primer do?"

"Well, before you paint a wall, you put on primer to smooth out the surface and…yeah. That way, the paint applies better…I guess? I really don't paint much."

She laughs. "What's next?"

"Um…" No clue. "Before you paint a wall, you should let the primer dry." I think. "So…let's do the eye primer, too."

"Okay."

I drag the wand out of the tube and slide it across her eyelids like I saw her do earlier. Then I spread that around. I think it needs to dry down, too.

But now what?

"Foundation?"

She shrugs. "Your decision."

"Hint?"

Masey shakes her head.

"A lifeline? Do I get to phone a friend?"

Her giggle lights up my heart. "Nope."

"You're mean. I'll make you suffer later. I know how…"

She blushes. "I know you do, but we're focused on makeup right now."

Maybe I can distract her. "You sure you don't wanna—"

"No." Then she turns a smile at me. "Well, later."

I sigh. "That will have to get me through. Okay, so… concealer. What would you be concealing with this tube of liquid? It's not going to hide a handgun."

She nearly spits out the wine she just drank. "Not that kind of conceal."

"Right. Um..." I don't see any blemishes or scars. I have a vague recollection that she put it under her eyes to cover dark circles I don't see, but okay. I take the wand from the tube. Masey is fair, but even this seems a little light. "Is this the right color?"

She shrugs unhelpfully.

"Okay, I'll just...put it here." I slather a bunch under one eye, dip back in, and repeat the process. "And here." I frown. It seems like a lot. "I'll let that dry down some so it doesn't smear everywhere. How about some foundation?" I pick up the bottle and pluck off the cap. "We just apply it like so..." It's got a pump, so I try to squirt some directly onto her face.

The drop plops straight into her cleavage.

She glances down at the running dollop, looks at me, and bursts out laughing.

"That did not go as planned." It's about to drip into her bra, so I reach out to scoop it up with my finger...then I have second thoughts. Should I do this on camera? She said nothing below the neck, but this is an emergency. I don't want to look like I'm feeling her up, so I draw my hand back. But the liquid is still running. What if this stuff gets into her bra? How will I get it on her face? "Crap. Okay. Not trying to be too personal on camera..." I curl my fingertip under the running droplet of pigment. "Sweep onto your face like this." I glide my digit across one cheek. "And voilà."

Wide-eyed and looking like she's trying not to burst out laughing, she nods. "Totally."

"I'll try the rest a different way." I squirt another pump onto my finger, dab that across her other cheek, then do the same for her forehead, followed by another for her nose and chin. "That should be enough to cover everything."

Now what?

The sponge thing, I guess. I hope it doesn't soak up too much product. If it does, I can get more, but this stuff doesn't look cheap, and I already used four pumps...

"Let's blend." I remember her using that word and I'm a little proud of myself. But when I drag the sponge through the first dollop of liquid, I realize quickly that a little of this stuff goes a *very* long way. "Oops. I used too much."

"You think?" Her tone tells me she *knows* I did.

This is going to be bad.

"Um...let's remove a little of the excess." I grab a tissue and try to wipe some off I've already spread, but when I lift the tissue way, her skin looks splotchy and uneven.

Shit.

With my finger, I transfer more from one cheek to the other and use the sponge to smear the product around. But that leaves her face looking streaky. "What am I doing wrong?"

"All right. One hint. *One*," she stresses. "Bounce the sponge. Don't drag it."

"Bounce." Like a ball? "Okay."

Hoping this doesn't fuck everything up more, I start bopping it across her skin.

It looks better...though not great. But at this point, I'll take any improvement. So I move to the other parts of her face, working the liquid over her eyelids, around her jawline, and down her neck since I have so much. I don't want to swipe it again with the tissue, so I just keep bouncing. But foundation oozes down my thumb and fingers. How does she wear this shit on her face? It feels like a coating of blech to me.

"What are you doing?" she asks. "Narrate for us."

"Blending. Blending…"

Finally, I step back to survey my handiwork. The foundation looks like a coat of shellac, thick and unnatural. What the hell? It says "natural" in the title. Either they lied…or I used too much.

Hoping it will sink in over time and dry down to something better, I smile. "The color looks good on you."

"Does it?" Masey sounds dubious.

"Yeah." She looks as if she's got a tan. Isn't that something makeup is supposed to do? It doesn't match her shoulders or the top of her chest, but maybe that doesn't matter?

"Let's blend the concealer now." It should be dry. I'm not sure how something so pale will look all right next to the darker shade of her foundation. Do they mix together?

I dab at the liquid—and I discover it's mostly dried in two randomly shaped blobs, one under each eye. So I rub harder. But it's not working.

"Fuck."

Masey lets out a hysterical laugh. "You can't say that."

"Family friendly. Right…"

I try not to panic. Maybe if I add some viscosity back under her eyes the concealer will spread. So I turn the sponge to the wet side. "Let's blend some foundation in with the concealer."

When I start bouncing the sponge there, she rears back. "Gently."

Right. *Don't give the pretty girl a black eye.* But hey, this method is working. Kinda. It's not perfect, but the shit is spreading. A little.

After a few minutes, I give up. It's all dried down again, and now it's not budging. It looks cracked and thick, but…

Time to move on.

"Let's do blush. We'll start with a brush and this compact of stuff by Glowtasmic in the shade…" I flip the package over.

"Climax. They seriously gave a blush that name? How are we supposed to keep this thing family friendly?"

Masey looks ready to burst out laughing. "It's just a name. Get back to my face, mister."

Vaguely, I recall that blush goes on with a brush, so I take a skinny, dense brush—the handle says it's a blending brush—and swipe it across her cheek. My eyes flare wide. The cheerful blush I chose to match her hot-pink shirt now looks like a dime-size, clown-colored swatch.

Shit.

Oh, well. I already suspected I would screw this up, so I might as well roll with it and deal with the cringe factor later.

"But you'll want the color diffused, of course." I grab a really big, fluffy brush from the stack. "So put the little blending brush down and get this thing that looks like a cat's tail and swipe it around the face." I make big circles on her cheeks, and thankfully the color starts to soften and spread.

"Perfect. Let's repeat the process."

I do. Her cheeks aren't quite even, but hey, it's not a bad first effort.

Before I do the next step, I get smart and take a brushful of bronzer and test it on a nearby white tissue. It's pigmented. I need to be careful with this.

"All right. Now bronzer. Masey doesn't need much since her foundation gave her a good tan." That seems to be getting darker by the minute. How is that possible? "So we'll just barely dip in with this big brush we used to blend the blush." I tap into the bronzer. "Let's sweep this across the nose and chin and dust it along the forehead. Yeah. And maybe this will make her chest look the same shade as her face, so some down here, too."

Her face looks artificially tan now, but that's nothing

compared to the seemingly splotchy dark shimmer over the fair swells above her breasts.

Since it looks terrible, I fake a smile of encouragement, glad she can't see this mess yet, then drop the brush. It's a lost cause.

"Now contour." But what the hell do I do with this stick that's a dark grayish-brown? No idea. "But she already looks so perfect, I don't think we need it. So…moving on." I toss it back in its basket.

She roars out laughing.

When I shoot her a quelling glare, she settles back into her chair. "Perfect. Keep going."

"Let's have some powder. They call this the Skin Perfecting Illuminating Veil. Why not just call it powder?"

"Because that doesn't tell you what the powder does."

I scowl. "Neither does Skin Perfecting Illuminating Veil."

"Sure it does. It's going to perfect my skin and add some glow, hence the word *illuminating* in the product name. And it's a veil, so it will give me a smooth canvas for the rest of my complexion products."

"If you say so."

She grins. "I do. Now hurry up or we'll be here all night."

"You want me to rush through the rest of this masterpiece?"

"Never."

I pretend I didn't hear her. "You got it. So let's apply this veil crap." I dust her face with the powder inside the compact. It smooths the harsh edges of her blush, tones down the too-dark bronzer, and makes her look almost normal…if a spackle consistency spread across the face is normal. "Let's move on to mascara."

Finally, something I know what to do with. Makuahine doesn't wear much makeup, but she has always said she loves a good black lash. So I pick up the tube I chose earlier. "This is

Purrfect Lash Mascara. I can't tell who makes it. You probably already know anyway, so let's just put this on the lashes." I glance at Masey. "Just the tip? I don't want to poke your eye out."

"Whatever you think."

She still won't help me, so I just need to keep making this the most glorious train wreck I can.

To that end, I sweep the mascara brush up her lashes a few times. How much of this stuff does she need? I've heard my mother talk about multiple coats of mascara, so… "Okay, we'll let that dry and do your eyeliner. Close your eyes."

I take the cap off the pencil, then turn to see she's dutifully complied. I draw a purple line from the inside corner of her eye to the outside. I think I'm supposed to get it close to the lash line, but my hand isn't that steady and I don't want to poke her, so it's more of a squiggle in the middle of her lid. Close enough.

"Open."

She does. Oh, that's horrible. Truly bad.

I sigh. "Let's do some cat-eye business. That's hot."

"Seriously?" Masey looks at me like I've lost my mind.

"Hey, it's my show, right? And the points or whatever out here"—I press near my temples—"are sexy. Close."

Dutifully, she drops her lashes to her cheeks. "They're not points; they're wings."

Good to know. "Okay, then. Wings are sexy."

Since I have no idea how to do this, I make it up as I go. Predictably, my wings don't match at all. Every time I try to make them look alike, I just make a bigger mess.

Finally, with thick purple strips just past her eyebrows, I shrug. "That's as good as it's going to get."

And another glance tells me it's horrific. Fuck the brown eyeshadow. This is too terrible to waste anything pretty.

Dayglow yellow it is.

While she's not looking, I hold my finger up to my lips in front of the camera, then put the Hawaiian Beach palette back in the bin. I grab the neon one instead.

"Let's go in with some color..." I have no idea what brush to use, so I just pluck up a small one and sweep the puke yellow shade all over her eye. "And spread this from her brows to her lashes." When I step back, I grimace. That's ugly and wrong, but... "Perfect. Now let's add because...why not? More is better." I grab a different brush and dip it into some neon green, then sweep that across her lid. I plop some orange in the middle of her eye. Yep, it's thoroughly terrible.

"Did you pick a brow product?" she asks, eyes still closed.

"No."

"Look over by the monitor."

I do. Oh, shit, there's another pile of tubes and pencils. "Grabbing a brow gel. I'll put it on now. Oh, it's got a brushy thing. Handy."

When I sweep it across her left brow, I realize my critical error. It's pigmented as hell and smears well beyond her brows, first. Second, the color is wrong. A glance at the bottom of the tube tells me the shade is honey blonde.

And on Masey's dark brows, it's beyond awful. So I add it to the other eyebrow.

I need to be done with her makeup before she hates me.

"Wrapping up with another coat of mascara and some lipstick." Which clashes terribly with everything on her face. "There. Let's finalize with setting spray. I think that's like hair spray for the face." And when I spritz her skin, it smells like someone puked in shit. "That is horrible. What the fu—"

"It's not one of my favorites." Masey looks like she's trying not to gag as she fans her face. I don't know if that's to dry the spray or dissipate the stench and I'm not asking. "Are you done?"

I study the damage to her look. I can honestly say I've seen intoxicated strippers who look classier than Masey right now. "Yes. And I will not quit my day job. Holy cow."

"I'm almost afraid to look."

"You should be."

She grins as I hand the hand mirror to her. "Drumroll, please."

Rhythmically, I tap my hands on the top of the desk, then point her way. "Time for the big reveal. And go!"

Masey raises her hand mirror to her face and gasps. She looks way beyond shocked. Dismayed might be a good description. Even disgusted.

"Ta da!" I beam. "Told you I could deliver an epic train wreck."

"This is even above and beyond my wildest expectations."

"You're welcome."

"I think as your penance—I mean reward—you should have to kiss me looking like this."

I can close my eyes. "You're on. Bring it over here, honey."

When I grab her face, she lays a fat kiss on my lips, then explodes into a fit of giggles. "I seriously don't think I've ever looked worse." And she sounds happy about it. "Also…watermelon lipstick isn't for you."

She holds up the mirror and shows me my mouth smeared with the dark color. "I'll remember that. You know, for the next time I'm tempted to wear it."

Masey laughs harder. "Thanks for joining me for this belated Boyfriend-Does-My-Makeup Challenge. I hope you enjoyed it as much as Trace did and learned a lot about what not to do. Watch for my upload later this week about some hidden skin-care gems. I'll get back to a normal release schedule after vacation, but until then, I'll be enjoying Hawaii and my time with Trace. Hugs and lipstick! And…aloha."

After she blows everyone a kiss, she turns off the camera, then faces me with a shake of her head. "That was perfect. I think I need to kiss you more."

"Please do."

CHAPTER ELEVEN

On Tuesday morning, Harlow and Noah volunteer to keep Ranger another day so Masey and I have more time together. Shortly after lunch, we drop off a few of my little man's things at my brother's place. Then Noah and I catch up in the kitchen, beer in hand, while the girls plant in a pair of chairs near the pool. Neither is smiling.

"That conversation looks deep," I say with a frown and a bob of my head in their direction.

"Yeah." Noah takes in the sight. "Harlow has been worried."

"She shouldn't be. I'm doing my damnedest to be good to Masey, make her laugh and—"

"Harlow isn't as worried about her as she is about you, bro."

I rear back. "Me?"

Noah scratches at his off-season scruff and grimaces. "We talked on Sunday night after you and I hung up. Harlow is surprised you're so serious about Masey."

"Not long ago, I would have said we just had good chemistry, but the last few days have been some of the happiest of my life. We're not on the same page yet, but I'm hoping we'll at least get to the same chapter soon."

"My wife isn't sure Masey is ready for anything lasting."

"I'm in love with her."

"Fuck. Have you told her?"

"Not in so many words. I'm looking for the right time, so I'm trying to get a better read on how she feels."

Sometimes, I think she's falling, too—hard and fast. Like Sunday night...

After we finished filming the makeup video, she scrubbed her face squeaky clean. Since I put on so many thick layers, it took a while. After that, she surprised me by initiating sex. We made love and laughed half the night. Everything felt perfect.

But other times, I swear she's pulling away. On Monday morning, she seemed inexplicably reserved, almost aloof.

"Any ideas yet?" my brother asks.

"No."

I feel Masey's caring in the way she looks at me, kisses me, and makes love with me. It's also in the way she laughs when I screw up folding laundry or she playfully kicks water at me when we take walks along the beach. I finally understand why my brother was willing to sacrifice his own happiness to ensure Harlow has the life she wanted, even if that was without him.

Since I can't blurt how I feel—I agree with Harlow—what can I do to prove to Masey I'm serious? I really don't fucking know. "Something's gotta give soon."

"It hasn't even been a week."

"Damn it, she was with Thom for years, and he treated her like shit. If I can't convince her I never will, she'll leave next week. And it will be over."

Noah nods as if he sees my dilemma. "You have to make her feel special."

"Don't you think I'm trying?"

My mother enters the kitchen then, walking slowly with the use of a cane.

I rise and help her across the room. "Makuahine?"

"Did you come down the stairs alone?" Noah chides.

"I'm slightly injured, not incapable of getting around." She tsks at my brother, then looks at me expectantly. "Noah knows what he's talking about, keikikāne."

"And I'm listening."

Yesterday, I returned some customer phone calls, giving Masey time to edit her recently filmed videos so she would know I can give her professional space. Then we cuddled on the sofa during a chick flick, followed by an action-adventure film, so she knows I can compromise. Then this morning, after I woke Masey with breakfast in bed, we strolled a local arts-and-crafts festival hand in hand, so she knows I want to spend time with her doing more than having sex.

Still, that's not enough.

My mother glances at Masey on the patio. "I have a sense for these things. Don't give up on her."

She had a sense about Noah and Harlow, too.

After I leave my brother a few more things for my napping son, I caress his downy head in the playpen and promise to be back for him tomorrow. The ladies join us out front.

"Thanks again, you two." I wave to my brother and sister-in-law, then kiss my mother's cheek. "Bye, Makuahine."

Masey turns to Harlow. "Thanks for everything."

"Don't forget what I said."

She nods. "I won't. Love you bunches."

My sister-in-law sends her a cheeky grin. "Of course you do."

They both laugh, then I take Masey's hand and lead her to

my truck, and we climb inside. "What did you and Harlow talk about?"

She doesn't move, but I feel her shrink back at my question. "She gave me some things to consider."

"Want to share? I'm happy to listen."

"Thanks, but..." She looks off in the distance, brow furrowed. "I need to work this out on my own."

My gut tightens. She's not leaving for the mainland tomorrow, but I feel her slipping away. In my head, I realize I've had four years to get over my two-week love affair. She's had less than one to recover from a decade. Still, I'm more than a vacation fling to Masey, right?

Maybe not.

Fuck, why keep fighting if winning Masey is a losing battle? Because I can't just quit. Noah said to make Masey feel special. I need to find more ways to *show* her I love her.

Since I owe her dinner out for watching Ranger, I take her out to one of my favorite seafood shacks. We have some drinks and some laughs, dance to the kitschy little band playing beachside. Once we're back at my condo, I tumble her into bed, filling her up with every desperate inch of my cock, kissing her feverishly, and telling her with my body that I've fallen for her. She answers in kisses and moans, scratches across my back, whispered pleas, and orgasms before sleeping in my arms, seemingly satisfied.

But I don't feel any closer to winning her over.

By Wednesday, I feel wound up. We start the day with sex. We finish breakfast with sex. We shower and have more sex. I can't stop touching her. I've already resigned myself to the fact that sex won't convince her of what's in my heart, but without blurting the words, I've got nothing else.

What we don't do anymore? Practice safe sex. I'm guessing

she's back on her birth control pills and doesn't see the point of condoms. Me? I don't want to trap her, but I hate not being as close to her as possible. I picture us raising Ranger and all our future children together. I see it so fucking clearly. Hell, if she's somehow miraculously conceived already, we could have our first baby together just before the New Year. That's mind-blowing. And a little scary…but I'd be thrilled.

I have no idea if she'll ever feel the same.

As evening approaches and we head out to retrieve Ranger, then grab an early dinner before I have to head to the marina for my sailing tonight, she turns to me. "What are you thinking?"

I'd love to tell her. I don't.

Instead, I shrug. "Anything in particular you want to do once I'm home from this sunset cruise? Finish that Netflix thing we started? Open a bottle of wine and talk?"

A smile creeps across her lips, then she leans closer. "Fuck on the lanai?"

The male part of me does a predictable happy dance. My goddamn heart wonders if she'll ever let herself think of me as more than a good time.

Dude, when has any female ever valued you for more than the way you make them feel?

Never. It sucks.

So why are you expecting her to be different?

"If you want," I finally murmur.

She frowns. "D-did that upset you? I'm sorry. I shouldn't have said it like that or assumed—"

"It's fine." What else can I say? None of my problems are her fault.

"It's not." She grips my hands tighter. "You've made me feel great these last four days. Tell me how I can make you smile."

The idea appears in that moment. Is it stupid? Probably. But

I've got nothing else. "You know, I've never had an actual girl-friend if I don't count Voldemort."

"Why would you count her?"

"Exactly. Just like you hadn't had an actual lover if you didn't count Thom."

"And I definitely don't anymore."

"Maybe what I need are boyfriend lessons."

Masey laughs. "You're crazy."

"I'm serious."

She shakes her head. "No. You're perfect. You're attentive without being smothering. You give space without being distant. You listen. You help. You're not selfish, moody, or insecure. You don't pay more attention to your buddies, your family, your job, or your phone than me. Despite me jumping to conclusions with Caitlyn, you don't flirt with other women. You don't disappear without explanation. You're a good sport. You're laid-back. You have a fun sense of humor. You build up the people around you. You're unfailingly kind and giving. Before you, those were all things I didn't think I'd find."

Then why don't you want them forever?

I want to scream the question at her.

She lays a soft hand on my arm. "Trace, you don't need anything I can teach you."

"But you think I need something?" I hear it in her voice.

"Yes, to stop falling for the wrong women. You gravitate to the ones focused on orgasms."

Just like Masey was when we met.

She shrugs. "If you want more out of relationships, you need someone who's looking for a good man to share her future."

"What about you? What do you want?"

Suddenly, she looks wary. "Why do you ask?"

"You don't have any guesses?" I challenge as we pull up in front of my brother's big-ass mansion.

Masey frowns. "Trace…"

Before we can say more, Harlow walks Ranger out to me. It's great to see my boy, but I fucking want to know what else Masey might have said.

With a curse, I shove the door open. My sister-in-law sets my smiling son in my arms and whispers, "Tread carefully with her."

I kiss Ranger and hold him close. As I glance across the truck, I see Noah carrying a diaper bag and a small suitcase of Ranger's things, making small talk with Masey.

"I'm fucking trying," I murmur to Harlow.

"She's afraid."

And I'm frustrated as hell. "Just tell me…is she anywhere close to letting herself fall for me?"

Suddenly, Harlow smiles and rubs Ranger's head. "The teething is getting more serious. I had to rub some stuff on his gums last night. But he was so sweet with Nolan, trying to pat him and share toys."

I glance at my brother, who's looking back at me. I give him an imperceptible nod. Yes, I need a minute more with Harlow.

"I'll keep that in mind tonight," Masey assures. "Anything in particular working well?"

"We packed what we've been using in the bag." Noah holds it up. "And if you freeze some of his teething toys…"

As soon as Masey gets engrossed in the conversation, I hold Ranger closer and stare at Harlow. "Is she?"

"She's hard to read, but I think so. She's quiet, which means she's thinking. That's good news."

Is it? "Thanks."

"Give her space and give her time to miss you."

I open my mouth to ask how that isn't counterproductive when I realize Noah and Masey have fallen silent again. My time to question my sister-in-law is over.

"Call me if you need pointers, okay?" She winks and rubs Ranger's cheek as if she's talking about him. "Auntie Harlow understands."

My son coos. He loves being the center of attention.

"Oh, and don't forget..." my brother pipes up. "Clint and Bethany's wedding is Saturday night at Keeley and Maxon's place. You two are coming, I hope. We'll have a couple of sitters up at the ohana for the kids."

I like Clint and Bethany. They've been down a tough road. And I'm glad to see them start their future together. They've finally finished wrapping up loose ends in LA. His family house is settled now, along with his younger brothers back in college. And Beth sold her condo in San Diego, so they're relocating to Maui and tying the knot.

"I'd planned to be there." I turn to Masey. "What do you say? Will you be my date? Save me from going stag and looking pitiful?"

The truth is, I'm hoping that something as romantic as a wedding will help Masey see what we could have. After all, if Clint could fall in love with Bethany, despite believing her responsible for his father's death, then winning Masey over should be much easier.

At least, in theory.

"I can't intrude," Masey insists.

"You wouldn't be," Harlow assures. "C'mon. It'll be fun."

"If you're sure, okay."

"Great." Harlow smiles. "Good thing they're tying the knot now. I've seen Bethany's dress. It's gorgeous but really figure-hugging. And she let it slip that she's pregnant."

"That's fantastic." But I wish it was Masey and me.

With a wave, we pile Ranger in the truck and drive off.

During our quick, casual dinner, Ranger seems more intent on squishing his jar of peas between his gums than actually eating. He does his happy sing-screech through the meal, pounding his palms on the high chair, seemingly glad to be back with me. That does my heart good, especially since Masey is really quiet. And she's barely eaten.

"Something wrong with your food, honey? Chicken underdone?"

"No. It's fine. I'll get the rest to go. I'm just not that hungry. Besides, who wants to eat when there's a really handsome guy around?" She lifts Ranger from his high chair and cuddles him. And she looks at peace.

That, right there. Every time I worry that Masey isn't ready for another relationship, much less a ready-made family, she proves she's really smitten with my son. She can be open and honest about her feelings for Ranger because he won't hurt her, just look to her for a snack, some entertainment, and affection.

She knows I want a whole lot more. And she's afraid I could hurt her in return.

That must mean she has feelings for me.

"What time do you have to be at the marina?" Masey asks as we leave the restaurant.

The sun is sinking toward the horizon. I don't want to go. But I can't cancel on Terry. He's a good guy who's nearly fifty and finally found the woman he wants to spend his life with.

"Thirty minutes. Can I ask you a question?"

"Okay." She sounds hesitant as she climbs in the truck.

Ranger talks from the back seat like he has something to say.

"What was the breaking point between you and Thom? What was the straw that broke the camel's back?"

Masey folds her hands in her lap. "It was a lot of things."

She doesn't want to talk about it. Thom hurt and humiliated her. But something precipitated that moment.

"General summary. It was about more than Betsy What's-her-name, wasn't it?"

"That was a lot of it, but…yeah." She sighs. "I look back now on that last month and realize how stupid I was. Instead of admitting the obvious—that we weren't meant to be, I didn't love him anymore, and he was cheating on me—I kept thinking that our troubles were about lack of commitment."

"So…you pushed him for more?"

Masey nods. "We'd been together for ten years. Everyone was asking when we were finally going to get married. At first, I laughed away the questions. But even my subscribers pointed out that, if he hadn't proposed to me after a decade, he wasn't going to. Coupled with the gossip and his sudden supposed last-minute business trips, I felt insecure and I wanted some proof of his commitment. So I gave him an ultimatum. The minute it came out of my mouth, I knew it would end ugly."

"He refused to propose?"

"Yeah. And he admitted to his fling with Betsy." She rolls her eyes. "I can't take any woman who calls herself Candy Kitty seriously."

"And that was that?"

"Yeah."

"If he had proposed?"

"In that moment, I would have said yes. And I would have told myself I was happy. I would have convinced myself our fairy tale was coming true." She shakes her head. "We would have ended up miserable and divorced in less than five years."

I suspect less than two, but numbers aren't important.

"You probably think I'm psycho." She tries to lighten the conversation. "Wanting a proposal from a guy I didn't love."

"No. I think you were confused."

"I'm not anymore. Getting away from Thom has been enlightening. Thanks for putting up with me."

"I'm not just putting up with you, honey. You make me happy."

She bites that pretty, pouty lip again. "I'm happy, too."

Yeah, with the status quo.

Maybe it is better that I'll be gone tonight.

A few minutes later, I drop her and Ranger off at the condo and head to the marina. Terry is nervous but excited. His girlfriend, Ainsley, is younger and very driven. Wednesday was the only night they were both free. But the good news is, the water isn't as crowded or choppy. With the sky full of oranges, pinks, and purples, my buddy drops to one knee and asks the woman he loves to spend her life with him. I melt into the background as she gasps, cries happy tears, and screams yes. They're both ecstatic; I can see it.

I want that—and I want it with Masey.

Proposing didn't work out for me the first time. Wrong reasons. Wrong woman. And I swore I'd never get down on one knee again. But maybe it's time to get over my abject terror of being humiliated and rejected.

It probably sounds crazy, but do I dare propose to Masey?

Saturday, April 14

The next few days pass in a blur. On Wednesday night, I returned home late. Terry and Ainsley insisted I come with them for a celebratory drink after we docked. I agreed since they were in the mood to party, and I wanted to give Masey time to miss me. But it hurt listening to them make wedding plans. And staying away from her was so fucking hard. Still, I hung out with them until nearly midnight.

When I made it back to my condo, the place was quiet. I palmed my keys so they didn't jingle. Masey was asleep in my bed, Ranger curled up beside her. The sight of them unraveled my heart.

After dropping a kiss to my son's head, I scooped him up, warmed him a bottle, changed and fed him, then stood over his crib and watched him fall back to sleep.

With a sigh, I tiptoed to my room and slid in bed, curled Masey against me. I tried like hell to leave her alone, but I couldn't stop myself from kissing her half-awake, then making love to her—twice—before watching her fall into a sated slumber.

What *would* happen if I proposed to Masey? After dozing off and on for hours, I couldn't come up with an answer.

The rest of the week, nothing went as planned. On Thursday morning, I got a last-minute booking. I took it since Masey and Ranger scheduled a playdate with Harlow and Nolan at the beach and the vacationer hiring me offered me a fortune. Plus I hoped some girl time would help Masey envision what living on the island would be like if she stayed.

Thursday afternoon, Masey's Boyfriend-Does-My-Makeup video went live. Apparently, it racked up views quickly, and the comments were overwhelmingly positive. Unfortunately, we didn't get to talk much about it, and I didn't have a chance to look because Ranger started vomiting. Five hours later, we took him to the ER and spent most of the night there, waiting to hear that he simply had a virus—nothing more serious, thank God—that would have to run its course.

Masey was supportive and by my side every step of the way —a helping hand, a shoulder when I got tired, an encouraging word when I was worried and trying to feed Ranger a barium bottle at two a.m. for tests. In short, she was the perfect helpmate.

Twelve hours later, my little guy was eating like a champ again. Go figure.

But Masey and I were exhausted. We slept most of the day in shifts, and that evening, we figured out what to wear to Clint and Bethany's wedding the next afternoon. One thing I noticed? The minute Ranger improved…she got quiet again.

Now, as we're dressing for the big event, she's barely speaking. I'm walking on eggshells, worried I'm going to say the wrong thing.

After I slip on my shoes, I approach her from behind, cup her shoulders, and kiss her crown. "You look beautiful."

She turns to face me, wearing a simple off-the-shoulder dress in a blush pink. She's slipped on pearls at her throat and ears, along with bone-colored sandals—and a tight smile. "Thanks. You look good. Wow."

Since I'm wearing roughly what I had on the night we met, it's nothing new. "Ready?"

She reaches for a little clutch, then sets it back down. "Maybe you should go without me."

Everything inside me wants to push her to come. An evening of hope and happiness would probably be good for us. But I don't.

"What's this about?"

"I feel like I'm crashing Bethany and Clint's big day. I've never met either of them."

"I RSVP'd for a plus one, and they were thrilled." Then I force myself to shrug. "I won't make you go if you'd rather not, but I'd love to have you by my side."

She turns to me. I see tears in her eyes.

My heart drops. "Honey?"

"Why?"

"Do I want you with me?"

"Yes."

I grapple to find the right answer. She's really asking something else, looking for an answer to a question I'm afraid to answer. Should I keep the conversation light and joke about looking way better with her by my side? Grumble again that I don't want to be one of the few single people at this wedding? Neither of those feel right. I know Harlow said Masey isn't ready to hear how I feel, but I'd swear she's begging me for something—reassurance?—without speaking the words.

"Honey, I need to tell you something. This"—I gesture between us—"isn't just about sex for me anymore. It hasn't been for a while."

She presses her lips together like she's stunned...but not really surprised. "It's not just about sex for me anymore, either."

And that's a giant goddamn relief. "You're scared?"

"Terrified."

I cup her face. "Don't be. We don't have to decide anything today. We just have to attend a wedding and have a good time."

Her small nod doesn't encourage me. "What about tomorrow?"

Masey is a doer, so of course she wants to solve every problem the minute she becomes aware of it, but that's compounding our issue. "That's a problem for then. For now, just come with me."

"All right."

I tip up her chin and press a long, soft kiss to her lips. "It's going to be all right."

Her uncertainty bleeds between us as we grab Ranger, dressed in his best shorts with smart loafer-like shoes, and head out.

About twenty minutes later, we reach Keeley and Maxon's Sunshine Coast Bed-and-Breakfast. The day is cloudless. The palms sway with the gentle tropical breeze. It looks peaceful. Perfect.

Not even close. As soon as we get out of the car, trouble becomes obvious.

Keeley is testing the malfunctioning sound system while trying to sing Norah Jones's "Come Away With Me." Evan curses as he tries to fix it while Britta and her mother, Eleanor, put the finishing touches on the catering. I hand Ranger and his gear to the sitters, settled with the handful of other kids in the ohana out back.

By the time I return, Masey is doing Bethany's face since the makeup artist she hired was a no-show. Harlow clucks over them while searching high and low for her shoes. Nia tries to help everyone, but she's winded and uncomfortably pregnant. Maxon and Griff are setting up chairs outside while Lono, the officiant, positions his podium at the plumeria-draped altar. Meanwhile, Evan's buddy Sebastian is directing the photographer and cake maker. Clint's two younger brothers, along with his friend Asher, all try to keep the impatient groom from demanding they get this damn show on the road.

In short, it's a barely organized shit show.

That leaves Noah and me standing together, shaking our heads.

"Glad you made it, bro." He claps me on the shoulder. "You okay?"

Not really. "Why?"

"You look like shit."

"What the fuck? I shaved and showered."

"I mean you look like a train wreck waiting to happen. But I know that because I know you better than all these other people, who will buy your BS smile. Nothing better with Masey?"

"Yes…and no. The elephant is finally out in the open between us, but neither of us knows what to do with it."

"Well, the night is young, and interesting things always happen after a wedding." He winks at me. "At least they did after mine."

He's trying to cheer me up, and I appreciate the effort, but… "Eww. Fuck off."

My brother laughs. "C'mon. Let's go see if we can help. And if you need to talk, you know where to find me."

Since being helpful is better than moping and wondering what Masey is thinking, I follow my older brother.

Jesus, I need to man up.

Evan isn't making any headway with the sound system, so I pitch in. Between the two of us, we get Keeley warming up to sing the bride up the aisle. Noah helps round up the attendants —Harlow, Nia, and Asher's fiancée, Samantha—and coaxes them into place.

One minute it seems as if pandemonium will win the day. The next, the sun inches near the horizon, lighting up the sky in a breathtaking riot of vivid colors, as if the universe knows the wedding of two amazing people is about to start. Then suddenly, everyone finds their place, a string quartet strikes up classical music, and the attendants make their way up the aisle to wait opposite Clint and his groomsmen.

Beside me, I feel Masey tense as Keeley begins singing Christina Perri's "A Thousand Years." I take her hand to soothe and reassure her as Bethany glides up the aisle in a white confection of lace and mesh that hugs every curve, reveals half her thighs, a good deal of her cleavage—and has the groom's eyes popping. And yet, she looks regal with her pale upswept hair, simple veil, and contented smile.

The ceremony is short and heartfelt. And other than Clint's brother Bret checking out his new sister-in-law's assistant in the second row and needing a nudge to pass the groom the ring, it goes off without a hitch.

After a moving tribute by Clint and his brothers for their father, who encouraged his oldest son to meet Bethany the day he unexpectedly passed away, the groom plants a longer-than-strictly-polite kiss on his wife's lips. Then, laughing to the strains of American Authors' upbeat number "Best Day of My Life," they run back down the beautiful petal-strewn runner, hand in hand.

Twenty minutes later, pictures are done, and everyone is assembling under the extended lanai out front, near the makeshift dance floor. As soon as Clint and Bethany have finished their first turn around the floor, the deejay invites everyone to join in. I pull Masey into the least-crowded corner of the designated dance space.

She tries to demur. "I'm not much of a dancer."

"I'm barely passable. I just want to hold you."

Thankfully, the music gods play along, spinning a soulful song I've never heard the deejay tells us is called "Best Part." It's perfect for this moment. Masey feels like my water when I'm stuck in the desert. Then Daniel Caesar begs his woman to say something if she loves him. Dude, I so, so relate. He goes on to croon that if she's a movie, she's the best part. I sigh. I'm still waiting to find out whether Masey will be my happily ever after…or my ultimate tragedy.

Fuck, I have to stop this maudlin shit.

Instead, I turn my focus on Masey, swaying to the beat, caressing her back, and pressing a kiss to her forehead.

"Trace?"

Her voice sounds like it's shaking, and I frown. "Yeah, honey?"

"What are you doing?" I hear her fear. "You're ruining me."

"Or maybe I just don't want you good for anyone else."

"Trace, what's happening with us? It's crazy."

"It is, but I can't stop myself."

She bites that pretty lip, and her blue eyes fill with tears. "I don't know if I can, either. I've tried. I've tried so hard…"

My heart stops. Jesus, I'm hoping this is it, the moment her walls break. I hope like fuck she's ready to admit she's mine. But I'm stuck in the middle of a goddamn crowd, at least an hour away from gathering my son, my car, and my woman and getting them all back to my place.

Fuck.

"Come with me." I lead Masey off the dance floor, toward the house.

"Where are we going?"

"Anywhere."

But she's got a good point. Where the hell am I taking her?

I scan the yard on my way up to the house. The wedding was a small one, but suddenly it seems as if there are people everywhere. I whisk her inside the main house, where I'm hoping like hell to find a romantic spot so we can tuck ourselves away. All I see is Britta and her mother prepping more appetizers. A few feet away, the bartender frantically mixes drinks. There's pandemonium everywhere.

Son of a bitch.

I must look frantic because Keeley pops out of one of the bedrooms and heads directly for us. "You okay, Trace?"

I debate. I don't want to sound rude or announce that we need privacy right now, but I can't let this opportunity go.

Masey saves me. "We need to be alone. Is there anywhere…"

Maxon's wife tucks a red curl behind one ear and motions my way. "Um…follow me."

Thank God.

She bustles into the kitchen, and we follow as she snatches a key off the wall, then continues out back.

The moon is rising as she guides us out by the pool. Between the shimmering water hugged by natural stone and a gorgeous waterfall on one side and the Pacific on the other stands a solitary structure.

At the simple white door, she turns and presses the key into my hand. "We've been renovating this pool cabana and making it a cozy cottage for two. We're not scheduled to open it until next month, but I think we have enough of the pieces in place to make it enjoyable. You can let me know when you're ready whether it's romantic or not."

"Thank you." I grab her hand. "Really. I owe you."

"No, you don't. I'll run interference if anyone is looking for you." Then with a wink, she's gone.

"Hurry." Masey turns and presses herself against me, kissing her way up my neck as I fumble the key into the lock.

Finally, it gives way, but I already feel like I'm shuddering and on fire. I'm dying to get inside this woman and stay forever.

I shove the door open, then flip on the nearby light switch. Fairy lights strung across the gorgeous koa-beamed ceiling illuminate the white canopy bed with padded headboard and pale quilts on a comfortable rug. On one side, a floor-to-ceiling window shows off the jewel of the ocean. On the other, there's a coffeemaker, snacks, a bistro table, and a clawfoot tub for two.

All I care about is Masey.

"Wow," she says as she meanders across the room and strokes the soft bedding. "It's beautiful."

"No, you are. Come here."

She turns to face me. My heart races as she slowly approaches, her stare never leaving mine. "Trace…"

Finally, she's close enough for me to touch, and I wrap an arm around her, bring her against me, and close my eyes, reveling in the feel of her pressed to me.

This can't be one of the last times I hold her.

"Please stop trying to resist. Just let this happen." I take her face. "Let *us* happen."

"I'm afraid."

"I know. I'm fucking scared to death, too. I didn't expect this."

"I didn't want it. I wasn't ready."

Damn it. My grip tightens. "Don't say that, honey."

"But—"

"I don't know if we're ever ready. I wasn't. But I'm done fighting it."

She wraps her fingers around my wrists, clinging to me with both her eyes and her touch. "I don't think I can anymore."

"It'll be okay. We'll figure it out. But I need to tell you something." I press my forehead to hers. "I love you."

CHAPTER TWELVE

$\mathcal{M}$ asey seems to stop breathing. She blinks at me, staring, searching. Unmoving.

My heart pounds. Is she going to run? Stay? Or is there any chance she'll say those three words back to me?

Finally, Masey swallows. "Oh, god. Trace…"

That's all she has to say? When it comes to love, why am I always on the losing side of the equation? "You can't be that surprised."

"I am. I've been awful. I-I had my best friend arrange for you to sleep with me. I cringe just thinking about that. And now that I know what your relationships have been like—"

"You mean my non-relationships?"

"How are you not mad at me for…using you? I can't think of another word, and that wasn't my intention but—"

I cut her off with a kiss, catching her mid-breath. Suddenly, she's silent under me. Stiff. I feel her worry.

When I brush my lips over hers again, she slowly goes pliant and slides her arms around me, rising on her tiptoes to meet me pucker for pucker.

Finally, she relaxes and sighs into my kiss. Slowly, I force myself to pull back. Keeley put us in a room with a bed, and I'd love to take advantage of it, but we don't need the distraction of sex now. It's tempting, but I have to know for sure that, unlike every other woman in my life, she wants *me*, even without it.

"Okay, so you're not mad."

"I'm not," I assure her. "How can I be? You didn't know my past, and we may not have met otherwise."

"True." She gives me a shy smile. "You know, all my subscribers think you're hot and that I should chain myself to your bed for the next twenty years."

"I wouldn't object." I kiss her nose and try to smile. But I peeked at some of the comments earlier this morning, too. "Some of them suggested you should grab me tight and never let me go."

She drops her gaze. Instantly, I miss looking into her blue eyes. I need to see what secrets she's hiding behind them.

When I lift her chin with my finger, I see her teeth sinking into her lip again. And tears rolling toward her cheeks.

"Hey." I dab at the drops with the sleeve of my coat. "I know how hard you worked on your makeup. No need to be upset. I'm really not mad. Anything else we can talk out, right?"

"Maybe."

That's better than a no. "I'm just glad we're talking."

"I've been so afraid to."

"Because everything happening between us is so sudden?"

She gives me a self-deprecating laugh. "You'd think so. Normal people would be concerned about that. Not me... I like to plan my life, and I never saw this—you and me—coming. But

I feel so good when I'm with you. I feel like myself. I'm sorry I've been quiet lately."

"Harlow said you were thinking. But that's all she said. She didn't break your confidence."

Masey's *Mona Lisa* smile makes her look even more beautiful. "That's why I usually talk to her. She's Fort Knox. But this time, I didn't tell her much. I honestly didn't know what to say."

"Tell me what's holding you up." I tuck a dark curl behind her ear. "If it's not that we've somehow developed these feelings in less than a week—"

"It's not. I could give you a lot of excuses. Mostly, it's about me." She sighs. "The thing is, if it took me a decade to figure out what an absolute douche Thom was and he *still* had to be the one to end it, have I learned enough not to put myself in that position again? And until I do, do I have any business putting someone else's heart at risk?"

That's her concern? That never once occurred to me. Maybe it should have. Masey isn't much of a risk-taker. "You don't trust your judgment, huh?"

"I don't exactly have a great track record. And neither do you. I mean, your first and only 'girlfriend' was Voldemort."

I laugh. I can't argue with that. "All this time, I've been thinking your objection was me."

"No." She looks at me like I'm spewing crazy talk. "I told you, you're great."

"Or my career."

"Of course not. You love it. It pays you and makes you happy. Why would I find fault with that?"

"Voldemort did."

Masey looks at me as if the answer is obvious. "That's why she's Voldemort."

"You got me there. What about my past? My choices?"

"With the opposite sex?" She shakes her head. "I can't judge you for whatever you did before you knew me."

"What about my son? Ranger is—"

"Precious! He's no problem at all. I love him to bits. Trust me, he has nothing to do with my reluctance."

"So...maybe stepping into a mother role someday doesn't bother you?"

"Not even a little." She smiles. "Wondering if you'd ever let me kind of has."

So she's thought about the future and what that might look like? I smile. "And I assume you wouldn't hate relocating to Maui?"

"I don't know. This place is terrible. Nothing pretty to look at. Nothing to do. No good food or amazing people or..." Masey rolls her eyes. "Stop. Like I said, I've just been a lot more worried about learning from the Thom debacle and doing better in the future."

"Honey, there's no way you spent a decade with Thom and learned nothing. Just like there's no way I could have spent most of my life playing the field and not learned something, too."

She shrugs. "Maybe. It's been a bit of a red flag to have feelings for a guy whose life was basically a series of one-night stands—"

"It wasn't."

"But, other than Voldemort, you didn't have girlfriends?" Masey looks confused.

"I didn't. But I had long-term friends-with-benefits. Take Caitlyn, for instance. We called each other randomly for hookups for four years."

"Four years?" She gapes at me. "How was that not a relationship?"

"Trust me, it wasn't."

"What did you two talk about?"

"Sex."

She rolls her eyes. "Other than that."

"We didn't. She had her life, and I had mine. Unless we were naked or getting naked, we had nothing to do or say to each other."

"So you never went on a date? Not once?"

"No." How do I explain this? "We had nothing in common."

"Except sex?"

"Except sex."

She looks genuinely perplexed. "But it's so much better when you're with someone who matters."

I grin. Does she realize what she just admitted? "You think so?"

Masey blushes, then meets my stare head on. "Yeah. The night we met… If your mother hadn't hurt her ankle, I'm sure the sex would have been good. After all, you're"—she sighs —"fantastic. But you know that. Practice makes perfect."

"That's the saying." And I used to care about being the best in bed. Then again, I had nothing else. Now all I care about is being the best I can be for Masey.

"But because we waited that extra day and I got to know you more, it was even better. And it's only blown me away more the deeper our connection has become."

"It has. And that's been a surprise to me, too." Another reason I'm trying so hard to break through Masey's barriers. I don't think I could go back to all the meaningless sex. I sure as hell don't want to. "Every day with you has just gotten sweeter, honey."

I caress her face, kiss her waiting lips, and make love to her mouth. Slow. Tender. Thorough. A thousand words of love without speaking at all. But when she reaches for my shirt buttons, I grab her wrists.

"Let's talk for now, okay?"

"You're right."

I lead her to a cozy, oversized chair in the corner, a plush off-white that's like a cloud the minute I sink down. Then I pull Masey onto my lap.

"Stop. I'm too big," she protests as she tries to stand.

I hold her tighter. "Pfft. No, you're not. Sit here. Let me hold you."

She stares at me, and I'd swear her eyes are telling me that I'm the beginning and the end of her universe.

Slow down, big boy. It's not as if she's said she loves you. Not even close...

Finally, she settles her head on my chest. "There's a whole beautiful wedding going on out there, and here we are in our own cocoon. I can hear the faint strains of the music..."

I can, too. And I'm not unhappy we're missing the B-52s. "I'm not going to apologize for it."

"And here we are, in our own 'Love Shack.'" She giggles.

"Really?" I lift my head and look down at her. "When you're nervous—"

"I tell corny jokes. I know. Sorry."

Actually, it's kind of cute. "Don't be nervous. It's just us. Keeley knew we needed to be alone. The truth is, I think everyone out there would understand. They've been through a lot, too."

"So much. OMG... Harlow has told me a bit about her brothers and their wives. All the pain, revenge, and betrayal. Those parents!"

"Real pieces of work, huh?"

"Holy cow. Harlow is so glad all that is behind her now. And she feels blessed that she and Bethany, despite not having met until just a few months ago, are really being sisters."

I nod and kiss the top of Masey's head. "And I'm happy for all of them. But I want to talk about us."

"Sorry. You're right." She sighs. "You want to know where we go from here."

"Yeah, but you're still thinking, aren't you?"

She nods. "I have to. Before I say anything, I want to be really sure…"

Because she's so cautious. I'm impatient as fuck to hear what she's feeling, but pushing won't get me anywhere. "I understand."

"You're trying to. And that's one of the things I—"

Love? I hold my breath. Stupid or not, I'm hoping.

"Admire so much about you," she finally finishes.

"Thanks." I try not to be disappointed. "I told my brother you and I weren't on the same page yet, but that I thought we were closing in on the same chapter, at least. Am I wrong?"

"No." Masey lifts her head to look at me. "You're not."

That's something. "Can you work with me here? You like me, right?"

"Of course."

"You *like*-like me?" I tease.

She laughs. "You know I do."

"Do you…like me a lot?" I caress my way down her arm. It takes everything I have not to pull up her skirt, reach inside her panties, and seduce her. But sex won't tell me what's in her heart.

"*A lot*-a lot. I feel like I'm in eighth grade."

"You liked someone in eighth grade that much?"

"I thought I did." She frowns.

Just like she thought she liked Thom. I can't let that thought fester.

"But you're not thirteen anymore."

"Thank goodness."

"You've learned a few things since then."

She sighs. "You'd think so, but why did I spend ten years with Thom? I've asked myself this over and over. My parents disliked him. My brother *hated* him. He put a wedge between me and my mom I still haven't fixed. It's getting better, but we're day by day. And why didn't I listen to my own heart? Every time I had the thought that maybe we weren't meant to be together anymore and I should break things off, I felt horrible and disloyal and talked myself out of it. I gave myself all kinds of reasons for my vague dissatisfaction and swore it would pass."

"So promise us both you won't bury your feelings. If something is bothering you, bring it to me. We'll talk about it. I'll do the same."

"You've never been in a relationship, and you know more about keeping one together than me." She shakes her head.

"Or maybe everything I know is academic and doing what makes sense will be harder in the thick of a problem."

"Maybe."

I cup her face. "Or maybe you're older and wiser now, and you know the pitfalls of stuffing down how you feel, so you won't do that again."

"I hope not."

Her lips right below mine are something I can't resist, so I plant a kiss on her pouty mouth, linger, savor, then pull back with a moan. "Any chance you like me more than a lot?"

"I think it's pretty much a foregone conclusion."

I can't stop the smile from spreading across my face as the giant gorilla of doubt finally climbs off my chest. "Is it now?"

"But I want to be sure."

"I want you to be sure, too."

"So...what now?" She bites her lip playfully, then glances across the room to the sumptuous bed. "It's awfully romantic here. And Keeley did ask us to let her know how conducive to romance the room was..."

She did, but... "I think she knows it's romantic. You and I know that, too. Just like you and I both know that sex doesn't equal romance and isn't always an expression of love. You know what is? At least for me?"

"What?"

I wrap my arms around her and stand. Her feet find the floor, her shoes landing with a dainty thud. I hold out my hand. "Dance with me."

Masey smiles and lays her fingers softly over my upturned palm. "You're trying awfully hard to make me fall in love with you, Mr. Weston."

We start swaying side to side to the strains of "Let Me Love You." I crack the French door open so we can better hear the song, then smile down at her. "Yes, I am, Ms. Garrett. You let me know when you get there, okay?"

"Okay."

We fall quiet, enjoying the music and each other. I close my eyes. I don't remember a moment I've ever felt more content. I've been more excited, more pumped, and more aroused—lots of times. But I've never felt a satisfaction that stemmed from peace rather than orgasm.

This feeling is far more sublime—and lasting.

"Trace?"

"Yeah, honey?"

"Don't worry. I don't think I'll keep you waiting too long."

Monday, April 16

"Where are we going?" Masey maintains a death grip on the catamaran's side railing.

If anyone should be terrified, it's me. Today is it. Make or break. I've got to convince her to stay with me. If I don't she'll be gone in forty-eight hours. Then she'll slip through my fingers for good. That will be it for us.

And I don't think my heart will recover from this blow.

You've got a plan, buddy. Stick to it.

"Not far," I assure her. "We're just going to hang out between Maui and Lanai, off to the west. You look adorable." I kiss her jaw, but it's hard to reach her around the orange life jacket.

"Adorable? I'm sure I'm green."

"Not even a little. Do you feel seasick?"

She shakes her head. "But I told you that water intimidates me."

That's just one reason we're here. "We're going to fix that. Once we reach the right spot, we're going to set down anchor and swim."

"Swim? You expect me to get off this boat—"

"Catamaran."

"Whatever. And jump in?" She shakes her head. "Uh-uh. No, no, no."

Despite my nerves, an indulgent smile makes its way across my lips. "Yes, yes, yes. I'll be right here with you. Every single second. Between me and the life jacket, you can't drown."

Masey glances longingly back at the harbor, then faces the

water again with a grimace. "But there's so much ocean out there."

"You like the ocean."

"I like looking at it. From afar. I never said I wanted to be *in* it."

"Honey..." I wrap my arms around her, hoping I get to do this for the rest of my life. "I promise. I'm going to keep you safe. I jumped into the scary world of makeup for you. Reciprocate just a little?"

"That's not the same! You can't drown in highlighter."

"Says you," I quip. "You also can't drown while you're wearing protective gear and you're with me. I swear."

She bites her lip. "I'm terrified."

"I know. But water is such an important part of my life, and I want to share it with you. Three hours. If you're still not enjoying it after that, I'll stop torturing you."

"All right."

"Thank you. You think I'd ever let you get hurt? I love you." It's getting easier to tell Masey how I feel, mostly because I'm convinced she's fallen, too. I just wish like hell she'd say the words and admit it. Once she does, I'm hoping she'll commit.

"Not on purpose."

"The water isn't going to jump up, pull you under, and swallow you whole."

"You don't know that for sure."

I don't mean to laugh at her, but I can't help it. "Yes, I do. Let me put it to you this way. I've brought Ranger out here many times, and he loves it."

"He doesn't know any better yet."

"But he's still alive not to know any better."

She sighs and tries to relax. "I'm being a wimp, aren't I?"

"This is a new experience."

"And I'm not handling it well." Masey drags in a calming breath. "It's fine. Fine. Everything is going to be fine."

"It will. Did I mention you look adorable?"

She nods. "You did. I still think you're lying. Panic is not charming."

I laugh again. "You and your family never did things like this growing up?"

"We never had time. My dad was a pediatric cardiovascular surgeon. He saw the cases most everyone else had given up on. We didn't have a lot of free weekends, and he never wanted to be out of the range of his phone or pager. Since my mom was a nurse, she kept weird hours, too. And my brother had a bunch of guy friends he did stuff with."

"They never invited you?"

"No. We're four years apart. Chase—sorry, everyone calls him Zyron now—used to go camping a lot in his last few years of high school. When you were seventeen, would you have wanted to take your thirteen-year-old sister with all your buddies?"

"Fuck no." The idea horrifies me. "They would all have tried to mack on you."

"I was thirteen!"

"Which tells me that you don't understand how horny teenage boys are. Besides, I'll bet you were hot even then."

"Gawky," she assures me. "Braces and freckles and not a curve anywhere on my body."

I turn her to face me, then look her up and down with a whistle. "Then things changed because you look amazing now. And I love your bikini. Nothing says Hawaii like a big plumeria over your pussy."

She swats my arm. "That's the first thing you notice about this suit?"

"Most of the rest of it is covered but…" I spin her around and stare. Yes, I love Masey, and she's an amazing woman, but I'm a guy and…wow. "The way these bikini bottoms show off your luscious ass ought to be illegal. Did I mention this catamaran has four bedrooms?"

She grabs my hands and leads me toward the interior. "Okay. Let's go."

I plant my feet. I'm hoping we'll get to enjoy that soon. But I've got other plans first. "Who's going to navigate the boat if I do?"

"Damn it."

Wrapping my arms around Masey, I bring her close again. "Really, it's all good. We're going to have fun."

She looks close to hyperventilating, but nods.

"Good." I press a soft kiss to her mouth and let her know I'm here for her. "I've looked at the charts, the wind, and the current. We're almost to the spot I'd like to put the anchor down. We'll be just over a sandy patch. I'm going to walk you to the anchor gear. When I give you the signal, you're going to release it—"

"I don't know how."

"I'll show you." And if I have my way, she'll have the hang of this in no time. "I'll be up at the helm, taking care of the positioning, okay?"

"If you're sure…"

I am. "When I give the signal, just release this lever. The hatch below should open. Because this ship has two engines, the anchor has a bridle and…" When I see confusion cross Masey's face, I stop. "You know what? It's not important right now. Just take my hand and tell yourself you've got this."

She nods, and it's obvious she's trying to put on a brave face

as I take her to the stern and show her how to release the anchor.
"That doesn't look too hard. I got it."

"You do."

"Will it stop when the anchor reaches the bottom?"

"No. And as soon as we've got enough chain, I'll tell you to
stop it."

"If you're not here, how do you know?"

"I'm a pro, honey. Since we're only staying out here a couple
of hours, we'll let out the scope about three to one. If we were
staying overnight, I'd have you let it out more like five to one."
When she looks at me blankly, I laugh. "Don't worry. Everything
will be fine."

She nods, and I kiss her until she loses a bit of her starch. But
with us, one kiss turns into another, then a few more. Hell, why
not make it a dozen? Then…who's counting?

Reluctantly, I lift my head to realize she's breathing hard and
turning pink. And since she's wearing sunscreen with SPF one
billion, I don't think she's getting burned.

God, everything about her fascinates me. Today can't be the
beginning of our end. It has to be the start of our future.

"Trace? Why are you looking at me like that?"

"It's time." I kiss her nose. "Just listen for my go and lift the
lever. When I say so, lower it again. That's it."

"Got it."

I kiss her one last time, then head to the helm. Once we're over
the spot I chose, I give her the signal. The anchor goes down on its
bridle, then I reverse the engines just slightly until the anchor
seats. I tell Masey to lift the lever, then I shut the engine down.

Now the fun can start.

"I did it!"

I jog down to where she's standing uncertainly and take her

hand. "You did. See? Now we're going to swim, and it's going to be great. I promise."

"I'm a little sad Ranger isn't here."

"Next time." If there's a next time. Just not now. I love my boy, but today is about Masey and me. "Besides, he's having fun with cousin Nolan. Snacks first? Or you just want to take the plunge?"

"Decisions, decisions. Do I want to throw up first or risk drowning?"

Now she's being melodramatic, and her silly smile tells me she knows it. "Stop with the worst-case scenarios. I want today to be special."

She's so fucking close to telling me she loves me, I can taste it.

"I know. And I'm teasing you about being terrified—mostly. Let's swim first."

"Let's do it."

One of my favorite things about this boat is the easy access to the water. We just have to walk down a couple of stairs—and jump right into the warm Pacific.

At the bottom step, I dive in headfirst. I've been out here a thousand times. I bring a lot of people here for sunset champagne cruises, so I know this spot well. It's warm and it's clear and it's deserted on a Monday afternoon.

When I emerge again, I swim up to the boat and hold out my arms to Masey. "Jump, honey."

She hesitates. "I'm afraid."

Eventually, I'll teach her to swim. Right now, I just need to prove that water isn't her enemy. "You trust me?"

"Yes," Masey answers without hesitation.

To some people, that might not be a big deal. To me, it's

massive. Masey doesn't trust easily, and it's another indication of how far we've already come together.

"I love you. Jump. I'll catch you. Always."

She drags in a deep breath, looking nervous as hell. Then she nods and takes a leap of faith, landing right in my arms.

I bring her close and reward her with a kiss. "The water feels good, right?"

After a pause, she cocks her head. "It does."

She sounds surprised, but I'm not. "Good. I work out here a lot, but it never feels like work, you know? I love the island and the breeze and the people who are all just loving life when they're with me. Take a deep breath and relax."

"I'm trying. When I was four, I went to a cousin's house. I was playing out by the pool when I tripped and fell in. If my uncle hadn't been right there to save me..."

Oh, shit. "Do you remember it?"

"Not the details, but I'll never forget the panic. And the water closing in over my head as I realized that I couldn't get back up to the air. Probably less than ten seconds later, Uncle Jeff plucked me out and that was that. But I had nightmares for weeks. After that, anytime any of my friends wanted to swim or hit the beach, I made up excuses. I just never confronted the water again."

And if I can get her to stay with me, she'll be surrounded by water all the time.

For now, I distract her with small talk. We play a few splashing games. Before too long, she's only holding on to me with one hand, then none at all. Once I point out how many places along the side of the boat she can grab if she panics, she joins me for a swim around the vessel. An hour passes. Then another. The sun starts to sink. I picture her living here, spending carefree days with me and Ranger, just enjoying

Hawaii and the life she and I build together. I picture her in this same bikini, belly rounding, cheering for my son as he swims between us.

God, that seems like the best life ever.

And she can make or break me with one word. I've got to do this right.

But no pressure, buddy.

When I finally help Masey back onto the catamaran, she seems perfectly at ease in the water with me. I'm about to burst with pride. I'm so damn excited that she let go and trusted me.

Does she trust me enough to know I'd never treat her like Thom?

After we've rinsed the saltwater and dried off, I call her into the galley and sit her at one of the barstools. I glance outside. Two minutes before the setting sun will be perfect.

Here goes nothing…

I pluck up two plastic cups and the bottle of champagne I've been chilling. "Would you take these out to the back? Let's sit at the table. I want to talk to you."

"Okay." But she looks suspicious. No, worried. "Everything all right?"

Fuck, I hope so. "Yeah. Be right there."

Masey nods and heads toward the stern. I change into my shorts and shove my hands into my pockets. Shit, I'm shaking. Am I crazy to think that a woman I've known ten days will uproot her entire life to come spend it with me?

Outside, the wind kicks up. I open the bottle and pour, doing my best to smile at her when, really, I'm so nervous I might puke. Flashbacks are a bitch. But this has to turn out better, right?

"You okay?" She looks genuinely concerned.

Unlike Voldemort.

I let out a breath. Masey trusted me today. Now I need her to trust in us.

"Honey, I've enjoyed every minute I've spent with you. From the second we met, I knew you were special. That became even more apparent to me when you helped me the night my mother sprained her ankle. Then again when you selflessly gave up your rental to come stay with me—a guy you'd known for two days—so someone else could be a bit safer."

"I've loved being with you. And you did star in my video. That meant a lot to me."

"Me, too. Thank you for trusting me with your audience and your passion. But the truth is, I don't want to be your ten-day boyfriend."

Her face falls, and she bites her lip hard, this time looking like she's about to cry. "I don't need a flowery goodbye, Trace. I get it. You never planned on me being underfoot and...I know love doesn't really last forever."

She thinks this is a kiss-off speech?

"It does." I grab her shoulders. "At least *my* love does, damn it." I'm barely aware of the sun's rich-hued glide toward the horizon or the salty breeze. I'm lost in her blue eyes and their pain. I had a speech prepared—and it's entirely gone. "You're it for me, honey. I don't want to be your ten-day boyfriend because I don't want to be your boyfriend at all. I'm not Thom. I don't need a decade to know whether I want to marry you. You've probably never thought of us as meant to be, but that's how I see us. There's a reason we came into each other's lives when we needed one another most. And I know as sure as I'm standing in front of you that my life will never be complete without you." I drop to one knee and pull out the ring I picked yesterday from my pocket. "Masey, honey, will you make me the happiest man ever and marry me?"

Shock crosses her face. Her eyes water and bulge. She covers her mouth with a trembling hand and starts to cry. "You're serious?"

"I'm down on one knee, offering you a ring, my heart, and my future. It doesn't get any more serious than that."

"Oh, my god." She searches my face, then drops to her knees beside me. "I never expected… I didn't think…"

"You thought I would just let you get on a plane Wednesday afternoon and fly away forever?"

"I've been afraid to hope for anything else."

"I want everything, and I want it with you. Just say the word."

She swallows, and I see her natural caution take over. Reservations set in. She frowns. "You haven't met my mother or my brother or…"

"Will their opinion really change your mind?"

"No." She shakes her head slowly. "Sorry. I'm so shocked I can't think. But no. They'll love you anyway. I just…didn't see this coming."

I try not to get frustrated. "I know. But can't you picture it? You and me and Ranger all together? You growing your business while I keep working mine? A new house? And someday more babies? Your best friend a few miles away? Staying forever in paradise?"

"It sounds amazing, like the most perfect existence ever." As tears roll down her face, she cups my cheek. "I love you."

Relief fills my chest. I grab her and pull her tight against me, pressing my forehead to hers. "Oh, honey, I love you, too. Is that a yes?"

She bites her lip. "I-I want to say yes. You have no idea… But I came to the island to bury my past. I wasn't thinking so much about the future. C-can I have twenty-four hours to think about it?"

I rear back. Is she serious?

Masey grabs me again. "This isn't about you, Trace. I don't want to be impulsive. Don't you want me to be sure I can genuinely come to you with a yes in my heart and make you happy?"

"I'm already convinced."

"I'm glad, but I need to catch my breath. When did you start thinking about this?"

"At Clint and Bethany's wedding," I admit.

"It inspired me, too. But you've had two days to wrap your head around this idea and what it would mean for us. I've had two minutes."

Disquiet rips at my guts. "You either love me or you don't."

"I do. Please..." She grips my face, and I try not to feel crushed. "You're asking me to move across an ocean and change my whole life. Shouldn't I think about that at least a little?"

I can't deny that I assumed she'd move here or that it's a sacrifice on her part, but if that's what's standing in her way... "I can move to LA."

I'd have to start my business over, and I'd miss my family like hell, but...

Love softens her face. "That's amazing of you to offer, but you don't need to. I'm not insisting on staying there, I'm just... I didn't let myself picture or hope or..." She gives me a self-deprecating smile. "If ten years wasn't enough to convince the last guy that he cared enough to marry me, why would I think the man I've known ten days would?"

Gritting my teeth, I hold in a curse and stand. I get what she's saying. Logically, she's right. Realistically, almost no one pledges to change their whole life so they can spend it with someone they've known less than a season, less than the flip of a calendar. Hell, less than a pay period.

I'm a level-headed guy, and not impulsive. But when it comes to love, I can get swept up and overly optimistic—and I fuck myself.

Apparently, I didn't learn much from Voldemort.

"Trace," she implores me as she stands. "Please. Twenty-four hours?"

"Sure." I shove the ring back in my pocket with my heart in the gutter and hope washing away. "We should get back. I told Noah I wouldn't be too late."

It's not true. I told my brother I would call him and let him know whether I'd be coming for Ranger tonight…or in the morning. I stocked enough provisions to stay out here at least that long, thinking that if we had something to drink to, I didn't want to put the celebration on hold.

Now, I just want to get the fuck out of here.

I swipe the bottle and the untouched glasses of champagne and take them into the galley. Every step feels like I'm dragging a ton of wretched regret.

And why is Masey right behind me? I can hear her. I can feel her. What the hell does she want, to see how much she's hurt me?

"Trace?"

I can't turn and look at her. I can't. Voldemort's refusal hurt my wallet and my pride. After a few weeks, I realized we would have made each other miserable. I wish the bitch had just been honest, but it should be no shock that Voldemort lies.

Masey doesn't have a dishonest bone in her body. She doesn't trust herself and she hasn't known me long enough to truly trust me. I proposed too soon. I fucked up. It's not her fault.

But she's going to rip my heart in two, probably forever.

I set everything in the sink, brace my hands on the counter, then take a deep breath before I face her. The tears streaming down her face are a stab to the heart. "Yeah?"

She takes my face in her hands. "I didn't say no."

"Let's be real. You're going to. You're just too nice to tell me to fuck off."

"No. I'm too afraid to throw caution to the wind and say yes. When I was with Thom, I never listened to my head. Ever. He said to trust him, so I did. He said he wanted what was best for us, and that wasn't getting married yet, so I believed him. My head told me the rela-tionship was all wrong, but my heart kept insisting we'd work it out. We were meant to be." She rolls her eyes. "When he left me, I swore next time I'd think with my head."

It's on the tip of my tongue to ask what the hell I've done to make her head doubt me. But it's not about me. None of this is. It's about her fear. It's about not being ready to commit.

"Then you should do that." I shoulder my way past her. I don't want to say something I'll regret.

After all, I can't blame her for not having healed enough to want to pledge her life to another man.

In silence, I guide the catamaran through the dusky twilight, back to the harbor. It doesn't take too long to dock, pack every-thing back up, toss out the trash, grab my gear, then motion to her with a head bob. "Let's go."

She looks hurt and chastened, and that's another stab in the chest. "Are you going to talk to me?"

"Honey, at this point, what is there to say? You've got a couple of days left on the island. If you want to spend them in bed, I'll indulge you." Though I don't know how I'll do that without falling deeper in love. "After all, you came to paradise for good sex. At least I can give you that."

As I head toward the parking lot to reach my truck, she grabs my arm. "Stop it. Right now. I'm so sorry I ever asked to meet you for sex. I didn't know you, but I realize it was an inhuman thing to expect. I wish I had asked to meet you simply to meet you. I wish I'd gone into our time together with a more open mind. I wish I could go back and do everything differently."

"Is this your goodbye speech?"

"No. It's an apology. It's a please-give-me-a-day-to-work-out-my-shit speech. It's a plea."

I could lash out with a dozen useless emotions, but I love Masey. She's obviously confused and struggling. I can't hurt her more. Besides, there's some preppy dude coming toward us like he's on a mission, and I'm betting the last thing she wants is an audience. "Okay."

What else can I say?

With a sigh, I keep walking. Masey has the keys to my truck in her bag. Behind me, I hear her digging for them. But once she finds them, we'll spend twenty minutes together in an awkward-as-fuck ride to Noah and Harlow's place.

Can't wait…

If I think I'm hurt and demoralized today, how much will life suck tomorrow when Masey turns me down for real?

Mr. Preppy closes in, staring at me. Whatever. I've got enough shit on my plate. Just beyond the overhead light is my truck. I'll count the seconds until I have Ranger back—and a buffer between Masey and me.

If you hadn't offered the use of her vacation rental to Amanda Lund, you could have just dropped her off…

But I'm a stupid schmuck. I still want every moment with her I can get.

As I approach the stranger, he closes in, knocking my shoulder with his. It's not a bump or a stumble. It's a wordless confrontation.

I glance up. The Ivy-League-looking prick snarls at me, clearly itching for a fight.

"What the hell?"

"Get away from her," he growls.

Masey?

Behind me, I hear her gasp, then her bag falls to the concrete. "Thom? What are you doing here?"

This is her ex?

"What do you mean, what am I doing here? I came here for you. To see you. To tell you I'm wrong and I'm sorry. To tell you that you can do better than this loser you put in your makeup video." He glares at me. "To tell you I love you and I want to make it up to you." I can't believe my fucking eyes when he drops to one knee and opens a box to reveal a ring that's blinding. "I want you to marry me, babe."

Is he fucking kidding? He wants her back now, after all these months?

Isn't this just perfect? Déjà vu all over again.

Fuck. Looks like I'll be spending my life alone.

CHAPTER THIRTEEN

Masey

*D*uring all the months Thom and I were apart, I rehearsed a hundred speeches to spew at him, all about how much he hurt me. I wanted him to feel guilty and ashamed. Mostly I wanted him to be contrite. Right now, I can only think of one word to say to my ex-boyfriend. "What?"

Thom was my first crush, my first kiss, my first lover. He was the first person I talked to each morning and the last person I spoke with each night. I knew his habits, his thoughts, his ambitions. I knew everything about him. But if anyone had told me even an hour ago that he would come back today on bended knee, ring in hand, I would have told them they were crazy and laughed myself silly.

I'm not laughing now. I'm totally confused. What changed for him?

And I can't help but glance at Trace, watching us, so unmoving and resigned it hurts.

"You heard me, Mase. Marry me. Make me so happy."

What about my happiness? "You chose Betsy. What about her?"

"She was a mistake," Thom insists. "A stupid snap decision I regret more than I can ever tell you."

A snap decision? "But you slept with her for months."

"And I was miserable without you. She isn't you. She's in the past. You, babe…" He stands and takes my hands, clutching them tightly. "You're my future. I was just too afraid to see it."

And he's way too close. I rear back. I don't want him near me. I don't even want him in the same zip code. "Don't touch me."

"Ah, don't be that way, babe."

Twenty bucks says Betsy broke things off with him. "Did she dump you?"

"What does it matter? I want to marry you."

So she did. "Look, Thom—"

"Hear me out. You always wanted me to propose. So here I am. And look." He shoves the ring under my nose.

It's a stunning round diamond; I can't deny that. Probably four carats meant to dazzle and blind me. I'm neither.

And what is Trace thinking about all this? Another glance at his sad face makes something in my chest pang.

"That doesn't make what you did okay," I tell Thom. "I can't be bought."

"Of course not. I just want you to see that I realize I made a terrible, colossal mistake. I'll gladly pay for that any way you want until the day I die."

"Thom, you can't just drop in and—"

"Don't do this, babe. I need you. C'mon. Give me a second chance. Like you always said, we were meant to be."

I don't love him, and I'm convinced he doesn't love me. I'm not sure he ever did. "I don't think that anymore."

"We have so much history together. I was wrong to think I needed someone else when all I needed was you, but…" He thumps a hand to his chest. "I was scared. You were pressing for more, and I was afraid of commitment. I wasn't sure what I wanted. But I know now. All I need is a second chance. It'll be better this time. We'll have more laughter and more fun. And I'll be so good to you."

I'm dumbfounded. I can only blink at him. He's saying all the things I wanted him to say months and months ago, when I was still nursing wounded pride and what I thought was a broken heart, but now? My bullshit meter is pinging.

What's more surprising? I don't feel a thing for him.

"Please." He grabs my shoulders before I can even speak. "Your heart is too good to say no. I don't deserve you, but I can't live without you. Just say yes. You'll see, I'm a new man."

No, what I'm seeing is that he's desperate because Betsy dumped his sorry ass. Thom is too insecure to be alone—he always has been—and he thinks he can come back to me, like I'm a consolation prize. I also see, now that I'm using my head, that he's a self-absorbed narcissistic slime who took advantage of my naiveté and my fairy-tale dreams to keep me by his side way longer than I should have let him.

"Hey, she told you not to touch her." Trace dumps everything in the bed of his truck, then closes in on Thom. "Take your hands off her."

"You're not her boyfriend. I am. I've got it from here. Get lost." My ex gives him a dismissive glare and a matching wave of his hand.

He thinks Trace is somehow beneath him?

Of course Thom does. He's a snob. But more than that, he's afraid.

It's so obvious now.

Thom always thought he had me in his back pocket, that he could come back to me at any time and I would be waiting. I don't know when Betsy dumped him. It doesn't matter. I wouldn't be surprised if he's slept with other women since then. But what spooked him was me going public with Trace. He's only here now because he wants to keep me in his sphere and under his control so I can be his backup plan, not because he actually cares.

I glare at Thom and wag a finger in his face. "Don't talk to Trace like that. How dare you? You don't know him. You don't know my feelings for him. You don't—"

Thom grips me so tightly I'm pretty sure his fingers will leave bruises. "I only want what's best for you, and it's not him. You've always been sheltered and too trusting, but let me tell you... I looked this guy up. He's not going anywhere in life. He's latching onto your rising fame. Prove to me you're not stupid enough to let him."

Trace steps between Thom and me, shoving my ex away. "Masey isn't stupid. She doesn't have to prove a fucking thing to you. And she told you not to touch her."

"What part of fuck off don't you understand, boat boy? You're not your brother. You're nothing but a man whore barely scraping by. Masey is mine, and I'll touch her if I want to. Go find another pussy. This one belongs to me."

I gape. Thom did *not* just say that.

Oh, but he did.

Before I can even open my mouth to let him have it, Trace hauls back and plants a fist in his face, sending Thom flailing onto his ass and howling. "I might be nothing, but I'm enough to stop you from hurting her again. She's not just a pussy; she's a woman with feelings and a heart you broke. If you're going to storm back into her life and marry her, at least care enough about her to treat her right."

I see it. In that moment, I see everything so clearly. I see more than my past and my present colliding—literally. Holding his bloody nose and staggering to his feet, I see Thom, the douche my girlish fantasies clouded me into believing was Prince Charming. And standing between us, I see Trace, the protector and lover my cynical heart wouldn't let me accept as the man of my dreams. Until now.

I see my future.

With my heart bursting, I set a hand on Trace's shoulder. "Thank you, but you shouldn't have done that."

He clenches his jaw and frowns. "Yeah. Sorry. I'll leave you two. If you'll just give me my keys…"

"And good riddance, asshole," Thom quips. "I'm going to press charges."

I whirl on Thom. "Shut up! Shut the absolute fuck up, Thomas Mazelton Wilmer. You're only here because Betsy got smart a lot faster than I did and dumped you on your snobby, egotistical ass, and you saw that Trace was man enough to be in the makeup video I'd begged you time and again to do with me. So you thought you could fly out here—I'm guessing Harlow told you where to find us?—and toss around a few words, flash a ring in my face, and after ten months, I would come crawling back. Ha! You're the stupid one. You're ten days too late because I met a man who's kind, who cares about my feelings. He compromises. He listens. He's funny. And he's smart—"

"Pfft. He sounds like a bitch."

Oh, I cannot stand this fuckwit shit-for-brains asshole anymore. And I'm ashamed I spent even ten seconds with him.

I march straight at Thom—and I don't stop until I shove him back on his ass. "He's a hundred times the man you'll ever be. Besides being a god in bed, he loves me. Really, truly loves me in a way I never really believed I deserved or would find. I choose him. I will choose him every day for the rest of my life. So get the hell out of my face and don't ever come back. Oh, and if you think you're going to press charges, think again. I'll tell everyone how you *really* got the Thurman account. All the gory details. And I have pictures…"

His face contorts. "You wouldn't."

That's his first concern—not that I love someone else, not that I'm choosing Trace, not even that I'm saying my ten-day boyfriend is a better man. Thom's first concern is about Thom.

How unsurprising.

"Try me."

He scrambles to his feet again. "I don't know who you are anymore, Masey. My sweet girl is gone."

"You're damn right she is. You killed her. In her place is a woman who knows exactly who she is and who she doesn't want anymore. So go." I give him the same dismissive wave of my hand he gave Trace. "Take your ring and your lies and your sorry ass away from me and off this island. I don't ever want to see you again. E-V-E-R. Do you understand?"

"Fine. I don't want to see you ever again, either." He looks at Trace. "She's all yours. Enjoy the whininess, the neediness, and the terrible sex."

Trace clenches his jaw and looks my way. "Can I?"

He wants to punch Thom again? "Be my guest."

There's no one more deserving.

Trace hauls back and plows his fist into Thom's stomach. I

nudge him aside and grab Thom's shoulders, then give my deserving ex a well-placed knee to the balls.

Thom groans and crumples onto his side, clutching his crotch.

Trace stands over him. "I might have been a man whore before Masey, but the two things I know? First, since you only ever put minimal effort into sex, you only ever got minimal return. I put in more—a lot more—and she's given me everything I've ever dreamed of. Second, love makes everything so much hotter and better."

I smile up at him. "It does. Take me home and prove it again?"

"Sure."

"You can't just leave me like this," Thom whines as we walk away.

I turn back to him. "I think I said the same thing to you the day you broke up with me. So I'll tell you what you told me. Yes, I can. And I'll add something special just for you. Hasta la fuck-off."

Trace looks like he's resisting the urge to laugh as I grab for his hand and we head to his truck.

After I press the fob to unlock the door, Trace slides behind the wheel with a laugh. "Hasta la fuck-off?"

"It just slipped out. You know I say corny things when I'm nervous."

"Yeah." He starts the truck, and we roll out of the parking lot.

I turn to see Thom through the back window, still huddled on the ground.

Good riddance.

"God, that was freeing." The oppressive weight of fear and failure is finally gone.

"You did amazing."

"Thanks for sticking up for me." His unwavering support showed me exactly the sort of man he is.

It also showed me that I'm an idiot.

"You're welcome." He shrugs. "I guess we should stop by and get Ranger. Do you want me to leave you with Harlow for the night?"

I know what he's thinking—and he's crazy. "No, I meant it. I want you to take me home."

"To my place?"

"Yes." It feels like home to me now. Probably because that's where Trace is.

"Look, Masey, I was happy to help you out back there with Thom. It was nice to be able to give you an assist so you could put the asshat in his place, but I'm not going to hold you to everything you said. I know you didn't mean—"

"Spend the night with me."

He swallows. "I can't, honey. I just…can't. If I do, it'll crush me."

My eyes well with tears. I feel horrible. "I'm sorry. You're right. I'm asking for too much again. No, I'm asking for the wrong thing. Let me try one more time, okay?"

He shrugs. "It's a twenty-minute ride. It's not like I can stop you from talking."

That's true; he can't. But I don't want him to feel as if he has no choice except to listen. I want him to want to listen because I'm going to say what he needs to hear most. "Let me rephrase that. Spend the rest of your life with me."

He stops the truck in the middle of the road and whips his stare over at me. "What?"

"I don't need twenty-four hours to know what I'm feeling or thinking. I need you. I want you. I love you. Spend the rest of your life with me." When he gapes at me, looking speechless and unsure, I lean in to kiss him. "I dare you."

"You can't do that."

"I just did. I'm sorry I messed up your perfect proposal and that I made you doubt—"

"You don't have to marry me to prove to Thom you're over him. Your knee in his balls did it."

"He deserved that, but he has nothing to do with the reason I'm saying yes. I want to marry you for you. Because you're the other half of me." I look into his dark eyes, willing him to understand and believe me, willing him to love me the way I see so clearly now I've loved him since almost the beginning. "Say yes. Please…"

He hesitates.

"If you don't, I'll have to double-dog dare you."

He gives me a short, acidic laugh. "Well, that is serious. You must really mean it, then."

"With every beat of my heart," I assure him softly, then prop my chin on his shoulder. "You have a ring for me, don't you?"

"Yeah." He digs into his pocket. His hands are shaking as he reaches for mine and slips the simple white-gold band with the oval diamond on my finger. "You're really going to marry me, honey?"

"Yes! Happily." I'm so sublimely ecstatic, I beam a smile his way and press my lips to his.

With this man is where I belong.

Behind us, brakes screech and horns start honking. Trace tears his mouth away. "Shit."

"We should probably get out of the middle of the road."

"Yeah." He presses his foot to the gas pedal and the truck lurches forward. "And I guess we should call everyone we know and give them the good news."

"Starting with your brother and my best friend so they can keep Ranger tonight. After that…well, everyone else can wait, because I want to lick you from the tips of your toes all the way to those lips I can't wait to kiss for the rest of my life. And I promise I'll focus on all the best parts in between until you scream for me."

He cocks his head. "You can't use my own lines against me."

"I just did. What do you say to that?"

"I dare you to love me forever."

"You know I can never resist a dare." I smile—and drop my hand to his thigh. "You got it."

Read on to see how sexy bodyguard Tanner melts the icy walls around single mom Amanda's heart…

Can I keep the gorgeous, gun-shy single mother safe—and prove I'm the man for her?

MORE THAN PROTECT YOU
More Than Words, Book 6.5
by Shayla Black
Coming October 6, 2020!
(Will be available in eBook, print, and audio)

I'm Tanner Kirk—Certified firearms instructor and mixed martial arts enthusiast. When I filed for divorce at the end of an empty marriage, all I wanted was a vacation in paradise, not another woman in my life. But how can I possibly say no to Amanda Lund, a young single mom desperate to learn self-defense? Or refuse the banked desire on the guarded beauty's face?

I can't.

So I seduce Mandy until we're burning up the sheets…and soon find my heart entangled with her bruised and battered one. But when a nemesis from her past tries to destroy our future by unearthing my secret, will she understand and forgive me—or give up on us forever?

Exclusive to Amazon for a Limited Time. Look for it elsewhere in January 2021.

Looking for more dangerous men in scorching contemporary romances that depict love on the forbidden side? HEA guaranteed!

FORBIDDEN CONFESSIONS
(available in eBook and print)

SEDUCING THE INNOCENT
Is she willing to give her secret crush everything to make him stay?

SEDUCING THE BRIDE
Can he persuade his best friend's daughter that she belongs to him?

SEDUCING THE STRANGER
Will a hot night with a stranger spark more than she ever imagined?

SEDUCING THE ENEMY
Once he takes his pound of flesh from her, will she steal his heart?

LET'S GET TO KNOW EACH OTHER!

ABOUT ME:
Shayla Black is the *New York Times* and *USA Today* bestselling author of roughly eighty novels. For twenty years, she's written contemporary, erotic, paranormal, and historical romances via traditional, independent, foreign, and audio publishers. Her books have sold millions of copies and been published in a dozen languages.

Raised an only child, Shayla occupied herself with lots of daydreaming, much to the chagrin of her teachers. In college, she found her love for reading and realized that she could have a career publishing the stories spinning in her imagination. Though she graduated with a degree in Marketing/Advertising and embarked on a stint in corporate America to pay the bills, she abandoned all that to be with her characters full-time.

Shayla currently lives in North Texas with her wonderfully supportive husband and daughter, as well as two spoiled tabbies. In her "free" time, she enjoys reality TV, reading, and listening to an eclectic blend of music.

Tell me more about YOU by connecting with me via the links below.
Text Alerts
To receive sale and new release alerts to your phone, text SHAYLA to 24587.
Website http://shaylablack.com
Reading order, Book Boyfriend sorter, FAQs, excerpts, audio clips, and more!

VIP Reader Newsletter http://shayla.link/nwsltr
Exclusive content, new release alerts, cover reveals, free books!
Facebook Book Beauties Chat Group http://shayla.link/FBChat
Interact with me! Wine Wednesday LIVE video weekly. Fun, community, and chatter.
Facebook Author Page http://shayla.link/FBPage
News, teasers, announcements, weekly romance release lists…
BookBub http://shayla.link/BookBub
Be the first to learn about my sales!
Instagram https://instagram.com/ShaylaBlack/
See what I'm up to in pictures!
Goodreads http://shayla.link/goodreads
Keep track of your reads and mark my next book TBR so you don't forget!
Pinterest http://shayla.link/Pinterest
Juicy teasers and other fun about your fave Shayla Black books!
YouTube http://shayla.link/youtube
Book trailers, videos, and more coming…

If you enjoyed this book, please review/recommend it. That means the world to me!

Wicked All Night (novella)

Forever Wicked (novella)

Theirs to Cherish

His to Take

Pure Wicked (novella)

Wicked for You

Falling in Deeper

Dirty Wicked (novella)

A Very Wicked Christmas (short)

Holding on Tighter

THE DEVOTED LOVERS (COMPLETE SERIES)

Devoted to Pleasure

Devoted to Wicked (novella)

Devoted to Love

FORBIDDEN CONFESSIONS (SEXY SHORTS)

Seducing the Innocent

Seducing the Bride

Seducing the Stranger

Seducing the Enemy

DOMS OF HER LIFE
(by Shayla Black, Jenna Jacob, and Isabella LaPearl)
Raine Falling Collection (COMPLETE)

One Dom To Love

The Young And The Submissive

The Bold and The Dominant

The Edge of Dominance

Heavenly Rising Collection

The Choice

The Chase

Coming Soon:

The Commitment (Early 2021)

THE PERFECT GENTLEMEN (Complete Series)

(by Shayla Black and Lexi Blake)

Scandal Never Sleeps

Seduction in Session

Big Easy Temptation

Smoke and Sin

At the Pleasure of the President

MASTERS OF MÉNAGE

(by Shayla Black and Lexi Blake)

Their Virgin Captive

Their Virgin's Secret

Their Virgin Concubine

Their Virgin Princess

Their Virgin Hostage

Their Virgin Secretary

Their Virgin Mistress

Coming Soon:

Their Virgin Bride (TBD)

STANDALONE TITLES

Naughty Little Secret

Watch Me

Dirty & Dangerous

Her Fantasy Men (novella)

A Perfect Match

THE MISADVENTURES SERIES

Misadventures of a Backup Bride

Misadventures with My Ex

SEXY CAPERS (COMPLETE SERIES)

Bound And Determined

Strip Search

Arresting Desire (novella)

HISTORICAL ROMANCE

(as Shelley Bradley)

The Lady And The Dragon

One Wicked Night

Strictly Seduction

Strictly Forbidden

BROTHERS IN ARMS (COMPLETE MEDIEVAL TRILOGY)

His Lady Bride

His Stolen Bride

His Rebel Bride

NEW YORK TIMES BESTSELLING AUTHOR

SHAYLA BLACK

Steamy. Emotional. Forever.

BOOK BEAUTIES
Facebook Group
http://shayla.link/FBChat

Join me for live, interactive video chats every #WineWednesday. Be there for breaking Shayla news, fun, positive community,

VIP Readers
NEWSLETTER
at ShaylaBlack.com

Be among the first to get your greedy hands on Shayla Black news, juicy excerpts, cool VIP giveaways—and more!

Made in the USA
Coppell, TX
27 November 2020

42181032R00174